SHAKEDOWNERS 2 - THE VINYL FRONTIER

JUSTIN WOOLLEY

LONELY ROBOT BOOKS

For you - thanks for coming back

CAPTAIN'S PROLOGUE_

Throughout history, even before Einstein came along, the concept of distance has always been relative. The faster you can travel, the less time it takes, the closer things seem. The idea of crossing a continent must have seemed incomprehensible to Stone Age man, but by the time humanity developed atmospheric flight, hopping from country to country became so commonplace that the staggering engineering required to lift several hundred people 11 kilometres into the air was reduced to little more than complaints about bad food and inadequate leg room.

Eventually, humanity took its first steps into space – to the moon and then to Mars and the other planets of the solar system – but it wasn't until the advent of the Bedi-Alcubierre-Millis-Formelge (BAMF) drive in the late twenty-first century that faster-than-light travel became a reality and other solar systems were finally within reach. In that moment two things happened. First, the trip from the Earth to the moon became the equivalent of backing out of your garage, and second, humanity discovered it wasn't alone in the universe. In fact, life was so abundant that the very idea that humanity might be the only sentient life in all the unending universe seemed laughably ignorant. Come on. The universe is probably infinite and you dummies think you're all that's out there? That's like picking up one grain of sand on the beach and thinking it's somehow more important than all the others.

Eventually, by the twenty-third century it wasn't unusual for people on Earth to take the ten-minute flight to Mars for their favourite cheese (there's a great cheese place near the base of Olympus Mons). At least, that was the case when Earth still existed – for more on that, see *Shakedowners*, the first book in this series because if you've come here without reading that then you've missed some stuff you might want to catch up on.

Point is, humanity had reached such speeds that all of the Milky Way galaxy was within reach. Let's be clear though, the galaxy is still huge. It would take the fastest ship in the Federation Space Command fleet just under twenty years to cross from one side to the other. Sure, that's longer than you'd want to spend on a road trip with your kids, but it's not outside of the realm of possibility. In fact, there were no less than a dozen long-term FSC exploration missions crossing the spiral arms of the Milky Way by the mid-twenty-second century. Most of them wouldn't make it back, for various reasons, ranging from the boring – disastrous ship malfunction and/or loss of life support – to the more exciting – being ingested by locust-like swarms of living asteroids. That's all part of the fun of space exploration.

So, distances that once boggled the human mind now seemed insignificant. Humanity may have conquered interstellar flight – to the point where people had once again started complaining about the food and leg room – but the distances beyond that, the distances between galaxies, were still stupidly big. Intergalactic distances meant hundreds and hundreds of years of travel on the fastest starship, just to get to the nearest galaxies. Humanity, and in fact none of the species in the Federation, had ventured beyond the confines of the Milky Way in any meaningful way. There'd been probes sent, of course, and some species had embarked on generation-ship missions, where the descendants of the original crew would continue the mission over many hundreds or possibly thousands of years, but it was well understood that these were one-way trips. Unsurprisingly, volunteers weren't always readily available, and then there were the ethical implications of creating an entire branch of your species who may spend their entire existence aboard a spaceship and would definitely end up worshipping a can of beans or something. All this is to say, the vast space between galaxies was, even in the twenty-third century, still the 'here be dragons' part of the map.

There might not have been dragons beyond the edge of the Milky Way, but there was something out there, traveling with incomprehensible speed through the unfathomable emptiness. Not too far (relatively speaking) beyond the spiral arm of the Milky Way, where a lovely if insignificant blue-green world had once orbited a G-class star, an entire civilisation was moving at speeds a million times faster than anything humanity had achieved. Their home-world was long forgotten, rendered inhospitable by the death of its own star when life on Earth was little more than fancy alphabet soup. They had thrown off the shackles of organic bodies billions of years ago, and were best considered a synthetic life-form, though they were not machines as any human would recognise them. Instead, they were consciousness embedded in matter, entities able to control single molecules as if they were their own appendages, and able to construct and move between bodies ranging from the microscopic to the cosmic. They were among the longest-lived species in the universe, and had passed through galaxies in the thousands, visited worlds in the trillions, and had been to each multiple times. Each time, they did so with the same purpose: to cleanse advanced life as one might disinfect a kitchen bench.

These beings were so ancient that no species in the galaxy knew of their existence, although there had been warnings. Peppered throughout the myths and legends of hundreds of sentient species there was a common thread of the cosmic evil, the unknowable horror from the depths of another dimension, the great cleansers, the old ones. They were the Devourers of the Stars, the Great Living Storm of Steel, the Lords of Interstellar Space, the Harbingers of Forever War. They were the Synth-Hastur, and they were entering the Milky Way.

If there was anything to make humanity wish they really were alone in the universe, it was the Synth-Hastur. There had been attempts to protect against this grave existential threat in the past. When the Synth-Hastur had last come to cleanse the Milky Way, one species now lost to time had created the Aegix, a swarm artificial intelligence that had been programmed to adapt all sentient life in the galaxy with bio-linked technology-controlling nanobots. That plan had not been successful, although I'll let you in on a secret: it had come close.

Half a million years later, a nondescript mining colony on Iota Persei E accidentally unearthed the Aegix. But in attempting to complete its original mission, the Aegix made a mess of things – a pink-goopy mess, leaving a trail of death and destruction. The Aegix had been stopped and mostly destroyed, but not before giving cryptic warnings about a galactic-level threat. There were those who believed there was something to these warnings, even if the Aegix had gone a little sideways after five hundred thousand years of programming errors. If the warnings could be believed, then the Aegix might still be the key to survival.

Unfortunately, as the Synth-Hastur breached the outer edge of the galaxy there were only two vestiges of the Aegix left. One was a probe that was days away from impact with the third moon of Geffet, a planet orbiting the red supergiant Betelgeuse. The other was in the body of one Captain Iridius B. Franklin,

CHAPTER ONE_

HELMSMAN'S LOG. *Galactic Central 2216 point 453 point 12. Lieutenant Benjamin 'Space Ace' Rangi, helmsman and most handsome crew member of the Federation Space Command vessel* Deus Ex, *recording. Another day aboard the Federation's most advanced stealth starship, another mission beyond the edges of Federation space, another day spent watching paint dry.*

Iridius Franklin, captain of the FSC *Deus Ex* and, in his opinion at least, significantly more handsome than Rangi, stared at his helmsman in disbelief. "Rangi," he said, concerned for a moment that his helmsman had succumbed to some kind of hitherto unknown space madness, "you're literally just speaking out loud. There isn't even such a thing as a helmsman's log."

Rangi spun around on his chair and Iridius made his seventh mental note to request some changes to the helm console chairs. Everything about the *Deus Ex* might have been several generations more advanced than the old rust-bucket he used to captain, the FSC *Diesel Coast*, but one thing was certainly better on that ship: the helm chairs didn't rotate.

"Captain," Rangi said, "there definitely is such a thing as a helmsman's log. I do one every morning after my coffee."

"Lovely," Iridius said. "Thank you very much for that image, Lieutenant."

"Besides," Rangi continued, "I was just making a point. This mission is another case of us floating around in space watching the Alliance do a grand total of fuck all. When are we going to get to save the galaxy again?"

Iridius drummed his fingers on the arm of his captain's chair. "Look, I know reconnaissance isn't exactly saving the galaxy, but most people never get a chance to do that. We're lucky we got to do it once. We can't expect to be saving the galaxy every week. This isn't some kind of space adventure series. Would you prefer to be back flying a hauler?"

"Well," Rangi said, "honestly Cap, yeah, sometimes I would. At least a hauler goes places, instead of hanging around listening to Alliance communications like a bunch of perverts."

"We're not perverts, Rangi," Iridius said. "We're the crew of a stealth reconnaissance ship tasked with keeping tabs on a threat to the Federation. It's important work."

"I know you'd rather be out there pushing the edges of charted space too, Cap. That's where the action is."

"Alright Lieutenant," Iridius said. "Your complaints are noted, but you can drop it now. Space Command has given us our mission. That's what we're going to do."

"Aye, sir," Rangi said, turning back to the helm. "I mean, if paint dries in the forest but no one is there to see it, does it really dry?"

Iridius sighed. This was something of a sore point. Rangi might have been the only one to voice his concerns, as he often was, but Iridius knew he wasn't the only crew member who felt this way. It wasn't prevalent in the newer members of the crew, Ensign Hal, Technician Grantham, Doctor Dooms and Ensign Herd, but those who had served with Iridius on the *Diesel Coast* or during his short but eventful time in command of the *FSC*

Gallaway – Rangi, Quinn, Junker, Greg and Latroz – all seemed bored or restless to varying degrees. He could recognise it in them easily enough because, despite what he'd said to Rangi, he felt it too. A monotony had descended on his starship, completing mission after mission of the same old thing, and he, like the crew, couldn't see an end to it.

Iridius had been excited about commanding the *FSC Deus Ex*. It was a highly advanced corvette, sleek and fast, and so different from the asteroid-hopper turned cargo ship he'd spent so many years on. The *Deus Ex* was also the only ship in the galaxy known to have complete cloaking ability. Other ships had managed adaptive visual camouflage, and used many and varied techniques to limit thermal and radiation signatures, but the *Deus Ex* was the first ship to manage complete stealth operations. The ship could render itself completely invisible, not only to the naked eye and optical sensors, but to thermal, electronic and radiation sensors too. How it managed to do this was so highly classified that even the crew of the ship, including Chief Petty Officer Samira 'Junker' Nejem, who was responsible for all maintenance on board the vessel, didn't know the secret herbs and spices. Iridius had argued until he was blue in the face that this was entirely impractical if something went wrong, but Federation Space Command had refused to budge. Although Junker was very evasive when he asked, Iridius had no doubt she had spent countless hours trying to pry open the sealed tamper-proof black boxes that housed the cloaking systems and figure out how they functioned. He expected nothing less from her.

Iridius and his crew had gone from the equivalent of space UPS to the shadowy ninjas of the Federation fleet, helming a secret reconnaissance vessel capable of infiltrating Alliance space, passing through and listening in on their most private conversations like an unseen spectre. This was another highly classified piece of information about the ship. While perhaps not as thrilling as a ship that could turn invisible, the *Deus Ex* was also fitted with another, perhaps even more galaxy-shaking, piece of technology: the latest in communication interception equipment. Any ship could perform the equivalent of sticking their hand out the window and intercepting radio signals – that technology had been available since the twentieth century, and encryption breaking machine-learning systems had been around since the twenty-first – but the *Deus Ex* went a step further. The real secret sauce with this ship was the fact that it was capable of intercepting quantum entanglement communication.

Quantum entanglement, the use of linked quantum particles that would instantaneously take the same state despite vast separation distances, was the only known method of communicating faster than light, and had become vital across interstellar distances. It was considered impossible to intercept because of the need for already established quantum particle dependence between two systems. But, some smart people somewhere in the Federation, probably wearing lab coats, Iridius assumed, had figured out how to make a system that could mimic a nearby quantum entanglement sending station. The only downside was that they could only intercept outgoing messages, not incoming ones for some reason. Iridius didn't understand the reason, and likely wouldn't even if the lab-coats explained it to him. Still, it was another advantage the Federation had that the Alliance didn't know about. Combine an invisible ship with the ability to listen in on communications thought to be secure, and you've got one hell of a strategic advantage.

Unfortunately, even with all that, Rangi was right. Ultimate ghost ninja ship or not, recon was extraordinarily boring. It was as boring as Great Uncle Pat's stories of being Procyon C's most in-demand washing machine repairman and, even though it meant agreeing with Rangi again, it did feel a bit creepy. Also like Uncle Pat. Iridius never thought he'd look back fondly on a cargo bay full of Endoplorean Land Whale dung or a trip wading knee-deep through Proxima Centauri C's out of control synthetic fertilizer plant, but here he was doing just that. There'd been a lot of shit involved with being captain of the *Diesel Coast*, but at least it was half-interesting shit.

As was often the way, he hadn't realised what he had until it was gone. It was human nature to think the planets were always greener on the other side of the solar system, but there had been something special about the *Diesel Coast*. Shame he'd only come to realise that after he'd flown it into an enormous dog-shaped spaceship housing a completely insane artificial intelligence bent on turning all sentient life in the galaxy into pink goo. He'd sent the rest of the crew to safety and only managed to escape a fiery doom himself because he'd been visited by a holographic projection of himself from the future. After Iridius managed to destroy an existential threat to the galaxy he'd been hailed as a hero and, for the most part, forgiven for his part in destroying the planet Earth. That had been one hell of a weird week.

"How long until we drop out of BAMF?" Iridius asked Rangi, mostly to get everyone's mind back on task – including his own.

"Seventeen minutes," Rangi replied.

"And that'll put us outside sensor range?"

"Aye, Cap," Rangi said, "assuming we're right about their range."

"It's not whether we're right, Lieutenant," Quinn said, "it's whether the intelligence we've been given on the ASS Locke is correct."

Rangi snorted, just as he did every time the name of their target was mentioned and, in fact, the name of any Alliance Space Station. Seriously, the Alliance couldn't have thought of anything better? They could have called them Alliance Orbital Platforms, AOPs, or even Space Stations of the Alliance, SSA, but no, they had to go with ASS. Iridius was sure the Alliance had named all of their space stations ASSes just so he'd have to put up with his immature helmsman giggling every time they were sent to do reconnaissance of the ASS Komet or the ASS Matron or now the ASS Locke.

"Let's just agree to call it Locke Station, shall we?" Iridius said.

"I do find it strange that the Planetary Alliance would name its strategically important stations after an anatomical part," Lieutenant Latroz said. "Still, I do not understand why you find it quite so amusing, Benjamin. Almost every species in the galaxy has some form of waste disposal system that could be considered equivalent to a human arse."

"Thank you, Lieutenant Latroz," Iridius said. "You see Rangi, you should listen to your girlfriend."

"Lieutenant Rangi and I are not friends, Captain," Latroz corrected him. "We are lovers."

Iridius took a deep breath. Despite the fancy new ship, some things had absolutely not changed. Even though they'd proved themselves highly competent, his crew still seemed like a bunch of misfits. He wondered whether April Idowu, captain of the *FSC Gallaway* (and Iridius's ex, but that wasn't why she came to mind all the time, honestly), had to put up with these kinds of inane conversations from her bridge crew. Plus, Iridius had never had to deal with a romantic relationship between his crew members before. Technically, because Rangi and Latroz were both officers of equal rank, they weren't breaching any FSC regulations. Early in the history of long-term space travel, Space Command had realised they had to be more lenient with inter-crew relationships than the terrestrial navy they were based on. When the crew of a ship were the only people you interacted with on a daily basis, sometimes for years on end, sparks were going to fly – both the good and bad. Still, in line with regulations or not, perhaps Iridius needed to rethink how openly they discussed Rangi and Latroz's ongoing relationship. FSC regulations allowed commanding officers to monitor relationships and intervene if they deemed those relationships detrimental to the ship's mission. Iridius wasn't going to go that far. He just didn't want their romance to be a distraction. Rangi and Latroz's relationship was something of a source of fascination for the rest of the crew, if only for the fact that Rangi was a human and Latroz was a seven-foot-tall purple Siruan warrior covered in organic carapace armour. It wasn't unusual, and was completely accepted, for inter-species relationships to happen throughout the Federation, but they usual happened between species that were, let's say, procreatively similar. Being human himself, Iridius was very familiar with the reproductive strategy of humans – although not as familiar as he might have liked over the last few years – but all he knew about Siruans was that the female of the species was humanoid like Latroz, while the male of the species was some kind of small sphere-like mass that was inserted into the female and absorbed during reproduction. What this meant for Latroz and Rangi he had no idea – and didn't want to.

"Girlfriend and boyfriend are human terms, Lieutenant," Quinn said. "Another term for lovers or mates."

"Ah, of course," Latroz said. "I have heard this before, thank you, Lieutenant Commander."

Lieutenant Commander Kira Quinn, Iridius's second-in-command, always stepped in when she knew Iridius was reaching the limit of his patience or knowledge – or both. Whether it was by quoting a specific Federation Space Command regulation or explaining some terminology or situation to one of the non-human crew members, he knew she always had his back. Of those who'd been involved in their galaxy-saving adventure against the Aegix, Quinn had probably been the most instrumental. Sure, it had been Iridius who'd valiantly sacrificed himself and his ship to destroy them, but Quinn had put her razor-sharp scientific mind to work. She had learned more about the Aegix, discovered the way they controlled technology, found the nanobots in Iridius's blood that allowed him to do the same, and helped put them in a position to stop the runaway artificial intelligence.

But it had been ten months and Iridius knew Quinn still blamed herself. She had developed a broadcast that should have disabled the Aegix but it hadn't worked. As a result, several ships in the fleet had been destroyed, and hundreds of crew members killed. No one considered this her fault, of course. They were facing a completely unknown threat that could rapidly evolve and they were scrambling to try and defeat it. Iridius had spent years trying to get Quinn, scientific genius but anxious mess, to come out of her shell in difficult situations. And when she finally had, it hadn't gone well. Now, though she tried hard not to show it, Iridius knew she was sinking back into fear of failure.

"Alright," Iridius said, "you all know the mission but let's be clear again. Space Command has received intelligence that a weapons development program is underway on board the, ahem, Locke Space Station that may pose a threat to the Federation. Since the destruction of Earth and that business with the Aegix, the Admiralty and Senate strongly believe the Alliance may take advantage of the disruption and attempt to seize Federation territory."

"Never mind that the Aegix would have wiped them out too," Rangi said.

"Indeed, Lieutenant," Iridius replied, "but we all know the Alliance hold a frankly ridiculous grudge over the loss they suffered in the Federation–Alliance war more than a hundred years ago. I don't think they're going to forgive us for that, even if we did ensure their ongoing existence."

"Seems dumb," Rangi concluded.

"Succinct as ever, Rangi," Iridius said. "Unfortunately, the logic of 'this seems dumb' never seems to permeate political differences. Latroz, what do we know about Locke Station?"

As tactical officer of the *Deus Ex*, Latroz's responsibilities were primarily situational awareness and operation of ship shields and weapons during combat, but she was also responsible for broader intelligence. She tapped at her console, bringing up the information they had on the ASS Locke. "Even for an Alliance base, Locke Station is a backwards water, as you humans say."

"A backwater," Iridius corrected.

"Yes, thank you, Captain. It is a backwater. The station is in orbit around Lentrani II, an uninhabited planet tidally locked to Lentrani, an M-class red dwarf. This station is operated by the Frost Norton Corporation. They seem to be a smaller member of the Alliance but one focused on advanced technological development, and with a large amount of wealth. The CEO of Frost Norton is a human named Devin Frost. We do not have information on him but he has recently taken over from his father. Federation Intelligence Bureau intelligence reveals that Frost Norton has made a breakthrough in weapons development, but we do not know what that weapon is."

"Thank you, Latroz," Iridius said. "So, we'll anchor near Locke for at least a week to monitor for anything that might be considered a weapons test, and to intercept and monitor communications for anything that may confirm this intelligence. The Senate and Admiralty have asked for any information we can give them so they can assess the risk. Should be relatively straightforward."

"Boring, then?" Rangi said.

"Let's hope so Rangi, because believe it or not it's best if we don't discover that the Alliance is developing advanced weapons," Iridius said.

"I s'pose," the helmsman grumbled.

Iridius had a suspicion that providing information to the Senate and the Admiralty so they could assess the risk was really code for providing a report that some desk clerk would file away, never to be looked at again. They'd spent ten months undertaking missions like this. Ten months looking for this greatly feared threat coming from the Alliance, and they'd never found anything. They'd investigated what was thought to be large-scale fleet movements of the Alliance but had turned out to be the migration of a space-dwelling race of enormous tentacled jellyfish. They'd been sent to monitor suspected Alliance weapons development on Graxen VI, which had turned out to be a corporation developing reusable space fireworks. They'd been dispatched to secretly monitor an Alliance space station rumoured to be developing their own stealth ship, but a week of monitoring their transmissions had revealed that the corporation, Exron, had been faking everything and pre-selling the non-existent technology. This pattern meant Iridius was plenty sceptical about yet another claim of a secret and highly dangerous weapons development program. Frost Norton was probably making pinball machines or developing some high-tech new soft-serve flavour. He had little expectation that they would find anything remarkable whatsoever.

CHAPTER TWO_

"THAT'S REMARKABLE," Quinn said.

"What's that?" Iridius asked, looking over at his executive officer, hoping that maybe after four days they might finally have intercepted something, anything, that could be considered valuable intelligence. So far there hadn't been a single ship coming or going from Locke Station, and they hadn't intercepted any communication of interest at all. There had been one message sent to another Alliance corporation, Trentham Limited, that was interesting, if only for the extremely colourful language used. The message insisted that Trentham pay a long overdue bill or Frost Norton debt collectors would be dispatched with 'weapons capable of genital inversion' and 'half a ton of Porlaxian Flesh Wasps in an anus-sized delivery package'. That message certainly conjured some interesting imagery and, despite Iridius thinking himself quite experienced, contained several curse words he'd never heard before. Still, they hadn't overheard anything pertaining to their actual mission.

Iridius waited a moment, but Quinn didn't look up from where she tapped at the screen of her console. When it became clear she was in one of her moments of scientific concentration, where the rest of the universe seemed non-existent, Iridius spoke again. "Quinn?"

This time she looked up with a jump. "Sorry, Captain, what?"

"You said something was remarkable," Iridius said. "Did you find something on the quantum entanglement interceptor?"

"Oh," Quinn said, "sorry, I hadn't realised I'd spoken out loud. Nothing to do with the mission sorry, sir."

"Right," Iridius said and when Quinn didn't offer any further explanation, he prodded. "Something I should know about?"

"No, not really," Quinn said, "just some personal study I've been doing. Nothing to worry about. It's fine. I'll get back to reviewing the quantum entanglement traffic Ensign Herd has intercepted. Not really anything worth mentioning."

Iridius stared at Quinn. "Quinn?"

"Nothing, it's nothing, Captain."

Iridius waited, slowly counting in his head.

One.

Two.

Three.

And...

"It's just, it's been six months since there's been a Franklin-ism, sir."

And there it was. He'd had a sneaking suspicion it would be something like that. "Keeping tabs on me then, are you?"

"Well, it's more like I'm keeping tabs on the ship, sir. It's quite a milestone to go this long without an issue. You had much less of an effect on the *Diesel Coast* due to its hard-wired system architecture, but even then we still had minor malfunctions at least every few weeks."

For as long as he could remember, technology had been badly behaved around Iridius. Given he lived in the twenty-third century, that was problematic. He hadn't had too many issues when he was younger, just the occasional malfunction of their apartment's weak AI and the unbelievable, according to his teachers at least, number of times his tablet computer had inexplicably lost his homework. The real problems had begun when he'd started spending long periods of time on board starships – something that was a pretty key part of his chosen profession as a Space Command officer. Perhaps because starships comprise hundreds of thousands of highly complex systems, the bridge of a starship seemed to react with even greater technological protest to Iridius's presence. At home, the television would occasionally flicker and his tablet would eat his homework, but on board starships the emergency backup generator would implode, the ship would attempt to launch its entire stockpile of nuclear anti-ship missiles and the ship-wide communication network would play Starship's 'We Built This City' on repeat without pause for seventy-six hours – all extremely dangerous situations.

It didn't take long for engineering staff to determine that Iridius was the common link. Soon after that, the bizarre and ongoing malfunctions that would occur in Iridius's presence were named after him: Franklinisms. Of course, at the time no one really knew what was going on, and no one could bring themselves to blame Iridius directly. He wasn't tampering with the systems in any way, and no one believed his presence could actually be causing these issues, because as a scientifically advanced society no one in the Federation would admit to anything as primitive as a curse. Though that was exactly how it felt to Iridius.

It had been Quinn who'd first theorised that Iridius affected technology in the same way as the Aegix. She then proved her theory by finding that Iridius didn't just have the same ability as the Aegix, his blood actually contained the Aegix's nano-sized robots. For some reason, unlike everyone else who'd been exposed to the Aegix, Iridius had not been melted into a pink puddle on the floor. Most mysterious of all, Quinn estimated the nanobots had been present in Iridius's body for twenty-five years, despite the fact that they had encountered the Aegix for the first time only ten months ago. It was this conundrum that Quinn could not resist. She'd been puzzling over Iridius, his powers and the nanobots ever since. She also knew he didn't want her to.

"Quinn," Iridius said, "you know how I feel about being your gronking science project."

"You're not a science project, Captain. You're a very important research subject for the Federation."

"That doesn't make it sound better."

"It's classic superhero stuff, Cap," Rangi said. "You've had your origin story, when you first get your powers and are forced to confront and destroy the big villain. Now you're settling in and coming to terms with your abilities. You're getting control of them. Techno-wizard part two."

"Stop calling me Techno-Wizard, Rangi, I thought we'd moved on from that."

"The problem is Captain, we don't actually know your origin story. I still have no explanation for how the Aegix nanobots got into your blood decades before we encountered them."

"That's not a problem Quinn. It's a curiosity. They're in there and that's that. Space Command had their concerns about them, but like you just said, it's been six months since we've had anything resembling a Franklinism – therefore, it's not a problem. We can all move on with our lives."

And that was what Iridius was trying to do. Quinn wanted to know why they hadn't had a single Franklinism and the fact was, Rangi was almost right. Iridius was learning to control his abilities. Perhaps it was the simple fact that he finally understood what it was that caused ships to go haywire when he was around. Now he actually had something to target his frustrations towards. It also helped that he'd discovered in moments of anger, fear or desperation he could, in fact, control the nanobots and use them to influence technology. He didn't want to, but Iridius could sense the invaders in his blood now, and over the last ten months he'd made a concerted effort to fixate on them. He'd begun to notice a slight feeling of agitation within him, subtle twitches of his muscles, an extra alertness to his body just before a Franklinism, and over time he'd begun to push back. It became easier and easier, and by now it had almost become second-nature. But this was where Rangi was wrong. Iridius didn't want to harness the power of the nanobots. He wanted to subdue them. His entire life, his career as a starship captain, had long been hampered by these nano-machines that lived within him, but no more. He was determined to stop their influence on the technology around him, and for the last half a year it had been working. Soon, he hoped, he'd manage to disable them permanently.

"Captain, don't you think it's important we understand where they came from? It could mean there are more Aegix out there. It could mean there are more people like you. We don't really know what the Aegix were trying to achieve."

"They wanted to turn everyone in the galaxy into slime," Iridius said. "Remember?"

"Sir, I'm not the only one who believes that wasn't the case. The Aegix clearly said they were trying to protect the galaxy from the Synth-Hastur."

"Yes," Iridius said, "by turning people into slime. Their actions caused the deaths of billions. If they were trying to help, then they're a bit like the little boy who throws mud at the girl he likes, but instead of mud it was missiles, planet-destroying weapons of mass destruction, and something that turned you into goop."

"Those of us studying the Aegix believe the effect they had on most life forms was an accident, a side-effect of whatever they were trying to achieve. They were a synthetic life-form using programming half a million years out of date. We believe they were attempting to alter sentient life to make it resistant to whatever threat the Synth-Hastur pose, but maybe life in the galaxy is now incompatible with what worked five hundred thousand years ago. Except, for some reason, with you. If the Aegix were trying to load nanobots into every living thing in the galaxy, we need to understand why it worked on you and nobody else."

"Okay," Iridius said, "if it's so important, why hasn't the Federation said anything to me?"

"Well," Quinn said, "there's been some turmoil in Space Command and the Senate and, even though a lot of the scientific community doesn't agree, they don't consider the Synth-Hastur a threat because there's been no evidence they exist at all."

"Well, I suppose that's that then," Iridius said. "We've got our mission. If the Federation thinks I'm fine to continue with that, then I will."

"Sir," Quinn said, "it's short-term thinking. They're worried about the Alliance, but what if the Synth-Hastur really does pose an existential threat to the galaxy?"

"Quinn, we've got our orders. I think reading the intercepted communications would be a far better use of your time," Iridius said. "So far all we've learned is just how far up someone's colon Porlaxian Flesh Wasps can manage to climb, and that Devin Frost is a big fan of someone called DJ Chromium, who's coming to perform at his fortieth birthday party."

"What?!" Junker, who was on the bridge undertaking maintenance, sat up so fast she smacked her head on the communications console above her. "Ow, gronking Jupiter's nuts!" She rubbed her forehead.

"Are you well, Chief Petty Officer Nejem?" Junior Ensign Hal, the FSC Deus Ex's resident android, asked. "Would you like me to administer first aid?"

Junker waved him off. "What did you say about DJ Chromium, Captain?"

Iridius looked at Junker, confused. "Uh, I don't know. Apparently the CEO of Frost Norton really likes him. There's been zero ships arrive or leave from Locke Station, but we intercepted a message confirming that DJ Chromium's ship would be authorised to land so Frost could have him perform at his birthday party. Security seems tight, but they're just letting this guy through. Frost must be a big fan, I suppose."

Junker stared at him.

"Is everything okay, Junker?" Iridius asked.

"Some guy," Junker said, completely aghast. "You just called DJ Chromium 'some guy'."

"Sorry," Iridius said, "I just assumed it was a guy. That was probably wrong of me. Is DJ Chromium a woman, or non-gendered? Wait, is DJ Chromium not human?"

"Oh my god, Captain," Junker said. "It's DJ Chromium. Most people think he's human and probably a man, but obviously we can't be sure."

"Okay," Iridius said, "why exactly can't we be sure?"

"Because he's never seen in public without his suit and helmet, obviously. No one knows what he looks like."

"Right, of course."

"I can't believe it!" Junker exclaimed. Iridius suddenly felt like he was a father being chastised by his teenage daughter. He looked around the bridge, searching for any likely allies, but apparently none of them had seen Junker like this before either and they weren't keen to get involved. "You don't know who DJ Chromium is, do you?"

"Um, no," Iridius said, now completely convinced Junker was viewing him as some old, completely out of touch grandpa. "Should I?"

"He's only the most popular DJ in the galaxy. An absolute superstar. I love him."

"You love him?" Iridius said, then he laughed. "You're kidding. You don't love anything except engines and beating me at cards."

Junker stared at him, stone-faced, with an intensity more terrifying than anything even Latroz, the seven-foot-tall alien warrior, could manage. "I *love* him. I love him more than engines."

"Fuck," Rangi said, "this *is* serious. But, I mean, you probably should have heard of DJ Chromium, Cap. He's a big deal."

"I guess I'm just not that into music," Iridius said.

"Obviously," Junker muttered. She continued muttering as she went back to her task. "Calling DJ Chromium 'some guy'. Best musician ever, that's what he is."

Iridius went quiet, wondering when it would be safe to speak again, before remembering that he was, in fact, the captain of this ship and didn't need to tiptoe around Junker. Though he would still be careful, because she did seem to have gone completely mad at the mention of someone who Iridius assumed didn't actually play any sort of musical instrument of his own. He probably just played albums for a crowd, not that Iridius was going to say that out loud, because there seemed a non-zero chance Junker would activate the *Deus Ex*'s self-destruct mechanism in an act of fangirl rage.

"As I was saying," Iridius said, "let's just go back to monitoring any communication from Locke Station. We've only got a couple more days, so let's make sure we don't miss anything."

That seemed to get everyone back on task, for the time being at least. A couple more days of this and then they could send in their report and head back to Tau Ceti for two weeks' shore leave. This was going to be yet another waste of time for a ship and a crew that could be out doing something important. Iridius and his crew were heroes. They'd saved the galaxy and now they were stuck floating in space gossiping about who Devin Frost was having at his birthday party.

"Hal?" Iridius asked.

"Yes, Captain?"

"Would you mind getting me a coffee?"

"Certainly, Captain."

The golden metallic android rose from his seat at the helm, turned and walked stiffly off the bridge. Iridius was glad the robotics engineers of the Federation had finally given up on their attempts to have realistic-looking flesh on androids, because no matter how advanced they'd become, they'd still never managed to claw their way out of the uncanny valley. Iridius really wasn't a fan of synthetic life-forms, but Hal seemed harmless enough. He was a new-model android sent to use his machine learning algorithms to study Lieutenant Rangi's flying techniques. Plus, Hal made excellent coffee.

"You shouldn't keep using him as a servant, Captain," Quinn said. "He's an advanced android, not a butler."

As if on cue, the butler re-entered the bridge carrying Iridius's mug.

"You don't mind fetching me the occasional coffee, do you Ensign Hal?" Iridius asked.

The android tilted his head to the side. "Of course not, Captain. It is my pleasure."

"See?" Iridius said to Quinn. "He doesn't mind."

Iridius took a long sip of coffee then sat for a moment, savouring the excellently brewed beverage. Hal's coffee was perfect every time – warm enough but not so hot that he couldn't drink it, the perfect amount of milk frothed almost identically every time. It was in tasks like this that androids excelled. They could always perform repetitive or well-defined tasks far better and more accurately than a human ever could, but in the hundreds of years they'd been developing, they were always missing that one trait that a human had, an unquantifiable intuition. Hal was here to see if he could pick it up from Rangi – a pilot who flew with almost nothing but intuition. Iridius took another long sip of his coffee. If being a pilot didn't work out, maybe Iridius could figure out a way to keep Hal on board as their official barista.

"Okay," Iridius said, feeling refreshed by the caffeine surge. "Let's—"

Iridius was interrupted by a beep and a flashing icon on the interface built into the arm of his chair. He'd received a personal message via quantum entanglement. It was from Captain April Idowu. Well, well, well, April had finally messaged him. They'd only spoken a couple of times since Iridius had been given command of the *Deus Ex*, and each of those times it had been Iridius who had reached out. After the last time, some three months ago, he'd told himself he wouldn't do it again. He couldn't continue trying to hold on to whatever it was they'd had. Besides, he didn't want to look desperate, because he was definitely not desperate to talk to her and it wasn't like it was extraordinarily hard to go a single day without thinking about her. And it also definitely didn't hurt that she'd never reached out to him the same way he'd reached out to her. She was probably just busy.

April was out there somewhere on the *FSC Gallaway* exploring the edge of known space, a mission that sounded far more interesting than his own reconnaissance work. She was learning about strange new worlds and new alien life-forms while he was stuck learning about strange Alliance invoicing techniques and some musical artist he didn't care about. He was sure she thought about him occasionally, and here, finally, was the proof. Normally Iridius would have waited until he was in his cabin to take a personal message but, feeling excited and more than a little satisfied that she'd finally reached out, he placed a communications earbud in his ear and listened to the message privately.

"Iridius, how are you going? I hope you're well. I know it's been a few months since we last spoke, sorry about that. I think I left our last correspondence hanging and forgot to reply. We encountered a new species, the Gallaway's first true first-contact, the Nereid, a humanoid species that lives an amphibian existence. They're almost identical to stories of mermaids from Earth, which raises all kinds of questions. Anyway, their whole race was enslaved as aquaculture farmers by an interstellar race called the Tassan and we happened to be there when the Tassan returned. The Nereid were desperate for our help, so we assisted in liberating them. Looks like the Nereid are going to join the Federation. So among all that, I forgot to send a reply to you, but I'm sure you're busy doing amazing things too."

Luckily this was not a two-way conversation, so Iridius didn't have to lie and try to make what he was doing sound exciting. April's message continued.

"Sorry, I'm rambling, I know. Maybe I'm trying to stall because I do have a reason for this message. Truth is, it's taken me a while to work up the courage to send this, but I just want to make sure you hear it from me before you hear it from anyone else."

Oh Jupiter's nuts, was she being promoted into the Admiralty already?

"I'm engaged."

Iridius felt as though he'd been snap-frozen in a Baklarvian Ice Crystal Bath. Did she really just say engaged? He was so taken aback that he missed the next few sentences before tuning back in.

"Teth has been on the Gallaway *in an advisory role since we left Tau Ceti and we've been in a relationship for the last six months. I know we've had our history but, I just...I wanted you to*

know. I hope you're loving your new command. You really deserve it. Talk to you soon, okay?"

Iridius stared straight ahead before giving voice to at least one of the questions clouding his mind. "Who the fuck is Teth?"

"Sorry, Captain?" Quinn said.

Iridius didn't reply. He was still reeling from the revelation that April had moved on. I mean, they hadn't been together for ten years, but they came pretty damn close to getting back together when he was on the *Gallaway* and they'd both said there hadn't been anyone else in all that time, and she was the one who tried to kiss him and she hadn't said anything at all about this when they'd spoken and who the fuck was Teth?

"Captain, are you well?" Hal asked. "You appear to have gone quite pale, which is often a sign of distress in humans."

"I'm fine. I'm—"

"Weapons launch from the ASS Locke!" Latroz shouted across the bridge. "Captain, they have fired something."

"At us?" Iridius asked, his attention suddenly pulled away from April by a spike of adrenaline.

"Negative, Captain," Latroz replied. "We are still fully cloaked. There is no indication we have been discovered. They are targeting a small freighter which appears to be derelict. It looks like some kind of weapons test."

"Holy shit," Iridius said, leaning forward in his chair. "Almost like they're undertaking a gronking weapons development program. What kind of weapon is it?"

"Unknown, Captain," Latroz said. "It's not nuclear and doesn't match any known spectral profile. No known explosive, not antimatter or quantum-reactive, but it's definitely not a solid projectile either. It's giving off some kind of signature, but it's unrecognised."

"How long until impact?"

"Ten seconds, Captain."

"Are we in any danger at this range?"

"Unknown, Captain."

Latroz had zoomed the view-screen on the small derelict freighter floating in space. Whatever weapon the Alliance had launched was too small to see. It didn't seem to have any propulsion system of its own, which often made missiles easier to spot against the black of space, but the impact of the weapon was plenty visible. A hole appeared in the hull of the vessel as the weapon punched its way through. Surprisingly, the freighter did not explode – at least not in the traditional sense. There was no great eruption, instead the vessel was enveloped in a strange violet light that burst outward like a rapidly expanding sphere, a shimmering energy wave unlike anything Iridius had seen before. One moment it looked like a sphere then, even as Iridius stared at it, it seemed to invert and appeared as if it were a hole in space, then it was back to an expanding sphere again. It expanded and expanded without slowing down. It became clear to Iridius that the energy wave was going to hit them.

There was no time to bring propulsion systems online and manoeuvre the *Deus Ex* out of the way – not without lighting up their systems to a level that would overwhelm their cloaking capability and give away their position. Even then, there was no guarantee they'd manage to avoid whatever was coming. If Iridius ordered a full propulsion power up there was a small chance he could ensure the safety of his ship, but a very big chance, almost a certainty, that Locke Station would spot them and the Alliance would know the Federation had a spy ship capable of entering their space undetected – something the Federation would absolutely not want to reveal. As a starship captain these snap decisions were what Iridius had trained for his whole life – no hesitation, no second-guessing, use the information on hand to make the best decision possible at the time. There was a beat of silence as the crew waited.

Iridius pressed the button for ship-wide comms. "All stations, brace for impact."

A handful of seconds later the FSC *Deus Ex* was struck by the strange wave of purple energy. When the light-explosion had first occurred it had been bright enough that Iridius had been forced to momentarily turn away, a stagnant after-image of yellow burnt across his vision. But he'd been certain that just before he looked away, he'd seen the purple wave pass through the freighter rather than tear it apart. As the wave of energy impacted the *Deus Ex* he realised he'd been right. The energy front did not destroy the *Deus Ex*. It didn't damage it at all. Instead, it passed right through the shields without them even registering contact. This alone was extraordinary because a ship's energy shields were not only designed to absorb the kinetic energy associated with physical objects such as railgun rounds or missiles, they were also more than capable of stopping highly charged subatomic particles such as when a ship dropped out of faster-than-light travel or even pure electromagnetic energy. Whatever this energy was passed right through the shields and then continued through the hull of the ship as if it wasn't even there.

Iridius saw the shimmering purple enter through the wall of the bridge and watched it pass right through his crew until it hit him. He was pleased to note it didn't tear them apart molecule by molecule or liquefy their intestines or wipe their brains or anything equally unfortunate. Iridius felt nothing as the wave passed over him, no pain, not even a gentle breeze; no physical sensation at all. Now, let's be clear, saying there was no physical sensation isn't the same as saying there was no impact. If one thing could be said for the great sprawling galaxy it's that there is some completely weird shit out there, weirder than anything humans ever dreamed up. Iridius had been privy to some pretty bizarre experiences himself, but what happened in that moment was up there with the strangest.

In the brief instant it took for the purple whatever-it-was to pass through Iridius, he saw what could only be described as duplicates of the bridge all around him, each laid on top of one another. Iridius saw Rangi moving, but with movements that seemed odd, fractured, almost like he was staring at a scene lit by a flashing strobe. There wasn't just one image of Rangi in front of him, there were dozens, maybe hundreds, all on top of each other, blurring into one another like echoes of reality. Not just Rangi but everything around him too. It was less obvious due to its static position but the bridge itself was duplicated just as many times. Iridius held his hand in front of his face and saw countless fingers, countless versions of his hand seeming to stretch out to infinity like fun-house mirrors reflecting each other. It took only a fraction of a second, Iridius had no doubt of that, but that moment seemed to last much longer than it should. There was enough time in that millisecond to look around the bridge and see that all around him the scene was the same, the bridge crew moving in stutter-step.

Then it was over. Iridius was looking out at the bridge and everything had returned to normal. Systems were running. Power was on. He could feel the gentle movement of air pumped by life-support systems. His chair hummed with the vibrations of an alive ship. Everyone on the bridge was wide-eyed. It seemed they'd all had the same disorientating, almost nauseating, experience of seeing reality piled on top of itself. It was, of course, Lieutenant Benjamin Rangi who gave voice to what they were all thinking.

"What in the fucking black was that?"

"Quinn?" Iridius said, immediately deferring that same question to his first officer because he had no fucking clue what that was and hoped she might have some immediate scientific explanation.

"Uh," she said, looking down at her console as if hoping the answer might appear on the screen. She was pale, whether from nausea or from fear he wasn't sure – probably both. "I, um, I don't know, Captain."

"Right, well, it's nice to know my scientific analysis of a situation is on par with yours for once in my life," Iridius said. "But see, here's the thing, I can't figure it out because I'm the dumb captain. You on the other hand are the smart one, so get me an answer please."

Quinn nodded. "Yes, Captain."

"The freighter is gone, Captain," Latroz said.

"So it was destroyed by that weapon? Put it on screen."

"It has been destroyed," Latroz said. "Debris is very small and already highly dispersed. There is not much left to see. But that is not the strange thing. There are always traces of the explosive destruction of a ship, residual thermal energy, radiation and so on. The strange thing is that the readings I am seeing suggest this vessel was destroyed several hours ago, perhaps as many as ten."

"Are you saying that weapon was launched ten hours ago?" Iridius asked. "Whatever that phenomenon was lasted ten hours?"

"We haven't had ten hours' worth of movement, Cap," Rangi said, turning from his console to look at Iridius. "We can't use full thruster anchoring when we're cloaked, so we drift a little but we haven't drifted that far."

"Sir," Latroz said, "according to this, that weapon impacted less than a minute ago, but the freighter was destroyed ten hours ago."

"That doesn't make any sense," Iridius said.

"Oh my god," Quinn said, looking up and down from her console as if checking something repeatedly before she spoke. "We've been temporally displaced."

Iridius stared at his XO. "We time travelled?"

Quinn nodded. "Basically, yes. About three or four minutes. Backwards."

"That lines up with the rotation of Locke Station relative to us, Captain," Rangi said. "It's in the position it was three minutes and sixteen seconds ago."

"That burst of energy was a temporal displacement wave," Quinn said. "They are theorised to occur if someone manages macro-state time reversal. It looks like the theoretical predication is true: a finite area of space has been exposed to decreasing amounts of temporal disturbance relative to another fixed observer out from the point of impact."

Iridius rubbed his temples with his fingertips. He could already tell this was going to hurt his grey matter. "You said something about time reversal?" he asked.

Quinn nodded. "Scientists have been investigating T-symmetry, the idea that time could be a reversible quantity, for hundreds of years. Most scientists don't think it's much more than a theoretical exercise, as the idea of spontaneous entropy decrease on the scale required is just so statistically improbable." Quinn must have noticed the incomprehension on Iridius's face, because she went on to explain. "Entropy is how we define time. Basically, things increase in disorder over time and irreversible entropic processes move in one direction, the direction we think of as time. Similar to the way we understand the statistical nature of quantum mechanics, entropy is also statistical. It's possible for entropy to decrease spontaneously, but only at quantum scales."

"Quinn," Iridius said, "do that thing where you talk to me like I'm an idiot?"

"Okay," Quinn said. "Imagine scrambling an egg. That's easy, right? That's increasing the entropy of the egg. Now, could you, if you continued stirring, somehow unscramble that egg?"

"No."

"Right," Quinn said. "That, broadly speaking, is what we

understand as the direction of time. Because of quantum mechanics it is possible that you could continue stirring and the egg would unscramble itself, but it's so unlikely as to be considered impossible. Macro-state time reversal is figuring out how to reverse the entropy of an area beyond quantum scales. It's all been theoretical, but it looks like the Alliance might have actually managed it. It requires a significant amount of energy to achieve, easily enough energy to have caused that level of destruction to a ship. In fact, there has been a theory that a time reversal event could be used as a weapon. The theory is that a weaponised reversal in time would cause an explosion that would actually happen before the impact event. I think they've done it. It's an incredible breakthrough. The Alliance just tested a weapon that destroyed a ship ten hours before the weapon was launched. It's—"

Iridius interrupted. "A fucking time bomb."

"More or less," Quinn said.

"So, hold on, we're three minutes ago?" Rangi asked, staring at the view-screen. "Does that mean we're out there? All of us, on the *Deus Ex* but from three minutes ago, not knowing that we're out here watching ourselves?"

"We must be," Quinn said, "although obviously we are cloaked and neither version of us can see the other."

"Goddamn it," Iridius said. "You know, in the Academy we were assured that, contrary to popular belief, there would be none of these time shenanigans because it wasn't possible."

"I know, it's amazing," Quinn said.

"No," Iridius responded, "it's already giving me a headache."

"Hang on," Rangi said, and Iridius could see the contortion of his face, revealing the equal amount of contortion that must have been going on inside his brain. "We went back three minutes before the weapon was launched, but the freighter is gone because it was destroyed ten hours ago, right? So what reason do the Alliance have to actually launch the weapon now?"

"See?" Iridius said. "Migraine inducing. Plus, it makes Rangi's constant barrage of questions even worse than usual."

"And why did we not see the freighter destroyed ten hours ago if that's when the weapon destroyed it?" Latroz asked. "We should have picked that up on sensors."

"Don't you start with the paradoxes too," Iridius said.

"And if they don't launch the weapon then how are we here? How did we get three minutes back in time when there will be no temporal displacement wave to send us back?" Ensign Herd chimed in.

"There's two copies of us in the universe now!" Rangi burst out. "Is that going to be permanent?"

Iridius squeezed his thumb and forefinger into his eyeballs. "Quinn," he said, "tell me there's some science to at least explain this and better yet, straighten it out, because a universe with two Benjamin Rangis can't be good."

Quinn took a moment, in that way she always did when her razor-sharp brain was working on something. "Paradoxes are based on logic," she said. "Temporal displacement immediately breaks logic. However, hundreds of years of scientific advancement have more than shown us that the universe doesn't care for logic. It's got to be the many worlds interpretation, or maybe superposition, like Schroedinger."

"I know this one," Iridius said, "dead cat guy."

"Superposition of two states," Quinn said. "The cat is simultaneously alive and dead until the waveform collapses, yes. But Schroedinger was talking about that on the quantum level. This is like superposition of timelines." She tapped her lip with her forefinger, stopping when she seemed to have reached a conclusion. "Maybe because we were inside the temporal displacement waves our experience of the universe is unchanged. Latroz, fix our sensors tight on the position the other *Deus Ex* would be in. Set for small variations in temperature against cosmic background. Ordinarily, cloaking would keep us hidden, but we know exactly where to look for tiny temperature fluctuations."

"Aye, Lieutenant Commander," Latroz said, and then after a moment, "Got us. There we are."

On the view-screen Latroz projected a faint outline of minor temperature variation from the ordinary temperature of space, 2.7 degrees Kelvin, in the location of the *Deus Ex* from before they were tossed three minutes back in time.

"Two Benjamin Rangis," Iridius muttered. "God help us."

"Let's wait," Quinn said. "It's just over a minute until the time reversal bomb was launched from Locke Station in our original timeline."

"And what are we expecting to happen?" Iridius asked.

"Not sure," Quinn admitted. "We're making observations."

The bridge crew waited in silence, watching the faint outline of the other *Deus Ex* as it floated in space.

Eventually Latroz spoke. "Impact would be occurring in three, two, one. Now."

On the view-screen there was something like a shimmer, a very faint, almost indistinguishable ripple in space. Latroz checked her console. "It's gone," she said. "The *Deus Ex* is gone. I mean, we are still here but the other *Deus Ex* just vanished, even though the missile was never launched."

"The freighter?" Quinn asked.

"Still destroyed," Latroz reported.

"Curious," Quinn said. "It seems like the timeline waveform has collapsed back to a single timeline. What happened inside the radius of the temporal displacement waves is the timeline we experienced, but outside of that the timeline is altered. It's fascinating."

"Right, but the universe has somehow cleaned up the mess

and the other us is gone?" Iridius said. "There's only one of each of us now?"

"Seems that way," Quinn said, "like the spacetime event of us going back three minutes is still part of the universe's timeline, despite the causality event not being necessarily present in the broader continuum."

"Got it," Iridius said, though he didn't really. "Moral of the story is, that was super fucking weird and I hated every second of it, but the Alliance still have a weapon they really shouldn't have?"

"Yes, sir," Quinn said.

"Right," Iridius said, standing. "I need to make a call."

CHAPTER THREE_

"SORRY," Iridius said, trying to keep the frustration out of his voice and failing dramatically. "Admiral Tullet, I don't think you understand what I'm reporting here. The Alliance have developed a weapon capable of being sent back in time to destroy something. Like, they launch it now, it hits something now but it destroys its target in the past, before the weapon was even launched. I saw it happen, my ship was caught in the temporal displacement shock wave, and I'm still having difficulty believing it. It's mind-bending to comprehend, but I can assure you we've witnessed it. They blew up a freighter ten hours before they launched the weapon that did it."

Iridius had retreated to his cabin to make his report to Federation Space Command via quantum entanglement. Finally, after almost a year of floating around in Alliance-controlled space, they'd discovered something, something of, it seemed to Iridius at least, utmost importance. For the first time in a hundred years the Alliance might pose a real, credible threat to the Federation, not just an annoyance to the outer colonies or a story old soldiers told about how they'd valiantly held back the threat of the crazed capitalist zealots of the Planetary Alliance of Corporate Holdings. Iridius had contacted the Admiralty and, much to his chagrin, had been put in contact with Admiral Edwin Tullet.

Iridius was already annoyed about the news of April's engagement, then he'd been unwittingly knocked three minutes back in time, and now he had to speak with this gronking muppet. Admiral Tullet was the epitome of an officer who'd been promoted through the ranks not out of merit but to get him out of the way. The embodiment of the Peter Principle, but instead of being promoted to his first level of incompetence he'd ascended dozens of levels above it. After the destruction of Earth, Tullet had been promoted to admiral to replace one of the many who'd been killed. Unfortunately, he was completely undeserving of the rank. Admiral Toilet, Iridius called him, at least in private. The man was completely full of shit.

"Do not speak to me like you believe me a simpleton, Captain," Tullet replied. "I understand what you've said. I'm telling you to leave the system and return to Tau Ceti."

"Admiral, we've discovered the Federation's largest enemy has a brand-new type of weapon and you want me to leave the site of its development completely unmonitored? It's my recommendation that I be permitted to investigate further. If we can get someone on that station, we can at least find out what they're planning to do with this time-weapon and maybe even stop its development."

"You've been given your orders, Captain Franklin. We will send another ship to deal with the threat you've uncovered."

"Another ship?" Iridius said, knowing he was failing in his attempt to remain diplomatic. "We're deep in Alliance-controlled space. The only reason we got in here unscathed is because we remained fully cloaked. The *Deus Ex* is the only ship capable of that. What mythical other ship is going to make it here without being attacked?"

"I'll advise you to watch your tone, Captain."

"Could I speak to Admiral Merritt please, sir?" Iridius asked.

"No, Captain Franklin, you may not speak to Admiral Merritt. Admiral Merritt is currently indisposed, and I'll have you know that much of senior Space Command disagrees with her treating you like some favourite pet. Admiral Merritt authorised you to be given command of the FSC *Deus Ex* before the complete Admiralty was re-established following the destruction of Earth. You remember that, Captain Franklin? The destruction of humanity's homeworld and the death of billions, something you were directly responsible for? The idea that the captain responsible for releasing the Aegix threat and delivering it straight to Earth, where it extinguished all life, should then be put in command of the Federation's most advanced starship is utterly preposterous. I'm not alone in thinking this, and have no doubt that when I make a motion to the rest of senior command at our next round table meeting, you will be stripped of your command in favour of someone far more worthy."

"Sir, I have been cleared of wrongdoing in that matter and I would appreciate if you would treat me as per the findings of the court martial. As you may be aware, it was determined that ultimately another ship would have responded to the situation on Iota Persei E, and they would have inadvertently released the Aegix as I did. In fact, my involvement resulted in a response that defeated the Aegix threat and possibly saved all sentient life. Basically, I helped save the galaxy, Admiral."

There was no video over this QEC link but Iridius didn't need to see Admiral Toilet's face to know he was scowling. He could hear it as clearly as if Tullet was one of the Fentrillians, who used vocal and body language in the complete opposite way to humans, moving their faces with complicated twitches and tics to communicate while vocalising their emotional state.

"Saved the galaxy, did you? You were lucky. You would never

have been able to do that without the support of far more accomplished captains in the Space Command fleet."

"Of course I wouldn't. Saving the galaxy is a team sport," Iridius said, his frustration with this absolute fungal-spore on the arse of Space Command growing rapidly by the second. "That's why I said I *helped* save the galaxy. But I was the one willing to sacrifice myself, willing to die to take down the Aegix in that final battle. That's why I received the Federation Star. You might have heard about that. Have you saved the galaxy, Admiral? Have you got a Federation Star?"

"You insolent worm," Tullet said. "Typical arrogance from you, Franklin. Typical starship captain who thinks he's better than everyone else in Space Command. I don't agree with you being given command of anything but why do you think you were given command of a stealth ship and sent to do recon? Even Admiral Merritt knew it was best to put you in a situation where you couldn't get involved and mess everything up. You're concerned about this Alliance weapon being developed, but you're the time bomb Franklin. Eventually you'll blow up again. Things will start going wrong and you'll cause chaos like always. You have malfunctions named after you. You *are* a malfunction. Best that you're left to float around recording communication and not getting in trouble."

Iridius knew he'd already crossed a line with his conduct, but now Tullet had struck a nerve and was really pissing him off. Why did he have to answer to this bureaucratic dipshit? Tullet probably hadn't set foot on a starship in years, because that would mean abandoning the comforts of foot massages and cucumber sandwiches. Iridius was self-aware enough to know that part of why he wanted to investigate Locke Station was that he was bored shitless with reconnaissance and desperately wanted to be involved in some action again. But he also had genuine concerns about what the Alliance were doing and what it might mean for the Federation. This might not have been as galaxy threatening as the Aegix, but as far as the Federation was concerned, surely it was just as much of an existential threat. The Alliance could do untold damage with a weapon like that time-reversal bomb.

Maybe if he was being told to stand down by Admiral Merritt or any of the other senior officers who had actual experience commanding a starship he might have listened, but Tullet's total experience of starship command was the one time he ceremonially brought the FSC *Lincoln* into dock after its final voyage, and even then he'd spent a large portion of the time giving orders that were completely ignored by the crew, who knew exactly what they were doing and didn't want to take orders from an idiot that would at best, make them look stupid and, at worst, see them collide with six different asteroids, two moons and possibly a star. Iridius had less respect for Admiral Tullet than Tantan megatapeworms have for even the strongest anal itch cream.

"Starship captains are not arrogant, Admiral Tullet. We are self-assured. You need to back yourself in the decisions you make out here in the black. You can't afford to second-guess yourself in a life-or-death situation. You'd understand that if you'd actually been a captain or been in a situation more dire than wondering where your next cream-cheese bagel is coming from."

"I will have you charged for this disrespect, Captain Franklin. I am a Space Command Admiral. I understand more about starship command than you ever will."

Iridius couldn't help but laugh. "Please," he said, "zooming toy ships around while you're in the bath making pew pew noises doesn't count."

"I'll have you back flying a hauler before you can breathe, Franklin! You're a sorry excuse for a starship captain. You and that bunch of idiots you call a crew."

"At least I am a captain," Iridius said. "And I'm not going to let your stupidity and jealousy give the Alliance an opportunity to destroy us."

"You will do as ordered and return to Tau Ceti or your command will be suspended immediately!"

"I'm going to stop the Alliance from deploying this weapon," Iridius said. "If you want to stop me you'd better send a ship."

"Oh, I will!"

"Maybe you should command it yourself, Admiral. You might learn a thing or two about what it's like in the real Space Command."

"Captain Franklin you will—"

Iridius shut down communication. If he wasn't still seething with rage he might have immediately regretted that conversation. His first thought was to wonder what April would say if he told her what he'd just done. Not that he should care what April would say because she'd moved on with Teth - who was probably a loser. The people Iridius really needed to talk to were his crew. If he was going to disobey a direct order from an Admiral and get his crew involved then he'd better give them the chance to object and hopefully save themselves, or at least put on a rain jacket to partially protect themselves from the shit storm they were about to fly into.

———

"Captain," Quinn said, immediately after he'd outlined his conversation with Admiral Tullet. "I'd just like to raise a point."

Iridius braced himself. Quinn was adopting the strategy known to executive officers and second-in-commands throughout the universe. She would tell him off, berate him even, but do so in a completely acceptable, advisory tone so that she didn't step above her authority or call him a complete gronking idiot in the way that, say, Iridius had just done with his superior officer.

"Quinn, you don't need to tell me it wasn't wise to speak to one of the Admiralty like that. I'm aware."

"No, it isn't that, Captain. Admiral Tullet is a complete and utter knob, I'm sure he deserved it."

Iridius smiled. "Well, nice to see even you are willing to speak out against the idiocy of superior officers when the situation demands it. I'll take it as a compliment that you've never called me a complete and utter knob then. You don't have to tell me which regulations I broke or which ones I'm planning to break, either."

"By my count 13B, 232, 413A and 413B, and you're borderline on 106 and 315, but that's not my point either. I don't care about the regulations."

Lieutenant Rangi, who was taking a drink from a water bottle, almost sprayed a mouthful across his console.

"Well," Iridius said, "those are words I never thought I'd hear from you. What have you done with Quinn?"

He might have been making light of her comment but Iridius really was shocked. Quinn's behaviour had changed since the battle with the Aegix. She blamed herself for the chaos of the fleet battle so sure, it made sense that she'd retreated into her shell somewhat, but what actually surprised Iridius was this new aspect to her behaviour, not so much rebellion but a disruption of her straight-edged view of the world. He couldn't imagine her previously having called one of the Admiralty a knob or saying she didn't care about Space Command regulations.

"I care more about what you think, Captain. I care about whether *you* think you're being reckless."

Iridius cocked an eyebrow. "No, I don't think I'm being reckless. I think it's reckless to leave this weapon development program unattended."

"That may well be, but I just want to remind you what

happened last time you decided we needed to intervene in something we probably shouldn't have."

"Yes, I remember," Iridius said. "Why is it people have to bring that up like they think I might have suddenly forgotten? Oh hey, remember that time you inadvertently destroyed Earth? Oh yeah, I'd forgotten about that. Silly me. Remember what happened after that though? I completely on purpose saved the galaxy so, you know, you win some, you lose some."

"I just want to make sure you've thought this through, Captain," Quinn said, "and you're not just running off to play hero again because you're bored with reconnaissance. That's the type of thing that might make an executive officer think their superior was being a complete and utter knob."

"Well, lucky I'm not."

Note: he was.

"Sometimes you don't get to choose the situation you find yourself in, Quinn," Iridius continued. "Sometimes things don't work out as expected and you've got to be willing to adapt. That's what Admiral Tullet doesn't understand. Yes, we were sent out here on a stealth reconnaissance mission but the situation can be dynamic. Things have changed, and now we have to stop a real threat to the Federation."

"Captain," Rangi interjected, "you know I'm as keen on a new adventure as anyone, but why can't you use your techno-wizard powers? If we fly close to the station can't you just use your nanobots to shut everything down?"

"No," Iridius answered. "I'm not using them. It's too dangerous. The nanobots inside me are part of what tried to wipe out all life in the galaxy, remember?"

"Yeah, I get that, but you can control them now right?" Rangi said.

"I'm not using the nanobots, Lieutenant," Iridius said. "That's the end of it."

"Alright, Captain," Quinn said, "let's say you're right and we really do need to intervene. We've already seen that Locke Station is, no pun intended, locked down. There's been no traffic to or from the station at all. Obviously now we know why. They are trying to keep their weapons development program secret, and no doubt CEO Devin Frost has ordered these strict controls."

"I too was going to raise this question, Captain," Latroz said. "I do not know Admiral Tullet, but if Lieutenant Commander Quinn believes him to be, as she said, a complete and utter knob then he must be what we Siruans would call a 'gonjiber', which I believe translates for you as a 'wanker'."

Iridius raised his hands in submission when Quinn looked at him. "I didn't say it," Iridius protested as innocently as possible. He turned to Latroz. "Consider yourself disciplined for using that language about one of the Admiralty, Lieutenant."

"Yes, Captain," Latroz replied.

"Even if he is a gonjiber," Iridius added, unable to help himself.

"I simply mean," Latroz continued, "if Admiral Tullet is so disagreeable that even Lieutenant Commander Quinn is willing to speak ill of him then he must be incompetent. I would therefore tend to agree with your assessment of the situation, Captain. We may need to engage in a mission to neutralise the threat to the Federation. However, I agree with Lieutenant Commander Quinn that it will be extraordinarily difficult to access Locke Station. Given the structure of the Planetary Alliance, CEO Devin Frost likely has near total control over what happens on the facility. He can mandate a complete lockdown of the station without exception. Even if we were to try and pose as citizens of the Alliance or representatives of the controlling Alliance Board of Directors, there is no necessitated mandate that he let us aboard the station. It is not like the Federation."

"I understand that, Lieutenant Latroz, and Quinn I recognise your concerns, but I wouldn't have pushed as hard as I did with Admiral Tullet if I hadn't already devised what I think is a plan that will get us onto Locke Station. We know Devin Frost is allowing one ship to dock with Locke Station, and that ship should be arriving in the next few days."

"DJ Chromium," Junker said, still unable to hide the excitement in her voice.

"That's right, Junker," Iridius said, "and what did you tell me about DJ Chromium?"

"He's the greatest ever?"

"Okay sure, but what I meant was the part where you said DJ Chromium always wears a helmet to keep his identity a secret."

"Oh, Captain Franklin," Quinn said. "You're not."

Iridius nodded. "That's DJ Franklin to you, Quinn."

CHAPTER FOUR_

CAPTAIN APRIL IDOWU's feet thumped in a constant rhythm against a treadmill in the fitness centre on board the *FSC Gall-away*. She had zoned out, letting her footfalls land in time with the beat of the electronic music that pounded in her earbuds. This song was one of her favourites to run to, 'Never Dance Alone' by DJ Chromium. The electronic instrumentation and driving bass seemed to make her run harder, and made the ordinarily uninteresting kilometres click by faster. April had never enjoyed running, not in the way she knew some people did. Teth was one of those people. He would run for hours at a time in complete silence, claiming to enjoy the way it cleared his mind. April couldn't think of anything worse. She had too many thoughts for that. The pressure of being a starship captain, the constant mind-noise of responsibility, meant that silence left her brain with nothing to do but parse the constantly competing priorities she had to sift through. Music was better than silence. Instead of trying to clear her mind she just pumped in extra loud, high-energy music to shove everything else out of the way.

Never. Never. Never.

The lyrics of the chorus repeated in her ears.

No, never dance alone.

As if these lyrics triggered something far down in her subconscious, thoughts of Iridius B. Franklin popped completely unbidden into April's head. That was just like Iridius. Even the version of him living in her subconscious would wander in unannounced, talking loudly, turning up when she least wanted him to. But was that true? Maybe it was fairer to say that he had arrived at an inopportune time. She couldn't honestly say she didn't want to think of him. She did. She would have like to see him too, but it was only four weeks until she had promised to marry someone else.

She also knew she couldn't blame Iridius for her own thoughts. It wasn't as if he'd chosen to appear all but fully-formed in her head. He would hate being blamed for that, in that light-hearted way he had of reacting with faux outrage to just about everything. He would complain that it wasn't her fault she couldn't stop thinking about him. April smiled, thinking of the times she'd woken up grumpy about something Iridius had done in her dream. He would be utterly indignant that she was annoyed when the real him had done nothing wrong. Of course, the real him had done plenty of things wrong. She had to remind herself of that before she started looking back through a rose-coloured space helmet.

"Do captains really have to face the black alone?" he'd asked her once.

Back then she'd thought the answer to that question had been yes, but since taking command of the *Gallaway* she'd come to realise that she didn't want to spend her life alone. Being captain of a starship was a lonely job. She was surrounded by a large crew and she enjoyed spending recreational downtime with them, but she was always the captain. That was something only other commanders understood. There was no one on board who was your equal, no one you could completely relax around. You could never have friends among the crew of your ship, not real ones anyway, and you could certainly never have a romantic relationship with a crew member. But Teth was different. Although he was serving on board the *Gallaway* he was a Cultural Attache Advisor, a Federation diplomat on board in the event of first-contact scenarios.

April hadn't sought it out. It had happened naturally after spending time together. He was sweet and generous and he cared for her and, importantly, they were free to have a relationship. She could be the captain of a starship and not have to face the black alone. She could never have that with Iridius, not unless one of them, or more realistically both of them, gave up their dream to command a ship among the stars. Maybe she should have considered that.

No. Neither of them would want that.

She shook herself free of her thoughts about Iridius, guilt setting in. This was normal, though. Everyone had cold feet before they got married, thought about their old flames, considered the might-have-beens. Everyone did that. Right? She loved Teth. She had no doubt she was going to be happy. Still, was it possible to love two people at once?

Two beeping tones cut through April's music and, thankfully, through her thoughts. The alert meant she was about to receive a communication tagged as urgent. She reached out and pressed the stop icon on the treadmill's projected holoscreen. The tread began slowing and April reached out to pluck her towel from where it was draped over the nearby handle. She wiped her face, clearing away the sweat from her forehead before tapping the earbud in her ear.

"Yes?"

The voice that spoke was Commander Mul's, her Executive Officer, second-in-command of the *FSC Gallaway* and currently Officer of the Watch on the bridge. "Captain Idowu," the Zeta

Reticulan said, "I'm sorry to interrupt your exercise time but you're needed on the bridge."

"Do I have time for a shower, Mul?" April said as she rubbed the towel over her sweat-soaked hair. Her grey standard-issue Space Command exercise singlet was dark with sweat and was clinging to her back in a way that quickly became uncomfortable as she cooled down.

"We've received new orders from Tau Ceti," Mul responded. "A priority one redirect to Betelgeuse to respond to a distress call from a colony on Acacia, one of the moons of Geffet."

"What?" April asked. "Why us? There must be someone closer to Betelgeuse than we are. We're at least a couple of days away."

"Yes, Captain," Mul said. "Travel time from here to Geffet is eighty-six hours. The hauler *FSC Clarence* has already responded to the distress call, but Space Command have asked us to respond as well."

"And what about our meeting with the Nereid ambassador? We're supposed to be there for the Nereid's Federation entrance negotiations."

"Yes, Captain," Mul said. "It's been delayed. I think you should just come to the bridge please, Captain."

April stopped midway through towelling down her under arms. If she wasn't going to get a shower she at least didn't want to smell too bad when she went back to the bridge. Mul had slipped into second-in-command arguing mode when he'd said 'please', but April knew he was losing his patience. That, in and of itself, didn't bother April. Mul was a grey, they famously had about as much patience as a Rafikan ultra-cheetah – a creature with such high-speed reflexes that they experienced time differently – stuck behind two elderly women pushing trolleys side by side down a grocery store aisle. Mul was always a grouchy little grey, and after almost a year under April's command he was more comfortable being grumpy with her. No, what bothered April was the undertone of concern, maybe even fear, in his voice.

"What is it, Mul? What's happened?"

"Acacia colony Agri-1 first reported an incoming unknown projectile. Scan data confirmed it as a probe of unknown origin. It impacted 48 kilometres from the colony. Within hours they had sent a distress signal."

"Let me guess," April said. "Whatever was released from the probe started turning people into pink goo?"

"Yes, Captain," Mul replied. "I think we've found our missing Aegix probe."

CHAPTER FIVE_

"INCOMING FTL SIGNAL DETECTED," Latroz said from where she'd been watching her console. "It's transmitting an identity beacon. A private transport called the *Interstella*, sir."

"Finally," Iridius replied. They'd been waiting days for the appearance of an incoming ship – DJ Chromium was expected to arrive at Locke Station any time now. "Any chance we can confirm it's definitely DJ Chromium's ship?"

Latroz worked at her console for a moment and then, in something unseen in the Siruan except when she was discussing the most efficient approach to disembowelling every known species in the galaxy, she smiled in amusement. "You could say there is a chance, yes Captain. I'll put it on screen."

The view-screen at the front of the bridge changed from the view of ASS Locke they'd been holding for the last week and switched to a highly amplified view of a ship arriving from BAMF. The shields around the vessel crackled orange as they caught the discharge of particles associated with dropping out of faster-than-light travel, and when the light show had cleared the ship was revealed as a sleek white Gulfstream Executive transport – a common private transport ship used by celebrities and wealthy business people in the Alliance. It was the type of private ship rarely seen outside the borders of Alliance space. This particular Gulfstream was even more customised than the few others Iridius had seen before. The outside of the ship was completely covered in what must have been hundreds of thousands, if not millions, of small RGB LED lights. The lights pulsed and flashed in epilepsy triggering patterns of colour, and Iridius had no doubt that if the vacuum of space had been capable of transmitting sound he would have been forced to hear the chest-pounding thump of heavy bass. The lights on the exterior hull of the ship seemed to vary from eclectic collections of spiralling shapes to waves of rainbow with complete randomness, but there was one steady constant through the whole thing. Along the length of the small transport ship the same words would flash constantly, over and over: DJ CHROMIUM ON TOUR.

"Ah," Iridius said, "I see this guy is fond of making his presence known then."

Iridius heard what he was certain was a high-pitched squeal. He spun in the direction of the sound, ready for a life-support check or to ask what other system might cause a squealing sound on failure. Instead, he saw Junker. Knowing they were waiting on the arrival of DJ Chromium, she'd snuck onto the back of the bridge. The only system that had failed was her self-respect as she squealed at the sight of the obnoxious Gulfstream. Junker was a tough, rebellious, grease-smeared wrench-monkey and a damn intelligent woman, so the sight of her hiding at the back of the bridge barely managing to suppress her desire to audibly scream was causing Iridius no small amount of cognitive dissonance.

"Junker," he said, "what are you doing?"

Junker pointed at the view-screen and mouthed the words, *it's him.*

"You know, when I was growing up we used to get warnings about the danger of succumbing to the cultural influence of the Alliance of Planetary Corporations. I thought it was bullshit, but maybe this is what they were warning us about. An apparent complete loss of reasoning skills. Yes, Junker," Iridius said, "I know it's him, I can see the giant words on the side of the ship. Why are you on the bridge and not down in engineering?"

It took her a moment, but eventually Junker seemed to return to borderline normalcy. "I just thought I could help, Captain."

"How is this," Iridius gestured in her direction, "helpful? Be honest with me please, you just wanted to see him, right?"

"Yes, sir," Junker admitted, "but I do think I can help."

Iridius wasn't happy with Junker arriving on the bridge unannounced, but it had been her ingenious alterations to the *FSC Diesel Coast's* propulsion system that had made it possible for them to avoid an onslaught of missiles that would have seen them peppered like a Procyon Hot Steak during the Federation's final stand against the Aegix. If Junker said she could help then Iridius had no doubt she could.

"Alright Junker," Iridius said, "what have you got in mind?"

"Well Cap, you're going to intercept that ship, capture it and then pose as DJ Chromium, right?"

"Yes, that's the plan."

"Well, as you've said, you didn't even know who DJ Chromium was until a couple of days ago and you still haven't heard any of his music. What do you know about being a DJ?"

"Nothing, Junker. I know nothing about being a DJ but that doesn't matter. I don't intend on getting myself into the situation where I actually need to know anything about being a DJ. I'm just using the DJ Chromium identity to get aboard the station, then I'll find the weapons development area and destroy the whole place if I have to."

"Okay," Junker said, "but what happens if you run into fans

who start asking you questions? What if you have to meet Devin Frost and he asks about music?"

"I'll wing it."

"You'll wing it?"

"Yes, Junker," Iridius said. "Believe it or not, I'm quite good at improvising."

"DJ Chromium," Junker said, putting on a voice that Iridius assumed was supposed to be a journalist of some sort, "many people say your first record, *Stars Above Us,* is still your best work. How do you feel when people disregard the continuing development of your style over the eight albums since then, and does it frustrate you that people constantly cling to your earlier work?"

"I'm just happy to have fans, man," Iridius replied in a slow drawl he thought might fit a musician.

"What do you think is your best album?"

Iridius paused. "Whichever you think, man."

"When you play live do you use the full suite of tools on your control pad and mix multi-channels in real-time or do you fake it with pre-recorded sets?"

"I'm a DJ," Iridius replied. "I mostly play pre-recorded stuff but I mix it live and I sometimes press buttons."

"Oh," Junker said, faking surprise, "even when you're playing the drums, keyboard or guitar live on stage?"

"I play instruments?" Iridius asked.

Junker stared at him.

"Fine," Iridius said. "Point taken. What do you suggest, a crash course in DJ Chromium?"

"I suggest that you let me teach you about DJ Chromium and the basics of DJing, yes."

"You can DJ?"

"I've always been interested in technology, Captain, and music made from technology is no exception. I wanted to be a DJ, and even performed under the name DJ Ratatat for a while before I joined Space Command, but there's not much future for underground music in the Federation."

"DJ Ratatat?"

"I was fifteen."

"Alright, I'm working under the assumption that DJ Chromium won't be travelling alone. I'm sure he'll have an entourage. I was planning on using that as cover for an away team. You can come on the mission as resident DJing consultant."

Junker beamed, smiling from ear to ear.

"But," Iridius quickly added, "you need to keep it together. We don't need you turning into a super-fan. I don't want your behaviour to ratatat us out."

Junker stared at him.

"Ratatat us out," Iridius repeated, but Junker still didn't seem amused. "Like rat us out, but...never mind. If I'm going to pose as DJ Chromium we first need to capture that ship, get aboard and take his place without Locke Station noticing anything is amiss. Latroz, ideas?"

"We do have the ability to remain completely cloaked during a docking sequence with the *Interstella*, Captain," Latroz replied, "and that way we would remain undetectable to Locke Station. Our advanced boarding systems should allow us to jam shields and communication of a basic transport like that, but if they have more advanced security systems and manage to alert Locke Station to a suspected attack, our cover would be revealed. There is a way you could ensure their communication is jammed, Captain, but you will dislike it."

Iridius sucked his tongue off the front of his teeth. "Nanobots."

Latroz nodded. "I'm afraid so, Captain. If you want to dock completely undetected I can see no alternative other than using your abilities to remotely disable the *Interstella* and allow us to dock."

Iridius stayed silent for a long beat and then shook his head. "No. We don't need them. I'm not using nanobots. We are a Federation starship crew. I won't have us relying on dangerous and misunderstood alien technology. We'll force dock in full stealth and try and jam their systems using our ship. Rangi, set us on an intercept course. Latroz, prepare to temporarily disable the ship's shield and comms."

"Yes, sir," Rangi said. "Moving onto an intercept trajectory now."

"Good. Okay everyone, listen up. You all know I was ordered not to do this. Admiral Tullet wanted us to return to Tau Ceti and leave the Alliance and this weapon completely unmonitored. I'm not going to do that. I believe the safety of the Federation is at stake and that trumps those orders. I am choosing to enact FSC regulation 12, 'Space Command personnel must obey the orders of superiors unless the order is of such a nature that a reasonable individual would know it to be unlawful or against the interests of the Federation and its peoples.' I believe this situation falls under the intent of that regulation. Admiral Tullet was very vocal about his dislike for us and I believe that has clouded his judgement. You all saw what happened with that weapon. It would be against the interest of the Federation to leave. That said, I am the captain of this ship and I'm able to make that decision, but I'm not the only one it's going to affect. Everyone on board this vessel will be disobeying the Admiralty, so this is your chance to state your objections for the record if you choose to."

The bridge was quiet.

"Nah," Lieutenant Rangi said. "We're always with you, Captain."

"Captain," Junior Ensign Hal said, "I believe I should interject with a contribution here."

"Yes, Hal," Iridius said, regretting what the android might make of the situation, "go ahead."

"I am unswayed by any emotional content in either yours or Admiral Tullet's assessment. I make purely logical determinations by analysing the known facts, and my conclusion is that you are correct. On the balance of known information, I determine that we should intervene."

"Well, there you go," Iridius said. "Logically speaking, we're on the level." Iridius turned to look at Lieutenant Commander Quinn in particular when he said, "Last chance before we proceed for any objections."

Quinn remained quiet.

"Alright, continue on intercept course Rangi."

"Aye, sir, four minutes from intercept."

"Sir," Quinn said, "may I have a word in private?"

Iridius looked at his first officer. "Quinn, I just gave you a chance to raise any concerns."

"In private please, sir."

Iridius relented. "Alright, step off the bridge with me. We've only got a minute."

Iridius rose from the captain's chair and walked to the rear of the bridge, Quinn trailing behind him. Once they were out in the corridor and the door to the bridge had slid shut behind them, Iridius turned to her.

"You know I like to keep open communication on the bridge, Quinn. Whatever your concerns with going against the Admiralty, you could have raised them in front of the others. We aren't a married couple trying not to fight in front of the kids. I'd prefer you make known your opinion that I'm being reckless and have it noted on the record, if only for your own protection."

"I don't have a concern with going against the Admiralty on this, Captain," Quinn said. "I would have said if I did. I agree with Hal – on the face of what we know, we shouldn't return to Tau Ceti."

"Alright," Iridius said, "then I'll admit I'm a little lost. What's the problem?"

"Iridius," Quinn said. He couldn't remember a time Quinn had called him by his first name, but he was pretty sure it meant this wasn't going to be an easy conversation. "We've served together for almost five years now. We, and several members of this crew, have been through some of the craziest stuff Space Command has ever seen. As Executive Officer I'm hoping you and I have honest communication."

"Yes," Iridius said, still not sure where this was going. "I'd like to think we have that."

"Then I want you to be honest with me. Why are you doing this?"

"You know why I'm doing this, you even agreed with me. We need to intervene for the good of the Federation."

"No, I said we shouldn't go back to Tau Ceti. I never said I agree with kidnapping a musician, posing as him and going aboard the station. A much more reasonable approach would be to simply hold position here and keep monitoring the station, reporting back anything to Space Command. The good of the Federation is not the reason you're doing this, it's your justification. Why are you going on board that station? Because you want to be a hero? I know you wanted to prove yourself, Captain, show Space Command what you're capable of, but you did that already. You saved the galaxy. That's enough."

"I'm just doing what I think is right, Quinn."

"If you won't be honest with yourself then I'll have to be honest for you. You always push too far, Captain. If you keep pushing, things will eventually break. What if things go wrong this time?"

Iridius took a deep breath and sighed. "Is this about what

happened with the Aegix? I told you not to blame yourself, Quinn. Sometimes things go wrong, but that doesn't mean we don't try. I'll admit I've pushed you harder than anyone on this crew, but that's because I see your potential. I see what you're capable of. I only push you to be better because I know you can be."

"You haven't asked me though, have you? You haven't asked me if I want to be pushed. Maybe I'm happy being quietly in the background. I was going to wait to tell you this but I've requested a transfer, Captain. I've put in a request to move to a non-operational role. I'm leaving Space Command ship crew and moving into a Federation science role."

"Quinn," Iridius said. "You don't have to do that."

"It's already been approved. I'm being given a role leading the investigation into the Synth-Hastur threat. I can't handle being here anymore, Captain. Not all of us want to be the hero. All I'm asking is you be honest with the rest of the crew about the fact that you do."

Iridius didn't know how to respond. He'd thought he was doing the right thing trying to push Quinn out of her shell. He'd never stopped to consider that she might not appreciate his efforts. He didn't want to lose her, though. She was an excellent first officer and she was his friend. April was getting engaged and now Quinn had requested a transfer off ship. He'd been blindsided by both. But Quinn wasn't right about everything. He wasn't being a hero just for the sake of it. He was being a hero because the Federation needed him to be. Right?

———

As Iridius walked back onto the bridge Rangi turned to him. "Approaching the *Interstella* now, Captain. We're ready to attempt a forced docking."

The bridge's view-screen was now filled with the image of DJ Chromium's colourfully pulsating ship. The lights that covered the ship's hull erupted in a visual cacophony that was really, given the ship spent most of its transit time in a completely separate universe generated by a BAMF bubble, a complete waste of money, but Iridius supposed it was all about the entrance. When DJ Chromium approached a planet there were bound to be a few people who might catch sight of a confusingly overactive star. He was a DJ, after all, and from the little Iridius knew about DJs he assumed they used as many lasers, flashing lights and smoke machines as logistically possible at all times.

Civilisation had progressed a lot from the twentieth century, when electronic music first became popular, but even after several hundred years some things had remained the same – humans, in fact sentient beings of most species, loved shoving borderline poisons into their bodies and having a party. In fact, once a civilisation reached the advent of faster-than-light travel and found themselves connected with the vast wealth of knowledge and resources presented by the many advanced civilisations of the galaxy, it wasn't greater understanding of the physical universe or a deep spiritual awakening that first made its way to their homeworld. It was, almost without fail, alien swear words, bizarre new foods and crazy party drugs that initially spread through the populace. Even hundreds of years since the birth of the rave, the crowds might now have been made up of a variety of different sentient species, and the gigs may have taken place on asteroids and space stations and planets humans had barely heard of, but all those partygoers completely strung out on all manner of chemical intoxicants still loved nothing more than thumping music piped into their ears and flashing lights shoved in front of their vastly dilated pupils.

Iridius might not have known about DJs but he'd put significantly more effort into partying at the Academy than he had into studying, so he was familiar with some of the galaxy's most popular drugs. *Ectopic-Mind* was a pill made from purple flowers originating on Lacaille III that caused the user's consciousness to seemingly leave their body and hover several feet above their head, generating feelings of inhibition, freedom and a sense of confidence at being much taller than they actually were. *Stink-pingers*, which were actually small portions of the atmosphere of the planet Gleet sealed in glass vials and ingested through the olfactory glands, resulted in a high, causing feelings of emotional warmth, love and togetherness that lasted on average seventy-six days in humans. But it was *Improv* that had been the most popular recreational drug over the last several decades, a small tablet that caused the user to at least partially believe they were another person. It came in a number of 'flavours' based on celebrities from throughout the galaxy. Iridius himself had enjoyed a particularly memorable night when he'd simultaneously taken both an Albert Einstein and an Iggy Pop.

Iridius pulled himself back from reminiscing about his misspent youth and focused on the task at hand. They hovered right above DJ Chromium's ship. It still amazed him they could be this close to another ship and remain completely invisible. He felt like he was outside someone's window and any minute they would turn around and see him standing there staring in at them, scream and then slam the shutters closed before calling the police. But no, every ship was constantly scanning, constantly monitoring the space around it and the *Interstella* would be no exception. The *FSC Deus Ex* all but hovered in front of the *Interstella*'s bridge blowing raspberries and making faces, and they had absolutely no idea they were there.

"Alright," Iridius said. "Attempt to jam their systems."

"Aye, Captain," Latroz said. She worked at her console for a moment. "Attempting to jam their systems." There was a pause full of anticipation. If the *Interstella* detected the jamming attempt and it didn't work, there was no doubt they would send a distress call to Locke Station, and possibly even further. After a tense moment, Latroz spoke again. "The *Interstella*'s shields are down. All point defences offline."

"Have they broadcast any comms?" Iridius asked.

"No, Captain," Ensign Herd answered. "No radio communication and no intercepted quantum entanglement."

"Good," Iridius said. He felt sudden relief. That had been a risk. He had no doubt the rest of the bridge crew was wondering why he hadn't used his nanobots. Thankfully this had worked out, so he wouldn't have to address that question. He wondered how long he could go without telling them the truth. "Good. So we can dock?"

"The *Interstella* still has no shields, external communications, weapons or propulsion control, sir," Latroz said. "It is ready to accept us. We can mount the enemy vessel the way the Siruan Flying Worm mounts its prey. The prey often remains unaware of the worm's presence until the worm ejaculates, filling it with poisonous sperm."

"Lieutenant Latroz," Iridius said, "remember we talked about you not trying metaphors?"

"Sorry, Captain."

"Hal, go ahead and dock us with the *Interstella*."

"Aye, Captain," Hal said. "Initiating forced dock with the *Interstella*."

The *Deus Ex* accelerated ever so subtly as the low-power thrusters fired a super-cooled silicate powder – this allowed the ship to manoeuvre while cloaked without producing spikes in either electromagnetic or thermal signature. The *Deus Ex* moved from a velocity-matched trajectory above the *Interstella* to bring itself into a position to dock. Iridius heard the clunk and mechanical drone as the *Deus Ex*'s telescoping docking interface extended from the rear airlock.

"*Interstella*'s docking systems are green, handshake for forced docking accepted," Hal said.

"*Interstella*'s weapons systems remain down," Latroz confirmed.

On the view-screen the flying epileptic seizure that was DJ Chromium's overpriced transport ship grew larger until the enormous screen resembled a kaleidoscope on acid. The two ships slowly came together until, with a gentle thunk, they joined.

"Contact established," Hal said. "Airlock extending and pressurising. Good seal. Docking complete, Captain."

"Excellent," Iridius said. "Well done, everyone."

"Makes me feel a bit gross," Rangi said. "Does anyone else feel gross? Feels a little, I don't know, non-consensual."

"It's not sex, Rangi," Iridius said. "Why does everyone always equate spaceship docking with sex? It's no different than any other boarding exercise. We just did it with more stealth than usual."

That said, Iridius wondered what the crew of the *Interstella* were thinking. Their systems had gone completely unresponsive, shields down, defences down, propulsion control disabled and now their systems would be telling them they'd been docked with. Except there was no other ship appearing on their sensors, and even if they looked out the window they wouldn't see anything. It would be easy to think it was some massive system-wide malfunction, except for the fact they would have heard, and felt, the clunk of contact as a docking interface connected.

"Rangi, Latroz and Junker," Iridius said, "you're with me as the away team. Rangi, you'll pilot the *Interstella* in. Latroz, I've got no doubt that DJ Chromium would have some muscle as protection, so you'll pose as that while also, you know, being my actual muscle. Junker, like we said, you're coming along as our resident DJ Chromium and general DJ expert. You can pose as, I don't know, my tour manager or something."

"Sure thing, Cap. Does that mean I get to tell you what to do?"

"No."

Junker made a finger gun gesture at Iridius. "Got it. Just happy to be here, boss."

"Quinn," Iridius turned to his XO, "you've got the conn. All good?"

Quinn took just the briefest moment too long before nodding. "Aye, sir."

―――――

Iridius gathered with Rangi, Latroz and Junker in the ready room, standing just outside the airlock that connected them to the *Interstella*. Iridius had ordered them to gear up in full hard suits and have AR-80 pulse rifles armed and at the ready. They weren't going to take this boarding lightly. Iridius didn't intend on breaching the *Interstella* fast and loud like a bunch of para-military maniacs kicking in the door behind a cloud of gas, but he knew if it was his ship that had been docked with by a mysterious invisible entity, he'd have defences up and be ready for whatever was going to come through the airlock. He had to expect the security team for DJ Chromium would be doing the same. Iridius could feel the buzz of his nerves, the adrenaline-fuelled trepidation and excitement that preceded any sort of dangerous off-ship mission. Leading an away team into danger was always fraught, but this was what being a hero of the Federation was all about.

"Alright," Iridius said, "we need to do this fairly quickly so the *Deus Ex* can break dock and fall back. We open the airlock ready for possible resistance but I will be declaring our intention for a non-violent outcome. I do not want you to open fire unless your life is genuinely at risk. We take DJ Chromium and the crew of this ship into custody as gently and calmly as possible. I don't want redshirts, understand? On their side or ours. Non-lethal only."

From the corner of his eye Iridius saw Latroz flick the switch on her rifle from the AR-80s high-powered assault rifle to the non-lethal microwave ray option. She was the only one who had to do this. Iridius could see the disappointment in her eyes.

"Once we've secured DJ Chromium and the crew of the *Interstella* we bring them on board the *Deus Ex,* keep them as temporary prisoners, and then we take the *Interstella* to Locke Station."

"Right, excellent," Rangi said, "and then?"

Iridius looked at the helmsman. "And then we find the time bomb, Rangi."

"Oh, yeah, but I thought, you know, you might have a plan for that too, given that's probably going to be the hard bit, isn't it?"

"I have the seed of a plan, Rangi," Iridius said. "I'll have it fleshed out once we get some intelligence about the station. First things first: let's get this ship. Latroz, lead the way."

Latroz stepped forward to the airlock door with her weapon raised and shouldered. In the sudden quiet of the ready room, Iridius heard the capacitors in her AR-80 hum as she charged her microwave incapacitation ray. It was an ominous sound, but better than hearing the even more sinister and much deadlier click-clack of a projectile round being chambered.

"Benjamin, pull the airlock," Latroz said with her eyes fixed forward, never wavering from the hatch in front of her. Like every Siruan, Lieutenant Latroz was intense in the same way that water was wet – it was just fundamental to who they were. But when it became clear that either ship-to-ship or personal combat was imminent, Latroz froze over. She was still Latroz underneath, still water, but in combat she underwent a state change to ice. Once a fight broke out Iridius wasn't sure a Siruan understood the meaning of a non-violent outcome or was able to fathom the concepts of gentle and calm. He just had to hope this wasn't going to get messy.

Still, leading a team onto an unknown ship, even the equivalent of a space tour bus, Iridius had to take the precaution that things might go sideways, and if that happened there wasn't another species he'd want covering his back. Averaging seven to eight feet tall, their bodies coated in semi-flexible plates of organic carapace, the Siruan race evolved on a planet where everything tried to kill you, from animals like the multi-fanged Siruan Flying Rattle-Spider to plants like blood-sucking Leech Lichen and razer-leafed Death Ivy. Even the planet's air was filled with toxic microbes that managed to take hold in any Siruan with even a slightly compromised immune system. The result was a world that produced some of the hardiest life forms in the galaxy. The Siruan race had also spent several million years in a state of constant war with three other dominant species on their world. At least, there had been three dominant species. Now there was only the Siruans and a whole bunch of fossils. The Siruan race had been the ultimate victor in that planet-wide struggle some five to ten thousand years ago – relatively recently, by galactic standards. The invisible hand of evolutionary biology had moulded the Siruans at the DNA level and sharpened them for millennia into the ultimate fighters, both against their environment and every other living creature unfortunate enough to meet them in a fight. Many historians and anthropologists will present theories about the tribal birth of humanity, debate whether homo-sapiens took their place as the dominant species on Earth through peace or violence, and discuss ad nauseum the warring-states phase of history through the twentieth century, but when lined up alongside the Siruans the idea that humanity was a war-like race was laughable. If Siruans are a sword then humanity is a pair of those plastic-coated scissors you give to toddlers.

Rangi pulled the black and yellow hazard-striped handle next to the airlock hatch. It flipped down with a clunk and engaged the airlock compression and unlocking sequence. With a faint hiss, air rushed in to fill the short tunnel joining the *Deus Ex* to the *Interstella*. An orange light above the doorway flashed, warning that the vacuum of the airlock tunnel was still being equalised with the ready room. After a moment a white spray filled the tunnel, decontaminating the walkway, and then the light above the door blinked from orange to solid green. A panel on the wall beside Rangi switched from a red cross to a green circle as the hatch unlocked. Latroz nodded to Rangi and he pressed his thumb to the circle. The hatch opened inward on motorised hinges.

Latroz was the first to move, her rifle still trained forward as she stepped out into the airlock tunnel. Iridius made sure he was next. He would let the ship's tactical officer lead the way because that was her job, but as captain he needed to be next. He might have graduated bottom of his class at Space Command Academy and been voted most likely to first lose a starship – which, for the record, he wasn't; Captain Dave Sinclair, a fellow command graduate in his year, had his ship, the *FSC Cobalt,* stretched to seven hundred and twelve times its normal length when he flew too close to an artificial black hole at least a year before Iridius had crashed his own ship into an enormous flying dog – but, despite his rocky schooling, Iridius had always held true to some fundamentals of leadership he learned at the Academy. First and foremost was that he always put the wellbeing of his subordinates ahead of his own. Sometimes that meant letting them use the shower first so they'd get the last of the hot water, and sometimes it meant positioning them after him when heading into a dangerous situation so that, in this case, he'd be first into hot water.

Iridius followed Latroz out into the airlock tunnel. The tunnel between the two ships was made up of the telescoping section of the *Deus Ex*'s docking mechanism. It was only 5 metres long, had no windows and was structurally sound and sealed tight to the *Interstella*, but in that short stretch of walkway Iridius couldn't help but feel exposed. Whenever he walked down a docking tunnel between two ships he felt very close to that vacuum and the enormous blackness of space outside. It felt like he was on a rickety rope bridge over a chasm, walking over rotten wooden planks that might snap underfoot at any moment and send him plunging into an infinite drop below. Of course, in the scheme of things this was a completely irrational view and he knew it. The airlock tunnel was not some treacherously thin connection between two places of safety. It was just as well built as the rest of the ship, and whether he was on the *Deus Ex* or the *Interstella* he was still on board a tiny metal box floating in the vast, unending and completely uncaring cosmos. No point worrying about the rope bridge when what's on either side is just as damn dangerous.

As Latroz, Iridius, Junker and Rangi all moved into the docking tunnel, the hatch back into the *Deus Ex* closed behind them, sealing the airlock to avoid exposing the ship to any explosive decompression, biological hazards or rampaging DJs when they entered the docked vessel – standard operating procedure, but it was still the moment an away team felt properly away.

Latroz stepped in front of the external hatch into the *Interstella*. Even the door was coated with lines of small circular LED lights that pulsed with colour to match whatever pattern was being broadcast on the side of the hull. Iridius tried not to look at it for fear it would leave bursts of after-image seared into his retinas, but it was difficult to avoid when that was the only way in. Latroz waited until Iridius was beside her and Rangi and Junker were stacked in formation behind them. Latroz might have been the only soldier on board, but they each knew how to handle themselves and had been repeatedly drilled on breaching a ship during a forced boarding. Hopefully the almost year of doing nothing but listening in on other people's conversations hadn't left them completely devoid of that knowledge. Each of them had their rifles raised, so it at least looked like they knew what they were doing. The moment of breach was the most dangerous part of a ship-boarding. It was impossible to dock with another ship without them knowing and, when you wanted to leave a ship intact like they did, you basically had no choice but to come in the front door. That meant the crew on the other side knew you were coming and where you were coming from. When the door was opened there was a moment, however brief, when those on the ship had a distinct advantage. An advantage that amounted to just enough time to pump you full of highly uncomfortable bullets, microwave rays, grenades, gas or, depending on the race, rapidly propelled mucus, spat poison, or slime ejected from various sacs and glands.

Iridius reached for the external handle with his left hand while holding his AR-80 in his right, keeping the weapon raised as best he could. Latroz looked at him and nodded. Iridius pulled the handle. With a hiss of final pressure equalisation the *Interstella*'s entry hatch opened. Latroz swung out from beside the door to close the angle as the door moved inward, but there were no metal fragments or alien bodily fluids hurled their way.

"Down, down, down!" Latroz yelled.

Iridius swung around into the open doorway. What he saw was not at all what he'd expected. There was no security team. There was just an old man, bent-backed and leaning on a black metal cane.

"I am afraid I can't quite get down with the sort of pace you are demanding," the old man said as Latroz moved towards him. She swept her weapon around the room, a small airlock antechamber, but the man seemed to be alone. "It is my back mostly, but my knees and hips are not particularly responsive either."

"Room is clear," Latroz reported. "I will watch the door." She moved past the old man to the only door at the rear of the room, rifle still up and ready, unwavering.

"There is not a need for the weapons, I can assure you," the old man said. Though calling the old man a man wasn't quite right because no doubt, dear reader, you have the image of a wrinkled old white-bearded human in your head and this was not a human. This was, like the *Deus Ex*'s crew member Gr'lak N'hlarkic Tre'laktor, AKA Greg, a member of the malignant race, a humanoid tumour who had developed as a cancerous growth on an enormous planetary organism and then sprung free at maturity to wander around the galaxy. The malignant were one of the few examples of fully sentient diseases – even though Iridius was more than happy to put humans in that classification, too. There was also the rather odd race known as the Tubulorts, who had evolved from something not dissimilar to a fungus infection. While technically they were a member of the Galactic Federation, they tended to keep to themselves which, though they might not admit it publicly, most other races were happy about because it turns out even the very accepting races of the Federation still got a bit grossed out by eighteen-foot-tall pieces of walking, talking moist tinea.

So, not a human man, a malignant man. You were right about the beard though, and the wrinkled skin. Except the wrinkles were less from old age and more from the overlapping layers of scar tissue formed from the constant healing, reopening and healing again of oozing legions of cancerous growth. Every malignant was covered in sores like this, as their cells were basically mutating, exploding and reforming constantly. Iridius had served with Greg for years and so was more than used to the appearance of a malignant. Still, even if he hadn't been, no one was really turned off by the malignants. On a human or most other races with uniform skin or the equivalent dermal layer, a gaping, pus-leaking wound was pretty noticeable and generally considered unsightly, but because a malignant was basically covered in things like that, they all sort of blended together and didn't seem quite as disgusting. Besides, of all the races in the galaxy, malignants were just so peaceful and nice they tended to put people at ease.

"I'm Captain Iridius Franklin of the *FSC Deus Ex*," Iridius said. "I am requisitioning this ship for the needs of the Galactic Federation. We intend to do this peacefully. No harm will come to anyone aboard this vessel if you cooperate."

"My name is Kla'thak J'artekic Flenbak. I am DJ Chromium's manager. You understand that we are not in any way associated with the Galactic Federation and are not subject to your laws."

"I understand that," Iridius said. "But I need to insist you comply with our instructions. We will be taking this vessel and would much prefer to do it peacefully."

"Very well," Kla'thak J'artekic Flenbak said. "One moment please."

The malignant stepped to the wall and pressed an intercom. Behind him, Latroz had turned from the door temporarily to watch, presumably in case he was triggering a bomb or some other distress signal. "Sir," Kla'thak J'artekic Flenbak said into the intercom, "our guests are aboard. They intend to take your ship but wish to do so peacefully. I believe it is safe for you to come down." He turned back to Iridius and the others. "Please lower your weapons."

Iridius looked to Rangi and Junker and nodded. They lowered their rifles. "You too, Lieutenant Latroz," he said. "Stand down." Latroz hesitated momentarily before lowering her rifle and stepping away from the door.

"So," Iridius said, "Kla'thak J'arkeeteek—"

"Kla'thak J'artekic Flenbak," the malignant offered, correcting Iridius.

"Right," Iridius said. "Do you have another name I could use? I know some of you take shorter nicknames."

"No," Kla'thak J'artekic Flenbak said firmly, "I do not have a *nickname*. My name is Kla'thak J'artekic Flenbak. I do not believe I should alter that simply because your race finds it difficult to say."

"Sorry," Iridius said, remembering only after his mumbled apology that he was the one supposed to be in command of boarding this ship. "How many people are on this vessel? And where is DJ Chromium?"

"I'm here."

The door at the back of the room had slid open so quietly that Iridius hadn't even noticed it. He supposed everything on this Gulfstream was the height of luxury and that meant they had doors that didn't even make a swoosh sound when they opened. Even Latroz spun in surprise, and it took a lot to catch her off-guard. Not only was the door quiet but DJ Chromium must have moved all but silently, which, given he was wearing some sort of silky silver jumpsuit that drooped off him in cascades of fabric, was no easy feat. Latroz had her AR-80 up and aimed at him almost as soon as he spoke, though.

"I am Captain Iridius Franklin of the Federation Space Command vessel *FSC Deus Ex*. You are DJ Chromium I presume?"

"That's right," the man standing in the doorway replied. His voice was modulated with an electronic filter but it at least sounded like a human male. He was, as Iridius had already noted, dressed in an oversized silver jumpsuit that was some parody of an early spacesuit complete with fake mission badges and a name plate that read CHROMIUM. His head was hidden by a similar silver helmet, his face obscured by a curved black glass front-plate. The plate was lit up with a simple animated face of green lines that may or may not have been mirroring his real expression – the mouth at least moved when he spoke. If the outfit alone wasn't enough to give away who this was, the small squeals of joy that were coming from behind Iridius as Junker tried desperately to contain herself were. Iridius turned as nonchalantly as he could, shooting Junker a look that channelled all the times his mother had rounded on him with embarrassment during his childhood.

"You're on my ship," Chromium said.

"Oh my god I know!" Junker said, not quietly enough.

Iridius turned to her. "Junker, honestly. You're a professional."

"Sorry, Captain," she said, and then leaned out to give a meek little wave to DJ Chromium. "Hi, big fan."

"Thank you," Chromium replied in his flat electronic voice.

"Listen," Iridius said, trying to pretend his dramatic ship boarding hadn't descended into absurdity. "We aren't here to chat. This is a boarding and seizure as authorised under FSC regulations in time of dire need." Iridius spotted the subtle movement of Latroz's thumb as she switched the rifle from microwave incapacitation to lethal assault rifle. "First word of warning," Iridius said to the shiny DJ, "don't sneak up on a Siruan." He looked to Latroz. "Stand down, Lieutenant."

"Aye, sir." Latroz lowered her AR-80 but Iridius noted she neither switched back to microwave nor engaged the safety. DJ Chromium's animated expression didn't change, but if he had any sense of how dangerous a Siruan could be, his forehead beneath that helmet should be leaking sweat like Greg during mandated physical training time.

"As I mentioned to Kla'thart J'atek—"

"Kla'thak J'artekic Flenbak," Chromium said. "It's not that hard to learn to pronounce malignant names."

"No, I know," Iridius said. "I've served with a malignant for years. He's on my crew."

"Is that right?" Kla'thak J'artekic Flenbak said. "What is his name?"

Iridius paused. "Greg."

"That is his simplified name for your benefit," the malignant butler said. "What is his true name?"

"It's Ger'lak N'hlakr Trac'tor," Iridius said, as confidently as he could.

"Captain," Rangi whispered under his breath but certainly not quietly enough, "it's actually Gr'lak N'hlarkic Tre'laktor."

"Alright Rangi," Iridius said out of the corner of his mouth. "That's unhelpful right now."

"Typical Federation shill," DJ Chromium said, "spouting the peace and harmony of your Galactic Federation when you're unwilling to even learn how to pronounce the names of another race."

"He likes being called Greg," Iridius said. "And we aren't here to critique my pronunciation of names. We're here because we need to temporarily requisition your ship."

"And if we refuse?" Chromium asked.

Iridius looked from the malignant to the oddly dressed DJ. "We have you at gunpoint. I'd have thought the alternative obvious. Do you even have a security team?"

"We can handle ourselves," Chromium said.

"Evidently not," Iridius replied. "Remove your helmet please."

"I can't do that," Chromium said.

Iridius raised his AR-80 threateningly.

DJ Chromium didn't move. "Look," he said, "it's a whole thing."

"It is his thing," Junker said.

"Quiet, Junker," Iridius said without turning around. "Fine, how many crew are on board?"

"Thirteen including us," Kla'thak J'artekic Flenbak said. "Master Chromium, Master Chromium's legal advisor Denrul, a pilot, catering, hair and make-up, roadies and myself."

"Call them all here, please," Iridius said.

Kla'thak J'artekic Flenbak looked to DJ Chromium who nodded before the malignant returned to the comm on the wall. "All crew and staff to the airlock antechamber immediately."

Latroz, Iridius, Junker and Rangi kept their weapons ready as a collection of people filed into the room. As Kla'thak J'artekic Flenbak had said, there were eleven more who came to join them. The half a dozen roadies stood around in their tight black t-shirts looking like a galactic biker gang. The young Terusian female who was clearly hair and make-up stood waiting, twirling her hair around an index finger and popping bubble gum. Two chefs in white outfits, a pilot in his flight gear and a Zeta Reticulan in a dark suit completed the occupants. Great, Iridius thought, a balloon-headed grey, just what he needed. The Zeta Reticulan was the last to walk into the room. Without hesitation, she looked at Iridius.

"You are the captain?" the grey said.

"That's right."

"I am Denrul. I'm DJ Chromium's lawyer. You know we've got a gig to get to, right?"

"I understand that's the case, yes," Iridius said. "I'm afraid you're going to miss it."

"I'll be lodging a complaint with the Federation and will expect full compensation for my client and extra for the damage incurred to my client's reputation."

"Sure," Iridius said. "No problem." Iridius turned to Latroz and Rangi. "You two escort this cast and crew to the *Deus Ex* please. Then come back here and we'll leave. Could you tell Greg to join us on the away team too?"

"Aye, Captain," Latroz replied.

"You're making a mistake," Chromium said as Latroz gestured for the occupants of the *Interstella* to head into the airlock tunnel. "I'm stating that now for the record."

"I'm sorry you feel that way, but I have bigger problems to deal with."

When the others had left, Junker turned to Iridius. "I can't believe I met DJ Chromium."

"Junker, we just took him prisoner."

"I know, so cool."

"And you acted like an idiot, again."

"Did you see he spoke to me?"

Iridius sighed. "Yes, Junker. I saw he spoke to you."

CHAPTER SIX_

THE *INTERSTELLA* DID NOT HAVE a bridge like a larger starship, just a small cockpit with two pilot's chairs. It didn't need much more than that and besides, Iridius thought as he looked around the ship, they had to make room for all the luxury add-ons like couches, a pool table, corner bar and an augmented reality massage bed. The bed was marketed as being used for simulation of any known form of massage in the galaxy but Iridius knew, without a doubt, that it was generally used for simulation of any known form of sex in the galaxy.

Rangi sat in the pilot's chair guiding the *Interstella* in toward Locke Station. The *Deus Ex* had undocked and fallen back to the nearest Lagrange Point, where it would maintain position and continue monitoring the station for quantum entanglement communication. The away team would not be able to communicate directly with the *Deus Ex* without giving away the ship's presence, but Iridius figured that if they were discovered there would probably be communication out to the broader Alliance. The *Deus Ex* could then alert Space Command with the pre-prepared message Iridius had recorded, taking full responsibility for disobeying orders.

"ASS Locke," Rangi said into the comms, having to stifle a giggle. "This is the *Interstella,* requesting clearance to land."

Iridius, Junker, Latroz and Greg stood behind Rangi, all jammed into the small cockpit, watching the station grow larger out the front window. They had changed out of their Space Command uniforms and into clothes to match the passengers of the *Interstella.* Rangi had slipped on a pilot's vest and wore a pair of extraordinarily old-fashioned aviator sunglasses, which he'd decided were exactly what his Space Ace aesthetic needed. Iridius had dressed in the utterly absurd silver outfit of DJ Chromium, holding the helmet in the crook of his arm. He'd already tried it on and was disappointed to discover that it had no heads-up display that would instantly teach him how to DJ. Latroz had found little that would fit her on board the *Interstella,* so they'd had to grab some of her personal clothes instead. She was going to play the role of a bodyguard, and her mostly dark personal clothing made her look the part. Junker had dressed like a roadie, and Greg had put on a suit belonging to Kla'thak J'artekic Flenbak. It was very possible that Locke Station was expecting a malignant to be accompanying DJ Chromium – luckily they had one on their crew, though Greg was far from pleased at being part of an away team.

"*Interstella,* this is ASS Locke, you are cleared to land in bay 75R. Light-up coordinates being transmitted to you now. On landing, please stand by for inspection."

In front of them Locke Station was growing larger by the second. It was fairly nondescript, comprising a common space station construction of an outer ring surrounding a tall central spire. The only thing remarkable about Locke Station was that it was perpetually dark. Lentrani II, the planet Locke orbited, was tidally locked to its star, which meant one face of the planet constantly faced the star while the other constantly faced away – a true dark side that received almost no light. That, in and of itself, didn't make Lentrani II inhospitable – there were dozens of tidally-locked planets that supported life in the galaxy, several even with advanced civilisations. The real issue with the Lentrani system was that the star produced very little light, and much of what it did produce was in the infrared spectrum. As a result, the star system was dark and cold. Not dark and cold like taking the trash out on a winter's night or the climate in a divorce lawyer's office, more like dark and cold enough to freeze the atmosphere off a planet. That meant the entire Lentrani system was an inhospitable wasteland a significant distance from a galactic centre or any major hubs of civilisation. On reflection, it was a perfectly excellent place to hide a secret weapons development program. Locke Station orbited Lentrani II and so passed into the light of Lentrani for half its orbit, but the low visible light meant even when the station was between the planet and the star, as it was now, it was still dark, and internal lights twinkled all around the ring and up and down the main spire. After a moment the holo display on the front window of the *Interstella* showed a simulated flight path to a flashing landing bay on the side of the station.

"Alright Rangi," Iridius said, "take us in."

———

"Prepare to be boarded for inspection."

The announcement was piped through the *Interstella*'s internal broadcast system as the ship sat waiting inside the landing bay they'd been directed to. Everyone on board had gathered in the airlock antechamber again, ready to greet the expected security inspection team. Having spent several years as captain of a hauler, Iridius was more than used to being boarded by security staff who would sweep the ship for any contraband, unlawful weaponry, suspicious personnel or cargo not on the manifest. Back then, of course, he was flying a Federation hauler to Federation worlds, so never received more than a cursory inspection. This was going to be different, and though he wasn't going to show the crew this, he was shitting absolute bricks.

"Time to get into character everyone," Iridius said. He slipped DJ Chromium's helmet on and locked it into place on the neck ring of the ridiculous silver spacesuit. The faceplate blinked to life with the anonymous green animated face. "It's hot in this thing," the green face said. At least the rest of the crew couldn't see his expression now, so he didn't have to be concerned about looking as worried as he felt. "Alright Greg," he said, "remember you are Klatak Jint..."

"Kla'thak J'artekic Flenbak, Captain," Greg said.

"That's right. He seems to be the voice of DJ Chromium around here, so try to act confident and take the lead."

"You want me to take the lead, Captain? I have never taken the lead before. I am more of a stay-behind-on-the-ship type."

"You'll be fine, Greg," Iridius said. "You remember what Commander Mul was like on the *Gallaway*?"

"Yes sir. I believe you called him a moronic balloon-headed grey twat, sir."

"Correct. Just act like that."

The external door opened and a team of four security guards in black armour thumped with heavy footfalls up the ramp and onto the ship. They wore half-helmets with visors that came down over their eyes but left their mouths exposed. Sure, helmets like that let them scowl menacingly and be clearly heard, but they certainly didn't serve the actual purpose of an armoured helmet. They might protect the top of your head, but Iridius imagined being shot in the mouth would still hurt.

Each member of the security team was holding a rifle not dissimilar to the AR-80s issued to Federation Space Command, though Iridius quickly noted that their rifles didn't seem to have any sort of non-lethal option. One of the guards, a Venusian by the look of his pale skin and elongated chin, stepped forward. Although referred to as Venusians, this was really a misunderstanding based on their first contact with humans. The Venusians were encountered during humanity's first manned mission to Venus, but they weren't actually from Venus – they were just passing through. The name stuck, thanks to the stubborn way humans managed to impose their names on things, like how people still referred to Native Americans as Indians, just because a ship captain hundreds of years ago got lost.

The security team's black uniforms were unmarked, with no name plates or insignia. In Iridius's experience, the amount of identifying features a security or law-enforcement unit wore was inversely proportional to the violence they were capable of. Plus, black uniforms were generally a dead giveaway for brutality. The Venusian had some chevron-like markings on his upper arm that seemed to indicate he was the highest ranked among them, but there was little else to distinguish them.

Greg looked to Iridius. Iridius gave a small nod as if to say, *yes, this is when you're supposed to take the lead, Greg.* The malignant stepped up to meet the guards. "I am Kla'thak J'artekic Flenbak. That is my actual name. What is it you want?"

Iridius cringed, but the Venusian guard just seemed to shrug it off as another strange alien speech pattern. "I am Guard Leader Meteon of the Frost Norton Security Force. We are here to inspect your vessel. You were instructed to have your entire ship complement ready for inspection."

"This is our entire ship compliment," Greg said, pausing as if thinking before continuing. He gestured to Iridius, but continued speaking to the guard. "Do you know who this is, you dumb idiot?"

Iridius cringed again. Maybe he shouldn't have told Greg to

act like Mul. He might have been laying it on a bit thick. The guard looked at Iridius and then back to Greg.

"Yes," Meteon said. "I know who that is, but unfortunately we need to perform an inspection even for famous guests of the CEO."

One of the other guards, a younger human, leaned forward. "Um, hi, big fan by the way."

The Venusian turned and shot him a look that, despite a visor covering his eyes, was clearly the same look Iridius had been forced to use on Junker. The lead guard returned his attention to Greg. "I expected a larger complement of staff. Don't you need people to set up for the show?"

Greg didn't reply for a beat so Iridius jumped in, the electronic filter reverberating as he spoke. "I'm planning a small intimate show for Mr Frost," he said. "Most of my crew are away setting up for my next show. I've got Junker here, my road manager, and the others are multi-talented. We've got enough hands to set up. Besides, Mr Frost promised us help if we need it."

"A small intimate show?" Meteon seemed puzzled. "My understanding is you're playing for ten thousand people."

"That's what I said," Iridius responded without missing a beat. "A small show."

"We were told you were bringing at least ten support staff," the guard said, the discrepancy clearly beginning to worry him. Iridius was about to make some other excuse, but unfortunately Greg followed orders and took the lead.

"You do not question DJ Chromium," Greg said. "We do not tell you how to conduct your business. You do not need to tell us how to conduct our business. Our business is doing music and that is what Mr Frost is expecting. We will be having words with Mr Frost about the state of his hospitality if this continues much longer. Now, get about your business, you white-faced skinny twat."

Guard Leader Meteon stared at Greg, and Iridius was convinced he was going to raise his rifle and blow the malignant's pock-marked face off. Instead, the guard turned to the others and waved for them to move into the ship. "Right then," the guard said. "We'll just take a quick look around."

When the guards had moved off to search the ship Greg turned to Iridius with a smile on his face. "I believe that went quite well, Captain."

"Shhh," Iridius hissed at him. "Don't break cover." He paused. "And when I told you to channel Commander Mul I just meant be a little bit arrogant. You didn't have to be a completely unlikable arsehole."

"Well, I decided to channel you instead, Captain."

"At least it worked so that's fi— Wait a second, what did you say?"

But Meteon and his team returned before Greg had a chance to reply.

"Satisfied?" Greg asked.

The Venusian nodded. "A quick sweep looks clear. Still, you've got a lot of gear back there for only a few people to cart in and set up."

"Like DJ Chromium said," Greg replied, "we aren't going to be moving it. You are."

"I have not been told—" Meteon started but Greg, clearly getting far too into his role, cut him off.

"Just leave some of your men to move all the things in the cargo bay to wherever the musical show will be. You can leave us now."

"I'm not..." He looked from Greg to Iridius and then sighed. "Fine. I'll have a team detailed to assist you, but I'm afraid DJ

Chromium and yourself will need to come with me. Mr Frost is expecting to meet you on your arrival."

"What, now?" Iridius asked.

"Yes," Meteon said. "You did agree to a meet and greet on your arrival."

"Yes," Iridius said. "Of course. I did. I just didn't expect it to be, you know, straight away right now. Any chance I could just have a quick stretch of my legs, maybe take a walk around?"

"I'm afraid not, Mr Chromium. Mr Frost is waiting for you. He was quite insistent that you be brought straight to him."

"Okay, yeah, sure," Iridius said. "My crew will accompany us then."

"No, just yourself and your manager – that was the agreement. The others can begin set-up for tonight's show. This way please."

"Right, okay." Iridius turned to the others. "You get set up for the show. When I'm done, we'll make sure there are no issues, particularly none related to *time*."

Latroz, Junker and Rangi nodded. Message received.

Iridius followed Meteon off the ship and onto Locke Station. The Venusian moved just ahead of them, and as they walked across the landing pad another of the guards followed behind. He didn't have his weapon trained on them or anything quite that overt, but the message was still clear. Iridius and Greg might have convinced the guards that they were indeed the people they posed as, but that didn't mean they could have free run of the station – not that he'd expected it to. They'd just have to get back to the ship and the others as quickly as possible to try and figure out where to start searching and how to go about it without drawing attention to themselves.

Iridius wasn't thrilled that he was being dragged off to meet CEO Devin Frost, but he had to look on the positive side. Perhaps, if Frost's guard was a little down, thinking he was meeting a famous DJ, Iridius might be able to trick him into revealing some information about the weapons development program. He wasn't sure exactly how he was going to do that because, not that he was willing to admit Quinn was right, he hadn't thought much past getting on board the space station. Still, if there was one skill Iridius had, it was making things up as he went along. He'd managed to get through childhood acting like he knew what all the fuss was about the whole time, he'd managed to get through the Academy by winging just about everything – he might have graduated bottom of his class, but at least he graduated – and he'd managed to save the galaxy by tumbling from one disaster to another. It might appear to an outsider that Captain Iridius B. Franklin was in way over his head, and they would be right. But he was going to go in confident and hope his galaxy-class improvisational skills came through with the goods.

The Venusian turned to Iridius and Greg. "We're going to make our way up the main street of The Burrows. There's a car waiting. It's the quickest way to Frost Norton Tower, where Mr Frost's office is. Just make sure you keep up with me. It can get a little hectic."

Space ports were a little like toilets. Iridius had visited hundreds of them throughout the galaxy and, assuming they were clean, well-lit and orderly, they all just kind of blended into one. It was only the ones that were covered in memorable graffiti, stunk with a particularly offensive odour or were riddled with substances best ignored that tended to stick with you. The space port of Locke Station was wholly unremarkable. With its line-up of landing bays ranging in size to accommodate everything from small transport shuttles up to haulers or long-range transports like the *Interstella*, to its hazard-striped open space buzzing with the movement of cargo lifts, to its corridors for travellers and workers, it could have been any space port anywhere in the galaxy. But, as

Iridius followed the Venusian guard out of the cleanliness of the dock, onto the streets of Locke Station and into what he assumed was the place the guard had referred to as The Burrows, things were suddenly a whole lot different.

They had headed radially inwards towards the centre of the station, away from any windows that might provide a glimpse of the space outside. On most Federation stations, the internal areas were lit with lights that would vary as the simulated day progressed from a cooler white light in the morning through to a warmer incandescence in the afternoon and evening. Space messed with the circadian rhythms of most species to some degree, depending on the star system, atmosphere, rotation rate and orbital period of their homeworld, among other factors. The variation in evolutionary environments meant it wasn't possible to create a simulated day that perfectly matched the natural needs of every species in the galaxy, but at least varying the light in some way seemed to be beneficial for most species, and avoided what had come to be called permanight psychosis, which caused symptoms ranging from insomnia through to murderous rage. This idea was apparently not used on Locke Station, or at least not in The Burrows.

As Iridius stepped through a doorway he was greeted by a scene reminiscent of much of Earth in the dark ages of the mid-twenty-first century, the period following the initial rise of trans-humanism and designer human-machine interfaces. What was it the historians called it? Cyberpunk? It was a time period that didn't last long, thankfully, due to the hideous environmental damage done to the planet and the eventual societal collapse that came from plugging social media networks directly into your frontal lobe. It was all over by, like, 2077 if Iridius remembered his high-school history correctly. Still, walking into The Burrows felt like stepping back to that time.

A long street stretched ahead of them, tightly bordered on

either side by storefronts and apartments. They were built into the walls of the station, but the ceiling was several storeys above them, giving the illusion of stepping out into a city. Alleyways and lanes split off at right angles to the main street, presumably leading to more streets like this one, some leading up to higher levels, some down to lower ones. Many of the buildings along the street seemed to spill their contents out, with shop vendors at stalls out the front yelling to the passing crowd or a mismatch of old furniture in front of the tenement blocks, usually occupied by teenagers crowded onto them. The street churned with activity as people moved in a thick, soupy crowd, heading in all directions without any semblance of order. People cut across the street or pushed their way through. Occasionally small tricycle-like vehicles, usually carrying people but occasionally loaded high with more goods than they had any right trying to carry, sounded short blasts of annoyingly pitched horns to force their way through the crowd on what Iridius assumed was supposed to be the roadway for vehicles, although it was kind of difficult to tell.

The lighting on the ceiling high above was nothing like the soft light Iridius was used to. It was stark white fluorescent tubes, each one running tens of metres long. But the white light from above was all but drowned out by the neon. That was what gave life to the scene. It seemed like every building was adorned with bright signs of illuminated green, pink, blue or orange. Some were animated, like the scantily clad species-neutral figure that spun around a pole and then beckoned for you to enter the Pleasure Emporium. Some were dull, flickering signs that mostly indicated one apartment building that was barely discernible from the others. Some of the displays, Iridius realised, were temporary projections blasted up onto walls from small boxes bolted to the ground, advertising everything from liquor to baby food to a greeting from your friendly CEO Devin Frost. Corporate slogans and unrelenting advertising were plastered with reckless abandon on what looked to be every spare surface. This truly was the capitalist dystopia he'd always been warned the Alliance was. The whole thing really was like a burrow, a warren dug into the station and decorated by an enormous corporate rabbit in the midst of a neuromantic nightmare.

"Come on," Meteon said, turning to Iridius and Greg. "The car is this way. Hurry before you get noticed."

"I don't know how anyone could notice anything here," Iridius said, standing and taking in the scene, his senses still over-whelmed.

"O to the S!" a voice shouted from somewhere nearby. "Is that DJ Chromium?!"

Iridius suddenly felt the attention of more and more people fall on him. Like a sudden surge of the tide in a river, he felt the crowd begin shifting towards them. Young people in particular were suddenly gravitating in his direction. "DJ Chromium! DJ Chromium!" They were shouting his name as if that would somehow reassure him, instead of making the swarm of giddy kids more terrifying.

"Can I have your selfie-graph?"

"I love you!"

"No, I love you!"

The Venusian guard growled under his breath. "Come on, quickly!" He lifted his rifle and moved off to the side of the street where Iridius spotted a low black vehicle, a sedan much larger than the tricycles he'd seen. It hovered on anti-grav plates. The guard behind Iridius and Greg shuffled forward, forcing them to follow.

"DJ Chromium!"

"Get out of the way!" Meteon roared. "Frost Norton Security! Move!"

By apparent sheer force of will Meteon parted the crowd. As they approached the black car the side door opened vertically and

Meteon waved for Iridius and Greg to get in. They obediently did so, and the two guards followed, closing the door behind them. The car began moving but it could only move slowly, as the crowd seemed nonplussed at a huge vehicle blasting its horn and bearing down on them. Fans slammed up against the side of the vehicle and began banging on the windows, still calling out for DJ Chromium to do everything from sign a picture to marry them. Eventually Meteon lowered the window slightly, stuck his rifle out and aimed it upwards, firing a burst of automatic rounds into the air, smashing one of the long fluorescent lights on the roof and apparently giving the crowd the warning they needed. Most of them scattered. The car turned down an alley and accelerated, moving onto another street far less crowded with people and continuing towards the centre of the station.

Meteon closed his window and sighed. "Fucking Burrows."

They drove through areas that were much the same for at least ten minutes, at one point swerving to miss someone who dropped from several storeys up and landed on the street. Luckily the most difficult part of a fall, the hitting the ground bit, was lessened by the station's safety mechanisms. Most large space stations had localised artificial gravity circuit breakers that could detect when an object was falling towards the ground at or near a terminal velocity. When that happened, the circuit breakers would lower the gravity in a localised area to soften the blow and prevent damage to either the station or any dropped equipment, or reduce the amount of injuries or the amount of death that would be suffered by a sentient being. Unfortunately for this particular sentient being, the large bullet hole through the centre of their face meant an artificial gravity circuit break wasn't going to do a lot for them.

At another point on the streets of the Burrows the vehicle they travelled in, presumably because it could be identified as a Frost Norton Security vehicle, was pelted with what Iridius at first thought were rocks but in fact turned out to be the eggs of Prycron Acid Chickens. Thankfully the vehicle's hardened body didn't succumb to the bubbling fluid inside.

But as they continued on towards the centre of the station, the streets around them grew less hostile and became more akin to what Iridius was used to seeing on a space station: long stretches of more or less the same-coloured walls that were a clean white, off-white or maybe a beige. Of course, being part of the Planetary Alliance of Corporations, the walls were still covered in massive arrays of advertising, but the further they moved towards the station's centre, the more expensive the goods being advertised became. The advertisements morphed from spruiking energy drinks, alcohol and cheap fast food to promoting the latest model tricycle, facial moisturising implants and ring view apartments. The advertisements here weren't quite as obnoxiously in your face, either, with bright animated neon giving way to more muted tones.

Eventually they reached the central spire of the space station, where they were stopped at a large circular door like a medieval portcullis by another Frost Norton Security team, wearing the same black uniforms and fashionable if impractical helmets. They checked the identities of the passengers and gave the vehicle a once-over with a device that was likely used to check for weapons or perhaps electronic or quantum listening devices. It was obviously not calibrated to detect large numbers of advanced alien nanomachines designed by an unknown race to protect against an existential threat to all known life in the galaxy, because when a guard swept Iridius it barely chirped. The security team waved the vehicle on as the circular door ahead of them rotated open with an iris-like twist.

The central spire was much like the cleaner, well-manicured areas of the outer ring, except here there was no advertising. Iridius quickly realised why –this part of the station was not for the people buying things, it was for the people selling things. He also had no doubt that what they were selling was the pipe dream that one day maybe you too could pass through the iris to the central spire; the same bullshit that had kept societies in line for hundreds of years.

The vehicle pulled to a stop outside a large elevator. This was the entrance to Frost Norton Tower, unmissable due to the enormous garish gold lettering over the doorway.

"This is it," Meteon said. "I'll take you up to see Mr Frost."

Iridius stepped out of the vehicle.

"If you'll follow me, please," Meteon said in the way guards, police, peacekeepers, guardians and basically anyone tasked with law enforcement the universe over always did. They made it seem like a request, they even used the word please, but you knew you had no choice in the matter. Iridius and Greg did as they were asked and found themselves in a small foyer. An android receptionist sat at a desk directly opposite them. The android, styled to look like a 1950s human secretary – which Iridius thought said plenty about the man they were about to meet – stared at them for a moment too long and then nodded. As she did, the horrendous golden doors to the elevator nearby opened. Iridius realised the android had been scanning them and was probably not a simple receptionist at all, but rather, a highly advanced security system. He wasn't sure what would have happened if the result of the scan had been negative, but he couldn't help but picture the manicured robotic woman in her pressed blue dress with the lace collar jumping up onto the desk, her eyes turning red and her arms becoming rotating saw blades. Instead, she smiled sweetly as Iridius walked by. *I'm not buying it lady,* Iridius thought, *I know you've got saw blade arms under that desk.*

Iridius, Greg and Meteon rode the lift up while the other guard waited with the car. When the elevator doors opened

Iridius was greeted by no less than seven enormous black-clad Frost Norton Security guards, all of them pointing rifles in their direction.

"It's alright gentlemen," a female voice said from behind the guards. "Let them through. DJ Chromium and Kla'thak J'artekic Flenbak are our guests."

The half-helmeted but fully-intimidating guards stepped aside. Behind them was an office that was, just like the foyer downstairs and its android occupant, styled like a mid-twentieth century New York high-rise corner office. An enormous wooden desk filled most of the space. It was probably made from authentic Earth mahogany. The desk looked like it probably had enough mass to produce its own gravitational field. Iridius wouldn't have been surprised to find out it was somehow being used to generate the station's artificial gravity. A drinks table loaded with bottles of top-shelf alcohol from throughout the galaxy sat in one corner, beside a couch positioned for optimum napping potential. There were even windows that, instead of displaying the planet Lentrani and a view of the rest of the station as they should, showed an artificial view of New York City dating from around the 1960s. It looked to be from before construction of the famous twin towers that had been destroyed in an act of terrorism, well before Manhattan was struck by the asteroid and obviously before Iridius had come along and destroyed the planet – but we weren't going to bring that up again. Leaning against the edge of the desk, dressed in a tight grey jumpsuit that very much fitted the twenty-third century despite the room around her, was a human woman with long black hair tied up in decorative braids along the side of her head. She stared at Iridius with dark eyes that might as well have been black holes in her face. Other than noticing that her jumpsuit was so figure-hugging it might as well have been spray-painted on, Iridius couldn't draw his attention away from her smouldering eyes.

"Welcome, Mr Chromium," she said. "Is that what I should

call you?"

"Yes," Iridius said, his voice failing him a little. He cleared his throat. "Mr Chromium is fine."

"Terrific," the woman said as she stood, or more accurately seemed to slither upwards like some kind of miraculously charmed snake. "My name is Gentrix Frost, I'm Chief Operating Officer of Frost Norton. Essentially I'm the second-in-charge around here, and responsible for much of the day-to-day running of the station." She glided across to Iridius and held out her hand. Iridius took her long dark fingers in his and shook her hand, thankful that his stupid DJ Chromium outfit hid not only his identity but also the amount of sweat pouring from almost every pore. "My brother, Devin Frost, CEO of Frost Norton, should be here momentarily."

"Great," Iridius said. "I look forward to meeting him."

"You say that now," Gentrix said, "but my brother can be quite, let's just say, intense." Gentrix turned and sauntered to the drinks table, where she lifted several bottles, inspecting each of them in turn before settling on one that seemed agreeable. She pulled the glass stopper from the bottle and tipped a couple of fingers of a stark violet liquid into a glass. She swirled it a few times, sniffed it and then took a sip before her eyes lifted to meet Iridius's. He might have been wearing a full face-obscuring silver helmet, but her gaze seemed to know precisely where his eyes were and they burned through his glass faceplate like two femtosecond lasers performing eye surgery. Iridius found it difficult to hold her gaze, even though he knew he had a helmet on. Gronk knows what the animated face on the front was doing. "Drink?" she said.

"Yes, please," Greg said at exactly the same time as Iridius answered for both of them, "No, we're fine."

Greg looked at him before looking back at Gentrix. "I'm fine," he said.

If this woman, who seemed like she would simultaneously freeze and set fire to the ground beneath her with every step, claimed her brother was going to be intense, then Iridius was suitably terrified. If Gentrix was second-in-charge, his mind raced with the possibilities of what it meant to be in charge around here. He could only imagine that CEO Devin Frost would probably be literal frost – some sort of human/ice hybrid. A tight-suited sociopath who likely had the same kind of presence in the room as his sister, maybe even more domineering. Iridius would have to be one hundred per cent on his game. If he was going to get anything out of Devin Frost he would have to outwit someone who was likely razor sharp, menacing of mind and body, a true nemesis for a Space Command Captain.

The elevator doors opened.

"Ah," Gentrix said. "Here's my brother now."

The man who entered the room had about as much in common with the mental image Iridius had conjured up as a child's first finger painting has with the roof of the Sistine Chapel. Devin Frost was not a tall, devilishly handsome man who strode with the same scintillating purpose as his sister. Instead, he rolled into the room like cookie dough, wearing an obvious hairpiece and a smile goofier than Lieutenant Rangi after a terrible joke. He did not cut into the room in the dark suit tailored from razor blades that Iridius had expected. Instead he wore an actual, multi-coloured flowery Hawaiian shirt that Iridius was certain had been banned under the 2156 Treaty of the Rights of Sentient Beings. He all but bounced over to Iridius, grabbing the tops of his arms with massive hands and squeezing.

"OMG you're here!" Devin Frost squealed. Then he grabbed Iridius and pulled him into an unexpected hug. "Thank you for coming, I'm an enormous fan. Your absolute biggest." Eventually Devin released Iridius who had, through the whole ordeal, remained in perfectly shocked stillness.

"I hear that a lot," Iridius said.

"Oh, I bet you do but I actually am your biggest fan. I've got all your albums pressed on actual vinyl. I've even got the original printing of the Android sessions, and there's only one hundred copies of that in the entire galaxy." Frost continued blabbering at Iridius in what seemed to be some sort of fast-forward, and he did so with his face uncomfortably close to Iridius's. "How was working with Graltax the Groovy? I have all his albums on vinyl too. Do you consider that your best duo work, or would you consider it to be what you did with Redux Rampage because that's what most people would think?"

"Uh," Iridius answered.

"Devin," Gentrix said. "Let's give our guest some space."

"Right, sorry," Devin said, taking a backwards step that still wasn't quite big enough to recover what Iridius would consider suitable personal space. "I'm just very excited you're here. You know she wasn't going to let me have you aboard for my birthday gig," Devin said, nodding towards Gentrix, "because she's a total meanie. Lucky I'm the boss, because then I get to say that you definitely are allowed. Why don't you come for a walk with me? I want to show you around my station. It's the best station."

"I told you he could be intense," Gentrix said. "Devin, you've got a few things you need to attend to this afternoon, but then you've got plenty of time later to catch up with Mr Chromium here."

Devin waved his sister's comments away. "You can take care of all that for me can't you Gentrix?"

"Devin, I—"

"Come on," Devin said, "please, Gentrix? You always handle the boring things better than me." Frost turned to Iridius. "She does a great job, my sister. A terrific job. The best. I couldn't run this place without her."

No, Iridius thought, drawing plenty of conclusions about

these two from just this small interaction, I don't imagine you could.

Gentrix sighed. "You are the CEO, Devin. There are certain matters you need to attend to."

"I am the CEO," Frost said, "but everyone knows you act with my authority. And as CEO I'm declaring that I'm taking DJ Chromium for a walk."

Gentrix stared at Iridius and Greg for a long, uncomfortable moment. "Fine."

"Come on DJ Chromium," Devin said, turning back to the elevator and continuing to talk non-stop as Greg and Iridius followed. "Should I call you that? Or should I just call you Chromium? Or wait, is it DJ?"

Iridius turned back to see Gentrix Frost, taking a sip of her noxious purple drink, watching him leave.

———

"Then I traded that for two copies of an original pressing of *Black Sky, Black Heart*, which as you know is very rare because I don't have to tell you that Vitalon Records really did not have enough faith in you to follow up after *Live a Little*, but of course we all know that was a huge mistake because it became a cult classic among not just Chromium fans and not even just fans of electronica but of all types of music. Do you think that was your break out into the mainstream?"

Iridius opened his mouth to answer. but Devin Frost continued after a pause so short that not even a Helixial, a tiny sentient extremophile species that lived their entire lives within the span of time it took to be ejected from a volcano and as a result conversed with each other at a rate of around one hundred words per femtosecond, could have managed to squeeze a word in.

"Doesn't really matter because I don't like the distinction between underground and mainstream. If you're successful enough that lots of people start liking you I don't know why people try and paint that as a bad thing. People love to say they were a fan of something before it got big, which is just stupid really. Of course, just to be clear, I was a fan of yours before you got big."

Iridius stared at Frost. So far he had taken Iridius and Greg on a tour of his office, his apartment and the recording studio he was having built in a section of Frost Tower, which had apparently once belonged to the Health and Safety Department before he'd closed it down. Then he'd taken them through to the Executive Restaurant, where they'd eaten. They hadn't stopped and sat at one of the many tables to have a meal though. No, they had wandered through and the wait staff had handed them preprepared brown paper bags of food which had probably once been plated delicately but had now become stuck to the bag in a way that Iridius thought would horrify the chefs, but was apparently the usual way CEO Frost took his meals. Through all this wandering around Frost had not stopped speaking. Not in the way people mean when they say, 'oh, he just didn't stop speaking' which really means 'he spoke a lot to the point where it was kind of annoying'. Devin Frost literally had not stopped speaking the entire time Iridius and Greg had been following him around.

Iridius stole a glance across at Greg, wondering if Devin's constant inane chatter was about to break him the same way Iridius thought he might snap at any moment. He didn't feel like he was going to explode with anger and scream for the man to shut the fuck up for all that was sacred and holy in the universe, though. He felt more like his brain was going to stop working; like Devin Frost was going to talk him into a vegetative state. Greg was walking beside Frost, his eyes fixed straight ahead. A malignant's face, already looking like a mottled, constantly mutating tumour, was sometimes tricky to read, but there was a far-off look in Greg's eyes as he walked, something akin to the look of a soldier who has seen too much.

"This way now," Frost was saying. Iridius had found it easier to simply tune in and out, or at least his brain had started doing that automatically. "You're probably not that interested in the sort of actual work we do here – it's not as exciting as being a professional DJ. I tried to see if I could make it as a professional VR gamer when I was younger, but it's just such a competitive field. I came close to making some pretty serious teams but I just do it as a hobby now, so I ended up taking on the family business after all."

From somewhere inside his boredom-anesthetised brain a part of Iridius screamed for his attention. Frost had just said something important. "Wait," Iridius said, interrupting Frost midway through an explanation of why he hadn't made the VR Space Combat team. Frost stopped talking and Iridius had that momentarily unsettling sensation one has when a loud, continuous noise suddenly stops, leaving only perfect silence. "You said something about what your company actually does?" Iridius said when the phantom ringing in his ears had subsided. "I'm interested in that. I'd love to know more about what you do here."

"Oh," Frost said. "Well, it's mostly just technological development of ship systems. We focus on more efficient power generation and sometimes branch into counter-measures for starships."

"Like what?" Iridius said. "Like weapons?

"Energy shields mostly, quantum stuff," Frost said. "I do have something very cool to show you if you want to see it? A real technological breakthrough for dealing with time. I shouldn't really show anyone...you want to see?"

"Yes," Iridius said. He looked to Greg, whose eyes also showed a sudden reanimation and interest. "I'd love to see a breakthrough to do with time stuff. I mean, I'm sure I won't understand it – I'm just a DJ after all – but it sounds interesting."

"Alright," Frost said. "It's under the tightest security we have on the station, so you'll have to stay close with me."

Iridius and Greg followed Frost out of Frost Tower and down to a nondescript doorway in a white wall. Frost pressed his hand to a panel beside the door, which chimed and slid open. Inside was an elevator with only two buttons, up and down. Frost pressed the down button and the doors slid closed. Iridius was suddenly very alert. He wasn't paying attention to whatever Frost was saying about collector's edition vinyl releases that had a mistake on the album artwork, but he was alert to his surroundings. He honestly couldn't believe how this enormous, Hawaiian shirted nerdy fool was in charge of this corporation. The longer Iridius spent with him the more he suspected that his sister, Gentrix, was the one running the show. It seemed obvious now as they descended the central spire in the elevator: Devin Frost was the CEO in name only. He had to be a cover for Gentrix. He was the public face of Frost Norton, which left his sister free to take care of the real business of the corporation, building weapons of mass destruction. Well, that suited Iridius fine because it had been easier than he'd imagined to talk this giant child into taking him straight to what he needed.

When the elevator stopped, the doors opened to reveal a corridor. At the far end was yet another door, this one an immensely thick vault door. Here Frost pressed a series of buttons on a coded entry panel. Iridius tried to catch sight of the code, but Frost's fingers flew with the speed of habit over the panel.

"This area is very secure," Frost said. "It's the most secure. You won't find security like this in most places in the galaxy."

When the vault door opened it revealed a circular room about 5 metres in diameter. All around the circumference of the room were banks of computer systems quietly humming, while in the centre of the space was a large terminal and what seemed to be a cylindrical tower of highly secure storage lockers. All of it, oddly, was hanging from the roof of the room rather than connected to the floor. Iridius looked up to find numerous scanners, sensors and cameras pointing down at them.

"Full biometric scanning," Frost said. "This room is constantly scanning your biometric data, and I mean all your biometric data. If an occupant in this room doesn't match biometric data held in the security database then the whole floor of the room explosively ejects into space, sucking the intruder out into the black. Luckily for you, my biometric data is authorised to have visitors."

This must be it, Iridius thought. This might not be the lab where the time reversal bomb was developed, but a room with this much security is definitely where you'd store one, or at least store the plans for how to build one.

"Here we go though," Frost said, moving to one of the storage drawers on the side of the central column. "This is what I wanted to show you. Engineers and scientists at Frost Norton have been doing excellent work in dealing with time."

Iridius and Greg stood either side of Frost as he placed his thumb on a scanner on top of one of the storage lockers in the room's central column. It chimed, flashed green, and a drawer slid out automatically. Iridius and Greg both leaned forward. In that moment Iridius realised he had no idea what a time reversal bomb would actually look like. He'd pictured some kind of shiny chrome cylinder with a countdown clock on it and a bunch of wires, red and green ones that you might be able to cut to disarm it if you knew what you were doing, although not until the last second, of course, if any of the movies he'd seen had been accurate. But that wasn't what he was looking at. He didn't know what the bomb would look like, but he did know what a collection of voidball cards inside a sealed clear container looked like. I'll let you infer which he was looking at.

"These are my most prized possessions," Frost said, smiling at Iridius, "other than my vinyl collection of course. Twelve hundred and sixteen rare and limited edition voidball cards. Many of them are rookie cards signed by players like Mattock Jensen, Charmeleon Brack and Leroy Brave. I've never had the collection valued, but it's probably worth as much as my whole company. I heard you were a voidball fan and used to collect voidball cards too, so I thought you'd be interested."

Iridius looked up at Greg and then looked at Frost. "Sorry Mr Frost," Iridius said, "I'm confused. Your voidball cards are a scientific breakthrough related to time?"

Frost smiled. "No, not my card collection, the box. This sealed container is actually our most technologically advanced breakthrough. For hundreds of years collectors of everything have used climate-controlled storage and all kinds of things to maintain the mint condition of their collections. What we've developed here at Frost Norton is a box that reduces entropy. It actually slows time in a very small area, which is what keeps the cards from decaying."

"Amazing," Iridius said.

"I know right?" Frost said. "I'll send you one for your own voidball collection as soon as we're ready to mass produce and get them on the market."

What Iridius didn't say was that it wasn't the technology he found amazing, though to be fair it was kind of cool, and he could see the application for his vintage comic book collection. What he found amazing was that he was pretty much convinced that CEO Devin Frost had absolutely no idea that his company had developed a time reversal bomb capable of all but destroying the Galactic Federation. He had to find out everything he could about Chief Operating Officer Gentrix Frost – she had to be the brains and, from looking at her brother, the brawn as well.

"I don't normally get them out of their containment box, but I'll show you what I've got in my collection," Frost said.

"No, it's fine," Iridius said. "I wouldn't want you to damage them on my account."

"No, I insist," Frost said, and to Iridius's horror he started with the first card in the collection and began working through the remaining one thousand, two hundred and fifteen.

CHAPTER SEVEN_

LIEUTENANT COMMANDER QUINN sat in the captain's chair on the bridge of the FSC *Deus Ex*, staring at the view-screen beyond the helm and watching the lights of Locke Station as it moved across the dark side of Lentrani. They hadn't picked up anything over the quantum entanglement interceptor that suggested the away team had been discovered, but that didn't mean it hadn't happened. They might well have been captured already, or maybe they were just on the verge of being captured. Perhaps Locke Station had uncovered their true identities and CEO Devin Frost had simply had them executed on the spot without bothering to tell anyone. Captain Franklin, Lieutenant Latroz, Lieutenant Rangi, Chief Petty Officer Nejem and Chief Petty Officer Gr'lak N'hlarkic Tre'laktor might already be frozen corpses floating in the dark of space.

Quinn knew she was catastrophising. She always did. She let her mind immediately pick the worst-case scenario. If she had to give a presentation she was certain the entire crowd would judge her as inadequate. Even after one-on-one interactions she spent days or weeks mulling over what the other person thought of her. And just like now, if there was an away team mission she was sure they'd all end up as redshirts. She knew exactly what her brain was doing as it launched itself towards the worst case, but that was the thing with anxiety, even if you understood it, it could still manage to control you.

Captain Franklin had a bone-conduction receiver implanted under his skin, just behind his right ear. This was a new initiative Space Command was rolling out across the fleet, a small emergency transponder and communicator that could track the location of prominent crew members and act as a receiver for emergency communication. Captain Franklin had reluctantly received the implant just prior to taking command of the *Deus Ex* under strict orders from the Admiralty. So, even in this situation, Quinn knew she could communicate with Captain Franklin if she absolutely had to but, because it was a high-frequency radio receiver, it would be noticed by anyone monitoring the airways and Captain Franklin had very specifically told her not to use it. Although she'd considered it more than once, just to check he wasn't dead. For someone with Quinn's anxiety it was cripplingly difficult not knowing what was going on aboard that space station. Heck, it was cripplingly difficult having Iridius B. Franklin as her captain.

She loved that man. She honestly did. She didn't think she could feel more affection for him if he were the actual older brother she'd wished for growing up as an only child. She knew he meant well, mostly, but his predilection towards wanting to be the hero was more than she could handle. Even if she hadn't been the anxious type, she couldn't help but think this desire of his to be a swashbuckling captain of old would see him, and perhaps all of them, walking the metaphorical plank one day.

She'd tried to tell him many times in the past, long before the *Deus Ex,* even before their time on the *Gallaway*, that she didn't want to be forced into the spotlight, didn't want to be an adventuring space explorer, but he'd continued to push her. He wanted the best for her, she couldn't deny that, but he only wanted the best for her as he defined it. Why couldn't he see that not everyone wanted to explore strange new worlds and seek out new civilisations? Some people were more than happy exploring strange new worlds from the safety of a lab or exploring civilisations through a video feed so they could take notes. At the end of the day, they might not have been as gloriously portrayed as the explorers out there on the fringe, but someone had to examine all the samples brought back. For Quinn, that was glorious. That was where the real work happened.

She had always known Iridius was the opposite to her. Where she saw only the misfortune that could befall every mission, Captain Franklin often struggled to see, or at least chose not to see, how his enthusiastic behaviour could lead to more danger than it was worth. So far, he'd skated through unscathed. But Quinn knew that eventually, breaking regulations and going off on half thought-out missions would lead to disaster.

What was she talking about? It *had* led to disaster. He had been cleared of wrongdoing in the end, but they were still the ones who had carried the Aegix to Earth. The encounter with the Aegix had been the final straw for Quinn. It was that adventure that had finally given her the courage to resign from active space operations.

It was Iridius who had held her back from resigning before. Despite not agreeing with how he tried to push her, a sense of misguided loyalty to him had stopped her from going through with it. She didn't want to let him down. In the end though, it had been the very lessons Iridius tried to teach her that had broken her. He had always pushed her to come out of her shell and then, when the galaxy was on the line, he had pushed her to come up with a solution. The solution she'd come up with had failed, and hundreds of members of Space Command had paid the ultimate price as a result. She had told Iridius she didn't blame herself, and that was mostly true. What she didn't say was that was because she blamed him. She loved Iridius Franklin, but she could not find it in her to forgive him for pushing her too far in the end.

Then there was the Synth-Hastur, the threat the Aegix had supposedly been developed to counter. The Aegix was not a malevolent entity, she was certain of that, it was simply doing what it had been programmed to do, but was faulty after so many hundreds of thousands of years. However, the Synth-Hastur might well have been malevolent. The Aegix called them the Devourers of the Stars, the Great Living Storm of Steel, the Lords of Interstellar Space and the Harbingers of Forever War. Nothing about that sounded promising. Most of the Federation had simply ignored the warnings, Iridius included. They considered the Aegix to be the threat, and that threat had been neutralised. They would say there was no evidence of the Synth-Hastur's existence, but Quinn disagreed. The very existence of the Aegix was evidence.

Luckily, she was not alone in her assessment. So many cultures in the galaxy had tales of cosmic-level, interstellar dwelling threats in their mythology and legends, the Old Ones, the Cosmos Eaters, the Unknowable Horrors. The warning from the Aegix of a galaxy-level threat had concerned enough people that the Federation had stood up a small team of scientists to investigate the validity of the claims and to prepare, in the event the Synth-Hastur, whatever they were, proved real. With her first-hand knowledge, Quinn's transfer request was readily granted.

"Lieutenant Commander Quinn." Technician Grantham's voice came over the comm.

Quinn pressed the button on the arm of her chair to respond. "Yes, Grantham, go ahead."

"I think you'd better come down here."

"Is everything alright? Are the prisoners still secure?"

"Aye," Grantham replied. "They're still secure but they're – well, they're making some claims you might want to hear."

———

Quinn walked out of the elevator, down a short corridor and turned into the brig. The *FSC Deus Ex* was a small ship, designed only for the type of secretive reconnaissance it had been doing lately, but still, as per Federation Space Command Regulation 211, it was mandated to have a brig for holding FSC personnel in the event of criminal actions, a serious breach of regulations or for the imprisonment of any neutralised external threats.

Regulation 211 didn't specifically mention the use of the brig to hold a famous DJ, but Quinn supposed he could be considered a threat to the Federation at a stretch. She was sure Captain Franklin would argue that while a musician and his roadies were not a threat in and of themselves, their temporary imprisonment was a requirement to save the Federation. He would probably be believed, too. She wasn't entirely sure how he managed it, really. She'd always believed rules and regulations to be fixed and immovable, but Iridius Franklin always found a way to bend them just enough that he could squeeze past. Quinn had realised soon after entering active service with Space Command that this phenomenon was not unique to Iridius Franklin. The most legendary starship captains in the history of the fleet, people like Roc Mayhem, Cathleen Jan-wei and Gertrok Siztil, had always been, if not on the verge of breaking regulations, absolutely shattering them. Regulations about first contact, interference with non-space-faring species and mandated diplomatic rules of engagement seemed to exist solely for these captains to ignore. Up until the events with the Aegix, Iridius wouldn't have been included in the category of 'famous starship captains' on *Galactic*

Jeopardy, but he'd still managed to talk himself out of consequences even when he'd been a lowly, often-ignored hauler captain. There was just something those in command seemed to have that Quinn absolutely didn't, a force of will and the ability to convince pretty much anyone that they were right. Humanity was not the only race that seemed built for people more outgoing than herself. It was true what they said: the galaxy was made for extroverts.

Quinn stopped beside Technician Grantham outside the holding cell. Normally Lieutenant Latroz or maybe even Junker would be left to guard a cell like this, but since Captain Franklin had taken Latroz, Junker, Rangi and Greg on the away team, they weren't exactly flush with personnel. The holding cell itself was only small, and was cramped with the thirteen people inside. As Quinn approached, DJ Chromium rocked forward from where he had been leaning against the cell wall and stepped up to the bars. Of course, the bars were only a holographic projection and weren't actually what kept the cell closed. The holding cell was actually sealed by a gravomagnetic quantum chromodynamic energy shield, much the same as the one that surrounded the entire ship, but on a much smaller scale. The holographic bars were there for two reasons. Firstly, they gave a sense of actually being imprisoned. Unless something collided with it, a gravomagnetic quantum chromodynamic energy shield was completely transparent, and there was a certain desirable psychological impact when a prisoner could see the bars of their cage. Second, the holographic bars indicated that the shield was active. Even accidentally touching the shielding would cause an energetic shock that resulted in sudden nerve impulses firing, causing those sentient beings that possessed one to immediately empty their bladder. This wasn't to protect the prisoners so much as it was to prevent crew members from embarrassment. It had been mandated across all FSC vessels after Fleet Admiral Staloz, a proud Siruan warrior, had backed into a holding cell shield and wet herself in front of several important dignitaries. She had become so embarrassed that she spontaneously exploded, a Siruan biological reflex called Gen-tri that usually happens when a Siruan general has been devastatingly beaten in battle. Judging from the stain down the legs of at least two of the roadies inside the cell, they had found this out the hard way.

"You are the first officer?" DJ Chromium asked. "Currently in command of this ship?"

"That's correct. I am Lieutenant Commander Kira Quinn, Federation Space Command, Executive Officer of the Federation Space Command vessel *Deus Ex*."

DJ Chromium grabbed the side of his helmet and unlocked it from his suit with a click. The green animated face blinked off and he lifted the mirrored chrome helmet from his head. Except Quinn had to make a rapid rectification as this happened, because DJ Chromium was not removing the helmet from *his* head, *she* was removing the helmet from *her* head. The person wearing the silver costume was a young woman, perhaps less than thirty, her dark hair cut short in military style buzz cut that was equal parts intimidating and kind of hot. It took a moment to register what seemed odd about her. She looked human but very thin and waifish, pale, and her irises were white.

Technician Grantham was equally shocked. "Wait," she said, "you're a woman?"

"No."

"No?" Grantham asked, confused.

"I am a human-andronia hybrid. We all identify as non-binary. But the question you were actually asking was whether DJ Chromium is a woman, and the answer to that question is also no. DJ Chromium is a human man named Mark Mudd. He's been an agent of the Federation Intelligence Bureau for almost thirteen years, about the same amount of time he's been a famous

DJ, so I'm sure you can put two and two together there. There's probably no better way to infiltrate the Alliance of Planetary Corporations than by using their own music against them."

"Are you saying DJ Chromium is a spy?" Quinn asked. "And who are you then?"

"I am Agent Electra Clix, Federation Intelligence Bureau." She turned and gestured to the others in the cell with her. "Everyone in here is an agent or asset of the Federal Intelligence Bureau."

"You're all with FIB? All spooks?" Grantham said.

"We prefer the term 'agents' for those of us who are employed by the FIB or 'assets' for those working with us, but yes, we are all affiliated with the Federation's intelligence service."

"Why didn't you say anything?" Quinn asked. "When Captain Franklin took your ship?"

"Our Senior Agent ordered us to maintain cover."

Quinn looked at the others in the cell. "May I speak with this Senior Agent?"

"I'm afraid not. Senior Agent Mark Mudd is not here."

"DJ Chromium is the Senior Agent?"

"That's correct," Agent Clix said.

"So he was never with you?" Quinn asked. "You were using the DJ Chromium identity?"

"He's not here," Clix said, "because he stayed on board the *Interstella* when your idiot captain decided to steal it and interrupt our mission. We know about the cloaking capabilities of the *Deus Ex* and we knew you were stationed here to listen in on the ASS Locke to ensure nothing happened before we arrived. As soon as we were disabled and realised we were being docked with by an invisible ship, Senior Agent Mudd ordered me to dress as DJ Chromium and then he hid on board the *Interstella*. It's been almost impossible to get aboard Locke Station. This operation has been in planning for months and you FSC idiots have jeopardised the whole thing."

"I need to contact Captain Franklin," Quinn said. "He's got an emergency communicator and—"

"You'll do no such thing," Clix said. "The Alliance will detect that transmission. They can't know Agent Mudd is on that station."

"What choice did we have but to act?" Quinn said, knowing there was absolutely another choice but feeling like she had to defend Iridius anyway. "Captain Franklin was convinced the weapon on board that station was a threat that needed to be addressed."

"It is a threat," Clix continued, "and you don't know the half of it. Our informants have sent us intelligence revealing that the Alliance has developed a very dangerous weapon."

"A time reversal bomb," Quinn said. "Yes, we know."

Quinn felt a touch of pleasure at the surprise on Clix's face. "Well, you're more informed than I'd given you credit for. Do you know what they're going to do with it?"

Quinn shook her head.

"The Alliance plan to use that weapon on major Federation targets, including Earth."

"Earth doesn't exist anymore," Technician Grantham interjected.

"Earth doesn't exist now, but the Alliance don't want to destroy Earth now," Clix said, "they want to destroy Earth over a hundred years ago, something they can manage with a time reversal bomb."

"Before the Federation–Alliance war," Quinn said.

"That's right. What better way to deal with a war you lost than by crippling your enemy back before it even began. The Intelligence Bureau had a carefully designed plan. DJ Chromium was going to sneak aboard, use the concert as cover to steal the plans for the weapon and disable their research capability. Now, thanks to your interference, most of that team is locked in this cell, our Senior Agent has had to stowaway on board his own ship and your captain is running around on Locke Station pretending to be a famous DJ with no idea what he's doing or how to steal that weapon."

"Yes, well, I understand there are some issues," Quinn said.

"Some issues?" Clix said. "Either the Alliance rewrites history or, if they discover Federation spies trying to steal or destroy their weapon, it could spark a major political incident that will probably kick off another Federation–Alliance war. This has to be handled delicately."

"Yes, well," Quinn said, struggling to decide whether to be annoyed at Captain Franklin or the FIB or both. She settled on both. "Seems like information we should have been given, doesn't it? Then Captain Franklin wouldn't have needed to go off half-cocked. But I'm sure our team are handling things delicately."

———

"Handle it delicately," Junker said as she watched Rangi guide a hovering cargo-lift down the offload ramp of the *Interstella*, banging it around on the way down. Junker walked over and looked at the crate. "It's the wrong one anyway. I said to get the crate with the synths in it." She popped the two latches and opened it. "See," she said, "these are the controllers and the holo-display manipulators."

Rangi looked inside the crate at the electronic devices, each covered with dozens of coloured buttons and twisty knobs. "I don't know what a synth is, what a controller is or what a holo-display manipulator is. These things have more buttons and sliders than the helm of a damn ship. You said get the green crate so I got the green crate."

"No, I said they were *in* a green crate. I meant the other green crate." Junker turned to the Frost Norton Security guards who'd been tasked with helping them unload DJ Chromium's equipment for the concert. "You three, go in and get the crate with the synths in it? That's the other green crate. There's only one left. You won't fail a 50–50 coin flip like this idiot here, right?"

Rangi waited for the three guards to head into the ship. As soon as they were out of earshot he turned to Junker. "Look, you know we aren't actually going to perform a concert, right? Who cares if we unload the syntho-jiggers instead of the whammy-jammers. It's not going to matter."

"It matters to me," Junker said.

Rangi looked over at Latroz who was standing near the front of the ship. "And why am I do all this? Latroz is stronger than me. She could probably carry all the crates out herself."

"I am on security detail, Benjamin," Latroz said, looking over her shoulder.

"Yeah, she's on security detail," Junker said.

The guards reappeared at the top of the ramp holding a green crate between them. Junker looked up at them. "That's the one. Come and put it here and we'll take a load to the theatre. Might as well take the crate this half-brained cephalopod brought down, even though I want to set up the synths first and it will just be in the way."

The guards did so, placing their crate on top of the one already on the cargo-lift.

"Go on then," Junker said, waving them on. "We're right behind you."

The guards exchanged glances and then began moving the cargo-lift across the landing pad.

Rangi turned to Junker. "One other thing. I know Captain Franklin has you posing as the tour manager, but I'm still a lieutenant and you're still a chief petty officer. You don't get to call me an idiotic cephalopod. I might be the laid-back funny guy on the crew but I'm still an officer, understand?"

"I'm just keeping in character, Lieutenant," Junker said. "I'm also conditioning the guards to think I have authority."

"Fine, just don't overstep the mark."

"Come on," Junker said, "we'd better catch up." She walked away and Latroz moved to walk with her. Junker looked back at Rangi. "Anyway, who said you're funny?"

"Excuse me, I'm the funny one. Everyone knows that."

Junker raised her eyebrows in a way that could only be interpreted as disagreement, then turned away.

Rangi hurried after her. "Everyone says I'm the funny one. Don't they?" Rangi increased his pace. "Junker? What do they say about me then?"

Rangi couldn't see the amused grin on Junker's face as she walked away.

"Junker?!" Rangi asked again. "Latroz? You think I'm funny don't you?"

Junker, Latroz and Rangi followed the security team moving the cargo lift off towards the theatre, leaving the landing pad around the *Interstella* empty and unmonitored. After a moment a small door hidden in the wall of the *Interstella*'s cargo bay slid open. Inside was a climatically sealed and electronically shielded safety chamber, a kind of space panic room that was an optional extra on luxury executive transports like the Gulfstream.

They had proven popular with the wealthy elite of the Alliance, who might need to travel through star systems prone to attacks from pirates – both the traditional type who attempted to steal ships and gene-pirates who stole the DNA of important individuals to on-sell to cloners or those interested in bypassing biometric security systems. However, those who used them faced one of two possible outcomes: either they emerged from the chamber and had to face the pirates anyway or they stayed in there indefinitely. There was one recorded case of a ship being seized by pirates, used by them for quite some time and then on-sold at a black-market shipyard. The new owner was startled to see a haggard, unshaven man emerge from the safety chamber claiming to be the CEO of the Twinkle Corporation. He'd been reported as killed in a pirate attack a decade earlier. Still, while not providing wealthy elites with the peace of mind they hoped for unless they were prepared to live for years in a small box, a safety chamber did provide an excellent hideaway for a well-respected super-spy turned DJ to stow away in when his ship was hijacked by well-meaning idiots.

DJ Chromium/Federation Intelligence Bureau Senior Agent Mark Mudd crawled out of the safety chamber in the *Interstella*'s cargo bay and brushed off his tailored jumpsuit. He couldn't believe that after months of preparation he was going to have to improvise this like a complete amateur. He wasn't an amateur. He was one of the finest agents in the galaxy and he had a weapon to steal – that hadn't changed. He just happened to also have an impulsive Space Command captain getting in the way. Mudd began heading for the exit of the ship but stopped just before the doorway as a thought struck him. He returned to his cabin and removed one of his iconic silver spacesuits and a DJ Chromium helmet from the wardrobe, shoving them inside a bag before turning to leave. He had a weapon to steal and a captain to stop, but he still had a show to do too.

CHAPTER EIGHT

"HAVE you ever heard of the Ganooshins?" Iridius asked as he, Greg, Latroz, Junker and Rangi sat around a table in the common room on board the *Interstella*. They had finally reunited after Junker, Latroz and Rangi had spent the entire morning carting crates of DJ equipment to the theatre for tonight's DJ Chromium gig and Iridius and Greg had been dragged around by Hawaiian shirt-clad moron Devin Frost.

"No, Cap," Junker said.

"They're a torture cult on the planet Inraki," Iridius said, "known for being masters of mind-manipulating torture. Apparently they use techniques of audio and visual stimulation that cause such profound feelings of boredom and malaise in their victims that it leads to instantaneous cerebral nerve shedding and a complete failure of nervous system function. They literally bore you to death. That's what an afternoon in the presence of CEO Devin Frost was like. I don't think he stopped speaking the entire time, but I couldn't tell you anything he said. He took us on a tour of the central spire and showed us everything from the plans for his own personal recording studio to every single one of his collection of twelve hundred and sixteen rare and limited edition voidball cards. I thought getting information about the weapons development program would be difficult because I'd need to battle wits with a criminal mastermind, but instead I didn't get any information because my brain was temporarily shredded into non-existence by the innate chatter of a child-man. I think it's pretty clear that his sister, this Gentrix Frost, is the real brains behind the operation. I don't think Devin Frost has any goddamn idea what's going on."

"Gentrix Frost does seem to have much more of your non-mutated human brains than her brother," Greg said. "She is also intimidating like Gk'gork Fr'nek Gren'trok."

"Your mother-in-law?" Iridius said, almost feeling a shiver. "Yeah, I remember."

"But," Greg said, "after this morning I think maybe I am more scared of CEO Devin Frost."

Junker chuckled. "It can't have been that bad. He just sounds like a dork."

Greg spun to her quickly. "You weren't there, man." His eyes bored into her. "You weren't there."

Junker held her hands up in submission. "Okay, sorry."

"Doesn't matter. Fact is we don't have any information about the time bomb or its location yet. We need to get out on the station, find out whatever we can and come up with a plan, and I think we'd better maintain character while we do it."

"I don't know if going out there dressed like DJ Chromium is a good idea, Cap," Junker said.

"I too believe it unwise," Latroz said.

"DJ Chromium is supposed to be on board this space station," Iridius said. "We're not. We should maintain cover. It'll be fine."

———

"Run!" Iridius yelled as the teen girls closed in on them, seemingly coalescing from every building and alleyway in the Burrows. They came from all directions, moving with the kind of purpose seen in predatory species the galaxy over – wide-eyed, fanatical, terrifying purpose.

"OMG! You're DJ Chromium! OMG!"

So, a heroic starship captain, an enormous alien warrior, a hard as nails mechanic, a hot-shot pilot and a sentient cancer all began running from a bunch of teenage girls. They were more terrifying than anything Iridius had faced before, and that included an insane artificial intelligence that had tried to turn every living thing in the galaxy into pink goop. They took off down the street back towards the space port, but soon saw another group coming towards them.

"OMG!"

Iridius and his crew had to rapidly change direction.

"Why do they keep saying O-M-G? What in the gronking black does that mean?" Iridius called as they moved.

"It's old Earth slang," Junker said. "It means oh my god."

"It's a religious thing?"

"No, it's just like how you say goddamn all the time."

"I don't say that."

"You do."

Iridius didn't get the chance to argue as another group appeared.

"It's really him, OMG!"

Iridius had been spotted seconds after they emerged from the space port onto the streets of the Burrows. As soon as he had stepped foot through the door in his silver space-suit heads had turned like gronking railgun turrets and locked onto him with the precision of the most advanced target acquisition system in the galaxy. He was shocked at how easily they'd been spotted among the chaos of the Burrows.

Many large space stations made an attempt to simulate some-thing of a cityscape, with enormous corridors masquerading as streets and protruding facades of buildings giving residents the illusion of being outdoors. Some even had simulated skies projected from holoscreens on the ceilings. But no matter how architecturally advanced or how clever the lighting and simulated surrounds on a space station were, Iridius had always been aware of a feeling of trickery. It was as though you were walking through one of those old Earth wild west film sets where they just had the fronts of buildings propped up on wooden braces.

However, the Burrows on the ASS Locke captured some-thing other space stations didn't. It felt like a claustrophobic, over-populated shit-hole of a city. The ceiling was low and blasted down nothing but stark florescent light that was forced to compete with the myriad of neon signs that pulsed and flashed and flickered. People moved in all directions, climbing up and down stairways and sharing the street with vehicles in a tangled mess. The press of the low ceiling, the looming buildings, the sprawl of furniture, carts, vehicles, overflowing garbage cans and booths for everything from instant makeovers to simulated sex, all combined to give you the feeling that you were indeed in a single tunnel of a vast burrow. The Burrows made no apologies that it was jammed along the outer ring of a space station in almost perpetual darkness, and as a result Iridius found it oddly more comforting than those Federation stations that attempted to make you feel as though you were walking the immaculate streets of an outdoor utopian paradise. Still, even among all this, it was as if Iridius was wearing an enormous arrow above his head proclaiming HERE IS FAMOUS DJ.

As if they were facing the calculated hunting patterns of Trandactil Megaraptors, the groups of teen girls had managed to all but pin them down. As one group came closer, Iridius raised his hands.

"Good evening, ladies," he said. "Nice morning isn't it?"

"OMG, nice morning, lol lol lol, you're funny."

Iridius turned to Junker.

"Laughing out loud," she said under her breath.

Iridius hoped his animated green face didn't look as confused as his real face surely did. "Why don't they just laugh?" he murmured.

"Can we get a holo-selfie with you?" one of the girls asked.

"I can't wait for your show. I've got tickets right up the front."

One of the girls lunged forward to grab at Iridius but Latroz moved, her reflexes matched only by the Erati monks who trained by opening a container of two hundred insects and skewering every single one of them on a toothpick-sized knife before they flew away – a feat itself matched only by the speed of a teenage boy flicking his computer monitor off when his mother entered his bedroom.

"Back off," Latroz growled.

The girl looked at Latroz and then, in a reaction perhaps never before seen by the towering, growling, organically-armoured warrior alien, she ignored her.

"I love you," the girl said, trying to grab at Iridius again. "I just want to touch your suit."

For a moment Latroz didn't know how to react. Apparently this reaction was completely foreign to her.

"I want to touch him too!" another girl said as she pushed forward. Latroz repositioned herself, getting ready to use physical force. They began crowding in now, a sudden sea of fans that seemed to be appearing from nowhere as if they were just spawning in like enemies in one of those virtual reality games Rangi was always playing.

"Look, calm down please," Iridius said. "I just want to ask some questions. Does anyone know—"

"I want to ask you a question!" someone shouted from the

press of bodies that Latroz was holding back. "Will you marry me?"

Another shout came from more teens, not just human girls now, but females and males and non-binaries from half a dozen different species.

"Where are they all coming from?" Iridius asked.

"I am not sure," Latroz said as she single-handedly held back the gathering crowd of Chromium-mania. "But I believe we should depart."

"DJ Chromium! DJ Chromium!"

Iridius turned to Latroz. "You're suggesting a tactical withdrawal then?"

"I'm suggesting," Latroz said as the crowd surged forward, shouting for DJ Chromium's attention, "that you run."

They began moving, Latroz forcing her way through the crowd, dragging Iridius along with her.

"Is this a zombie movie?" Iridius called. "This feels like a zombie movie!"

Latroz led the way as they headed for a small alleyway.

"How are there even this many teenagers on this goddamn space station?"

"Told you you say goddamn all the time, Cap!"

"Unhelpful, Junker!"

"I also tried to tell you DJ Chromium was super famous!" Junker added as they headed into the alley.

"Also unhelpful right now!" Iridius replied.

"ILU, ILU!" members of the crowd shouted as they followed.

"What are they saying?!" Iridius asked.

"ILU," Junker said. "I love you."

"Do they have to shorten everything in the Alliance?!"

When they were halfway down the dark alley Iridius felt something slam into his chest, like he'd just ran into a tree branch. His top half stopped while his bottom half continued and he landed on the hard floor with a slam that left him gasping. As he groaned, he looked over and saw Latroz similarly sprawled. He hesitated to look up, knowing that whatever had managed to lay Latroz out flat wasn't going to be nice.

When he did work up the courage, he saw a malignant standing over him. Unlike Greg, who was misshapen in places but mostly skinny and kind of weak looking, this malignant was huge. An absolute ogre with enormous muscles rippling beneath his mottled skin. Iridius had also been under the impression that the malignants were all pacifists like Greg, but this one gave off the opposite vibe.

"Don't move," the malignant growled. He raised a pistol. Iridius tilted his head to see Rangi, Junker and Greg standing behind him with their arms raised. Apparently they'd been spared the steel bar clothesline. "None of you move either."

"Yes," a more refined voice came from the shadows, "or we'll show you what else we shorten in the Alliance." Staring up at a buzzing fluorescent tube on the ceiling, Iridius saw Gentrix Frost's face lean over him. "We shorten lives." She smiled at Iridius and he felt a disconcerting mixture of both attraction and fear. She turned to the bulging malignant. "Bring them."

CHAPTER NINE_

Iridius stumbled as he was pushed into the room by one of the several identical Frost Norton Security Force goons.

"Hey, take it easy," he said.

"Shut it," the goon said from beneath the visor of his half helmet. His green skin tone and protruding jaw were enough for Iridius to recognise him as a Krug, a species that might have pipped the Siruans as the toughest and most war-like species in the galaxy if they weren't so thick they spent most of their time fighting with their own reflection.

"Actually, Mister Chromium is quite correct," Gentrix Frost said. "There's no need for that."

"But, you've got to shove 'em," the Krug said, his tone betraying his hurt. "How they know they're a prisoner if you don't shove 'em?"

"Thank you for that informative lesson, but DJ Chromium and his entourage are our guests, not our prisoners. We'll treat them as such."

"Fine," the guard grumbled, muttering under his breath.

They had been taken to the penthouse suite of a nearby tenement apartment building, one that looked indistinguishable from so many in the Burrows. Although 'penthouse suite' made it sound much more impressive than it actually was. It was a rundown apartment with paint peeling off the walls – the only thing 'penthouse' about it was that it happened to be on the top level. The main living space was empty but for a table and chairs, and a small desk in the corner. It looked like it had been set up as an office, but where Devin Frost's office had been styled after a mid-twentieth century New York office, this was styled after a dingy mid-twentieth century private eye's office, if it was styled at all. It seemed more likely the look had been achieved through general neglect and decay.

"This your office, is it?" Iridius asked, looking around. "Not as nice as your brother's."

Gentrix smiled, an expression that landed somewhere between crocodile and supermodel. "I've got an office in the central spire too, but I have to admit this is a little more my style. Besides, I need somewhere away from the glitz of Frost Tower to get the real work of running a corporation done – the dirty work. Shall we get down to it?"

"Well," Iridius said, "at least buy me a drink first."

Gentrix moved to Iridius and placed her hand on his chest, moving her face close to the mirrored glass front of his helmet. "You didn't need a drink last time."

The silver suit and helmet suddenly seemed very hot and stuffy, and Iridius had broken out in a heavy sweat. He tried to say something, but all that escaped his mouth was a muffled croak. He just hoped the sound hadn't escaped his helmet. Iridius's mind had gone so completely blank that he only marginally understood what she'd just said.

Wait. Last time?

Oh shit.

"I'll get you a drink," Gentrix said, slow and sultry, before her tone rapidly changed, "when you tell me what in all the black of

space you were doing wandering around the station in public."
She pushed off his chest, sending Iridius stumbling back a step.
"I'm not sure what you were trying to achieve. Or were you
trying to make some kind of point simply because I'd told you not
to do that?"

"We were just meeting the fans," Iridius said, managing to
find his tongue again. "Besides, we can look after ourselves."

"Don't be so naive," Gentrix said. "And for god's sake Mark,
take that helmet off."

Iridius swallowed, which was difficult because of the sudden
appearance of what seemed to be a concrete slab in his throat. He
glanced at the others. They weren't doing a wonderful job of
concealing their shock and concern either. At least he had a
helmet on. Rangi and Junker were just staring straight ahead, like
they wanted to be anywhere else in the galaxy but there. He
couldn't blame them, but they could have at least managed some
semblance of espionage skill and held it together. Iridius was
about to open his mouth and test the improvisational skills he'd
been banging on about when Greg spoke.

"Excuse me, you sensual black-clad human moron," Greg
said. "Do you know who you are speaking to? DJ Chromium does
not take his helmet off for anyone."

"Uh," Iridius said, "maybe not the best time to take the lead."

Gentrix looked at Greg as if noticing a buzzing insect for the
first time. "You can drop the act. I know exactly who I'm speaking
to. I'm speaking with Mark Mudd, also known as DJ Chromium
the Alliance assassin."

"The Alliance what-now?" Iridius said.

"I'm sorry," Gentrix said. "Is that uncouth? Do you prefer the
term 'operative'?"

Iridius's mind raced. "It's just, we don't usually go around
announcing it." He gestured to the guards who'd grabbed them
off the street. "Especially in the company of others."

"It's fine," Gentrix said. "Frost Norton Security are loyal to me, not to my brother. The problem is the rest of the company. Frost Norton is developing important technology for the future of the Alliance and my idiotic brother cannot be trusted. That's why you're here, remember? Not for this stupid show. You're here to kill Devin and grant me control of Frost Norton."

"Yes," Iridius said. "Obviously."

"It seems to me like you already had an opportunity," Gentrix said. "You were alone with my brother for several hours."

"Yes, I was," Iridius said, "but I couldn't do it then, could I?"

"Couldn't you?"

"No," Iridius said. "It would have been too obvious. Everyone knew he was with DJ Chromium. If he turned up dead then, all fingers would point to me. I'm a professional – I'm not going to shiv him in the back like some jail yard murderer."

"Fair enough," Gentrix said. "What's the plan then?"

"You'll know when it's been done."

Gentrix stared at Iridius. "Fine." She moved in close to him again. She was like a mixer tap, flicking from hot to cold to hot again. "That's enough business talk, don't you think?" She reached out and grabbed the sides of his helmet. "Now take this off."

Iridius put his hands on hers, stopping her. "Ah, my helmet stays on."

"Is this some weird kink?" Gentrix said. "Take it off."

"No."

"Take it off," Gentrix said, more forcefully this time.

"No, it's just, I—"

"He always keeps it on until the job is done," Junker said.

Gentrix raised her eyebrows at her and then looked back to Iridius. "Business before pleasure then, is it?"

Iridius nodded. "Yeah that's right. Exactly."

"Well," Gentrix said, "too bad. Call me old-fashioned, but I like to confirm the identity of any secret assassin ex-lovers I hire, just to be sure they are who they say they are. You see, my brother might be stupid enough that shoving a helmet on is enough to fool him into believing you're his favourite DJ, but it's not going to work on me." Gentrix gestured for her security goons to come forward. "Get that helmet off and find out who this is."

Latroz stepped forward, her fists clenched. She was unarmed and outnumbered, but the growl that rumbled in her throat said she wasn't going down without taking them with her. Iridius looked around for an escape route but there was nowhere to go. He considered several very high-level tactical decisions in that brief moment, from trying to dive out a window to dropping to the ground and wrapping himself in the foetal position.

As it turned out, he didn't need to worry because that was when the window exploded.

The dirty glass shattered with a barely audible high-pitched screech, the telltale sound of an acoustic window-breaching system – a forced entry technique. A scanner determines the resonant frequency of a pane of glass and then an emitter uses precisely tuned soundwaves to shatter the glass. Such systems were banned in the Federation due to the harm done to a number of sentient species who were more attuned to high-frequency sound than most, but the Alliance had little regard for such concerns.

As the window burst in a shower of diamond-like fragments, three small, almost silent hexacopter drones flew through the opening. They circled the room, focusing their small cameras on the surprised occupants like three birds of prey surveying their quarry. They would be processing masses of visual and auditory data using biometric algorithms to catalogue and identify everyone in the room.

"We're compromised," Gentrix called. "Let's move."

Like well-trained dogs, the Frost Norton Security team didn't hesitate. Four of them moved to the door with their rifles raised. Two stayed with Gentrix and began firing loud percussive bursts at the drones. The hexacopters responded rapidly, weaving out of the way. The bullets that missed punched holes into the roof, releasing small sprays of debris but eventually, after a cacophonous moment, the spray of bullets proved impossible for the drones to dodge and they dropped in a burst of sparks and shards of high-strength composite.

Gentrix spun to Iridius. "Come on. Whoever you are, you're coming with us."

"I don't think so," Iridius said. "What guarantee do—"

"Stay here and I guarantee all of you are dead," Gentrix said, interrupting Iridius.

"Let's go," Iridius said, because given the choice between certain death and maybe not certain death, he'd found that the latter was generally better. He and the rest of the crew followed Gentrix and the last of the guards out the door. "We're choosing to come with you," Iridius called as they hurried to the stairs at the end of the hallway. "Just so that's clear. We don't need your protection or anything."

"Okay," Gentrix said as they ran down the stairs.

"It's true," Iridius said, rushing to keep up as Gentrix and her security detail took the stairs two or three at a time. "I saved everyone in the galaxy once."

"Okay," Gentrix said again, in a tone that made it clear she didn't believe him. "Just get to the street."

At the bottom of the stairs Iridius came to a sudden stop with Rangi slamming into him from behind. Gentrix and the two security guards had stopped in the dingy foyer of the tenement building while the four guards who had gone ahead moved to the door with their rifles raised.

"Just to be clear," Iridius said as he watched the guards, their black uniforms glowing in the flickering pink of a nearby neon sign, "what exactly are we escaping from?"

"Not sure yet," Gentrix said. "But I can assure you it won't be anything good."

The guards at the door pushed their way out of the building, rapidly scanning their surroundings. Iridius wasn't sure how they could tell friend from foe in the neon-bathed chaos of the Burrows streets, but he supposed that was why they were so cautious. "It seems clear, Ms Frost," one of them called back. "We should move now."

"Come on," Gentrix said as she moved out of the building and onto the street.

Outside, the Burrows of ASS Locke suddenly seemed not only like an overly busy cyberpunk dystopia dripping with neon and crowded with sentient beings of all persuasions – including a frankly surprising number of teenage girls – but after Gentrix's veiled statement and the clear concern of her security team, it looked like the type of chaos that could hide a multitude of threats. Threats that rattled even the second-in-command of the Frost Norton corporation. As much as the Federation liked to consider itself much closer to a utopian society than the Planetary Alliance, Iridius knew there were plenty of people who did bad shit in the Federation. Still, he couldn't imagine the second-in-command of a Federation space station fearing for their life on board their own station. He suddenly had the realisation that maybe the settlements of the Alliance really were as dangerous as the Federations propaganda machine would have them believe. The rest of the away team looked to their captain for the go ahead, perhaps thinking the same thing. Iridius nodded, and they followed Gentrix and her goons out onto the street.

The hum of artificial gravity reversal engines immediately drew their attention up the street. That, and the sudden commotion of people scampering out of the path of two vehicles roaring in their direction with no regard for who they knocked aside. The two vehicles looked dark and sleek, very similar to the Frost Norton Security Force car they'd travelled in earlier, but these were a dark shimmering blue. They were clearly speeding towards the building Gentrix and co had just vacated. At first Iridius thought this was more Frost Norton Security coming to provide backup, but the way Gentrix's security detail put themselves between her and the approaching vehicles made it clear that wasn't the case.

As the vehicles approached, Iridius watched two long-fingered appendages extend from the open passenger-side window and wrap onto the roof. Then, like some cross between a snake and a spider, a figure slid out of the window and up onto the roof of the vehicle in a slithering, skittering movement that sent Iridius's brain into absolute hysterics. The figure, somehow stuck in place even as the vehicle swerved through the crowd, crouched low, its reptilian head tilted curiously to the side. It reached behind, pulling a pistol from a back-mounted holster.

"Shit," Gentrix said matter-of-factly. She turned to Iridius. "Grantakian assassins. We have to go right now."

"We'll hold them off," one of the Frost Norton guards called back. "Run, Ms Frost."

Iridius was stunned to see a long, articulated tongue lash from the mouth of the Grantakian on the roof and pluck another weapon from its back – this one a shining, curved knife. Gentrix, on the other hand, did not need another warning. She grabbed Iridius's arm, tugging for him to follow as she moved off with two of the guards, including the enormous malignant.

"Come on," Iridius called to the rest of the away team, who were already beginning to push their way through the crowd. Even Latroz, who Iridius had never seen run from anything, apparently didn't like what she saw.

As they ran down the sidewalk, the Frost Norton guards

who'd hung back to cover their retreat opened fire at the oncoming vehicles. The sudden burst of assault rifle fire was enough to make those who had not already fled realise this was not a situation they wanted to be around. The crowd screamed and ran as bullets pinged into the bullet-proof glass of the sleek black hovercars. The Frost Norton troops had targeted the vehicle the Grantakian rode on top of, bullets tracking up the windshield to the roof. But with its long, serpent-like tongue still gripping the hilt of its dagger and a pistol in its hand, the Grantakian jumped, tucking itself into a tight spiral to barrel-roll through the air before coming down to land on the vehicle beside it. It landed, limbs splayed, and raised its pistol, firing several quiet popping shots that were barely audible over the chaos. The heads of two Frost Norton guards snapped back in rapid succession as bullets punctured their cheeks right below the visor of their half-helmets. Iridius barely had time to gloat about being right about the terrible helmet design as they sprinted around a corner.

The vehicles were bearing down on the remaining two guards, who hurriedly turned their weapons to the Grantakian. Unfortunately, before they could shoot, a second Grantakian had slithered halfway from the window of the first car and fired several shots from an identical silenced pistol. One guard was struck just below the nose, levelling him, while the second took a bullet to the visor of his helmet. The impact forced his head back and the visor erupted into a spiderweb of cracks, but he survived. He thought briefly how thankful he was that their stupid helmets had saved one of them but then, as the hovercars sped past, the roof-mounted Grantakian flicked its disgustingly long, dagger-wielding tongue, slashing him across the windpipe. He fell to the ground, drowning in his own rapidly pooling blood, and wished he'd taken a bullet to the face like the others. At least that had been fast.

Iridius looked back to see the hovercars rounding the corner and a second and then a third Grantakian manoeuvring their way onto the roofs of the vehicles, each of them reaching for weapons with hands, tongues and tails. "Why are we being chased by assassins?" he called to Gentrix, who was navigating her way through the stampeding crowd ahead of him. "I thought I was the assassin!"

"Through here!" Gentrix shouted, changing direction suddenly and running into a shopping arcade.

Iridius and the away team followed Gentrix through the glass entranceway into the arcade. It was like a long pedestrian mall, lined with an eclectic collection of shops: food, household goods, doctors and pharmacies (though these were, of course, advertised with garish neon signs), alongside sex parlours, active nanochipping tattooists, bio-manipulation surgeries and gene-ripping clinics.

The centre of the arcade was absolutely packed to fire-regulation-breaching levels with individual stalls selling all manner of street food, trinkets and techno-gadgets. Gentrix had run them into a busy market. Shoppers and shopkeepers unaware of the impending mayhem turned to stare at the eight people running for their lives.

"I said, why are there assassins after us?!" Iridius shouted, feeling like this was something he was entitled to know. Generally, every time he'd had to flee for his life, he'd at least known why the pursuer had wanted him dead, and he didn't particularly want to die without some explanation.

"They're after me," Gentrix said, "but you were with me so they'll kill you too."

"Great, thanks for that," Iridius said, pausing to leap over a table of second-hand cybernetic implants out the front of a seedy-looking surgery. "Why are they after you anyway? This is your space station."

"This is the Alliance," Gentrix said, puffing as she ran. "There's always someone looking to end the career of a high-ranking executive in one way or another."

Screams sounded from behind them and Iridius looked back to see the entrance to the arcade burst inwards as the two hover-cars smashed their way inside. The first of the sleek vehicles ploughed into a stall of fruit that had been labelled as fresh but, judging by the bruised flesh that exploded in a shower of near-fermented juice, had actually been picked a long time ago in a galaxy far, far away. The second car came to a screeching halt when the driver realised they would be unable to navigate the busy arrangement of shops and stalls – which was obviously what Gentrix had hoped. Undeterred by the eruption of plate glass and rotten fruit they'd just come through, the Grantakians – there were five of them now – still clung to the roofs of the hover-cars. Their heads flicked in quick motions, tilting from side to side as their large black eyes tracked their targets through the crowd. Iridius watched long enough to see one of the Grantakians blink with a creepy sideways eyelid movement and then launch from its hovercar, landing on the wall with a thump and then sticking there. He saw flashes of movement as the other reptilian assassins leaped in different directions, another to the opposite wall, one to the roof and two bounding effortlessly, terrifyingly, from stall to stall.

"Captain!" Rangi said. "They're on the walls!"

"I see them," Iridius shouted back. "Just keep moving!"

"And the roof!"

"Yes, Rangi," Iridius said. "I know!"

The Frost Norton guards slowed, letting the others move ahead, and began firing at the Grantakians. The assassins dashed in serpentine patterns, dodging the bullets spattering the walls, but the guards managed to hit the Grantakian on the roof, proving they weren't completely inept. A geyser of blue-green blood sprayed as the creature fell, hitting the floor. It scampered to get up but the guards sent it convulsing with a barrage of bullets until it finally lay still. They turned their attention to the Grantakians on the walls, but they were moving too fast and had already passed them. As the guards turned, another Grantakian landed on one guard's back, swiftly opening his neck with a flick of his knife-clutching tongue. The other guard was quick enough to shoot, and struck the Grantakian in the side, but it had already buried its knife in the side of his neck. They both fell, clutching at wounds they were unlikely to recover from.

"The last of your security is down," Iridius called to Gentrix as they rapidly approached the end of the arcade.

"Yes," she replied. "When are yours going to cover us?"

Iridius looked at Junker, Greg and Rangi dodging through the last of the market stalls. Well, Junker and Rangi dodged. Greg mostly ran straight through things, not out of malice but because as a large cancer he wasn't overly nimble. He was calling apologies every time he broke something though, which was nice.

"That's not really their thing," Iridius said. Latroz had drifted back though, and Iridius could tell she was thinking of intercepting the last of the Grantakians. "Most of them, anyway." He turned back to her. "Latroz! Don't even think about it. Stay with us!"

"Captain, if I—"

"No," Iridius said, "no redshirts!"

As Iridius approached the last of the market stalls he looked back to see that Latroz had acquiesced, though she didn't seem happy about it, and was running at full speed to catch up – full speed for a Siruan being significantly faster than humans and malignants. The remaining Grantakians were gaining on them, skittering along the walls and leaping through the market. Despite knowing it would make him a target, Iridius jumped onto a table, scattering a collection of supposedly rare antiques from across the galaxy – the same ones he'd noticed for sale on at least three other market stalls – and waved his arms. "Hey! It's me, DJ Chromium! Over here for free holoselfies!"

Heads turned and the screaming began immediately – not the screaming of terrified vendors and patrons this time, but the screaming of fans who, just as he'd hoped, had materialised again, like particles and anti-particles just popping into existence. In seconds, fans were running in his direction. He jumped down and ran for the exit. Iridius, Gentrix and the others reached the end of the shopping arcade and burst out onto another of the Burrows' claustrophobic streets. Behind them, fans had swarmed, blocking the exit and hopefully slowing down their pursuers.

Gentrix glanced from left to right in a moment of consideration before veering to the right. "Come on."

The crowd of fans behind them must have caused enough of a blockage to slow the Grantakians, and after they'd made it almost a hundred metres up the street Iridius began to hope they might have escaped. But, because the universe doesn't like Iridius B. Franklin, immediately upon having this thought, the sound of shattering glass alerted them to a window breaking somewhere above them. Iridius looked up to see the shape of a Grantakian assassin, tongue flicking, silhouetted against the bright fluorescent lights on the high ceiling. It had burst from above them and dropped to the ground ahead, landing with splayed arms and legs to absorb the impact before flicking its head up to look at them.

"Fuck," Gentrix said as she was forced to come to a sudden stop. She went to turn back but saw the other two Grantakians coming out the arcade behind them, leaping over the fans, who were also still in frenzied pursuit despite what Iridius considered the very obvious danger.

The Grantakian in front of them lunged. Its tongue lashed out towards Gentrix, but Latroz was already moving. She plunged in front of Gentrix, pushing the COO aside and grabbing the Grantakian's wet tongue in her massive purple fist, catching it before the knife could whip across Gentrix's throat. The creature gave a squealing hiss of displeasure and raised its pistol. As it did so, Latroz yanked hard on its tongue, pulling it off balance and dragging it towards her. The Grantakian's pistol fired but the shot went wide, pinging off a wall above them.

Behind them, the other two Grantakians were approaching with deceptive speed. They seemed to cover more ground with each stride than should be possible, as if they were moving along one of those space port horizontal trav-o-lators. As the reptilian assassins drew closer, one of them pulled its pistol from the same back-mounted holsters they all wore. It lifted its weapon in a smooth motion as it ran, the barrel as steady as if it was on a tripod. Latroz was still busy tangling with a dripping reptile tongue when Iridius saw the assassin raise its weapon. It was clear Gentrix was the target. As the Grantakian fired, Iridius threw himself towards Gentrix, wrapping his arms around her and managing to shove her aside just in time for the bullet to miss.

They fell awkwardly, Iridius landing on top of her. His body was pressing into hers, her face close to the front of his helmet, her panting breath fogging his faceplate. He could feel shapes beneath him, shapes he should not be concerned with in the middle of an attack by reptile assassins, and yet there they were.

"Sorry," he said as he awkwardly rolled off her, glad once again for his opaque helmet and loose-fitting spacesuit. Gentrix, thankfully, said nothing.

With the sound of gunshots, the fans finally decided that perhaps a free holoselfie wasn't worth all this and scattered.

Latroz spun her arm in a windmilling motion, wrapping the tongue around her forearm and pulling the Grantakian into her. She yanked again and then lunged forward, driving her head into the Grantakian's green scaly face with a massive headbutt. The

Grantakian's eyes rolled back in its head but Latroz held the assassin in front of her like a human (well, reptilian) shield.

"Down!" she yelled at the others.

Iridius and Gentrix were already on the ground. Rangi, Greg and Junker dropped immediately to their stomachs, trained to know that when in a combat situation, the rule was to do whatever Latroz said.

Latroz grabbed the pistol from the Grantakian's limp grip and squeezed the trigger, firing on the approaching assassins. The two reptilians darted in sideways dodges but Latroz managed to clip one in the shoulder, slowing it enough that she could send another round through its chest. The second of the assassins began firing on her. The first of the bullets hit the Grantakian Latroz was using as a shield, but another went low and struck her in the upper leg. Latroz stumbled, dropping her shield.

Iridius looked up, expecting to see the Grantakian deliver the killing shot to Latroz. Instead, he saw the assassin's head erupt in a spray of blood and brain matter. A solo figure brandishing a high-powered pistol emerged from another of the side alleys. The figure walked over to the Grantakian on the ground, nudging it with the end of his boot to make sure it was dead. Then, he approached the group.

Iridius turned to Latroz, but as if anticipating his question, she spoke before he could. "I am fine, Captain. It is an injury to my dermal carapace only. Just a scratch."

"Hello, Mark," Gentrix said as their rescuer reached them.

Mark?

Oh shit.

The presumably real DJ Chromium was a man in his early forties, with dark hair silvering on the sides. He was handsome in what Iridius thought was an ordinary sort of way.

"Who's this then?" said Mark Mudd, AKA DJ Chromium, looking at Iridius.

"Federation," Gentrix said, "a starship captain by the sounds of it."

"No I'm not," Iridius said.

Gentrix looked at him. "Your team quite literally keep calling you captain."

"Yeah, well," Iridius said, waiting for his famous improvisation skills to kick in. "They weren't supposed to."

"You're wearing my outfit," Mudd said.

"Holy black," Junker said. "It's really you. You're him."

"Junker," Iridius warned.

"Look, we can't stay on the streets," Gentrix said. "I have a safehouse nearby."

"A safehouse?" Iridius asked.

"Yes."

"And is this safehouse safer than your last safehouse?"

"Yes," Gentrix said, not bothering to elaborate further.

"We don't intend on being your prisoners," Iridius said.

"Sir," Latroz said, "we've got incoming."

Iridius turned to look down the street. "Assassins?"

"No," she said, but Iridius had already seen the crowd of teenage girls gathering again, like some mechanical death-machine rebuilding itself from scattered pieces. "Worse."

Iridius looked to Gentrix. "Safehouse it is then."

CHAPTER TEN_

IN A WHOLE SEPARATE spiral arm of the galaxy, the *FSC Gallaway* popped out of BAMF travel and arrived back in reality in a way that must have greatly bothered the office responsible for upkeep of the space–time continuum. The ship was just beyond the gravity well of Geffet, the world around which the moon Acacia orbited – the moon where the lost Aegix probe had crashed.

"Ensign Wesley," Captain April Idowu said as the orange crackling glow of the overloading shields cleared, "bring us around to Acacia but keep us in a high orbit."

"The *FSC Clarence* is in standard orbit," Commander Mul said. "They appear to be fully operational, and life signs match registered crew numbers."

"We've dealt with the Aegix before, Commander Mul," April said. "We aren't risking this ship getting a hull full of laser-eyed dogs again." April turned to her comms officer. "Ensign Herd," she said, "open a channel to the *Clarence.*"

The Ensign Herd on the *Gallaway* was the original Ensign Herd. At least, he was the same Ensign Herd who'd been on the *Gallaway* when Iridius Franklin had been in command. His brother, the Ensign Herd who was currently serving on the *Deus Ex*, was the older of the two, by a year and a half. They looked a lot like twins though – to the point that one might put some credence in the rumours that the Babel transhumanist cult was secretly engaging in black-market cloning.

Cloning had been illegal under Federation law for more than a hundred years, ever since the short-lived War of the Steves, in which a maniacal planetary governor named Steve Vincent had cloned himself more than four hundred thousand times, creating an army of Steves with the aim of overthrowing several nearby star systems. The whole thing had lasted less than six days – the Federation had intervened – but, given the amount of infighting between the Steves over who was actually in command, it was unlikely they would have succeeded anyway. Still, it had been something of a wake-up call, and the Federation had finally put a stop to the cloning of sentient beings.

"Aye, Captain," Ensign Herd said, and then in that disconcerting way of the Babel cultists, who had communication feeds plumbed directly into their cerebral cortex, his face went blank. His eyes glazed over and he went momentarily cross-eyed before returning to the world around him with a visible twitch of the head. "Communication established with the *Clarence*, Captain."

"Open the channel," April said, "bridge-wide."

"Aye, Captain," Herd said, "go ahead."

"*FSC Clarence*, this is Captain April Idowu of the *Gallaway*. What's the situation?"

"Captain Idowu," came the reply, "this is Captain Jack Quaid of the *Clarence*, good to see you. Our orders were to remain on station until you arrived and not land on Acacia, and that's what we've done. I just want you to know we were following orders by not intervening."

"Okay," April said, concerned that Quaid felt the need to

confirm he was just following orders. That usually meant there'd been a turn for the worse. "What's happened?"

"There's been nothing leave the moon," Quaid said, "we've been making sure of that, but our communication with colony Agri-1 went dark over twenty-four hours ago. Up until then, we were in regular contact with the superintendent of the facility as the emergency unfolded. She was," Quaid paused, "she was desperate for her people to be rescued. There were fifteen hundred sentient beings working at the colony and they were rapidly being killed. We were on station for two days as they were whittled away."

"So there's been no further communication?" April asked. "None at all?"

"No," Quaid said. "I wanted to help, I swear I did, but Space Command was very specific that we shouldn't land. They were worried about whatever's down there getting off-world. It's the Aegix, isn't it?"

"We have reason to believe the last known copies of the Aegix swarm intelligence landed, or at least crashed, on Acacia. It's alright, Captain Quaid, you did the right thing not heading down to the planet. We can't risk the Aegix escaping again."

That was what Captain Quaid wanted to hear, and it was probably what he needed to hear, so it's what she told him. But was it true? Did he really do the right thing? April wondered what she would have done if she'd been the first responder to the distress call. She could sympathise with Captain Quaid's predicament. Should he try and save a few hundred or maybe a thousand people at the risk of possibly releasing the Aegix on the galaxy again? She really didn't know how she would have handled that conundrum. She wondered what Iridius or her old commanding officer Roc Mayhem would have done. She couldn't imagine they would simply sit in orbit, listening to desperate calls for help from a colony of people still alive but very much aware that they would die without aid. They would have tried to save people, no matter the risk. Who could say whether that was right or wrong? In this case, it was purely academic anyway. April had been called from fifty light years away; she was never going to arrive in time to make a difference.

"Life signs on Acacia?" April asked.

There was a pause from Quaid's end for a moment before he responded. "The last life sign we could pick up blinked out not long after their last transmission."

April sighed, feeling disappointment at first and then a spike of anger. "Captain Quaid, maintain your orbit and keep monitoring. I'll respond with a plan of action shortly. Herd, close the channel."

"Aye, Captain."

"Now open an immediate priority to the Admiralty."

After a moment Herd spoke again. "Ready, Captain."

"Put it bridge wide again," April said. "You can all hear this."

Herd nodded and then a moment later a voice came over the speakers.

"Captain Idowu, this is Admiral Tullet. You have arrived at Acacia then? You are to pro—"

"Why did you send us here?" April barked.

"Do not interrupt me, Captain," Admiral Tullet said. "I'm trying to give you your orders."

"We were three days away. Why in the fucking black did you send us? We were never going to make it in time to help these people. You could have sent anyone who was closer."

"You are not there to help anyone, Captain Idowu," Admiral Tullet said. "You are there to annihilate any chance of the Aegix escaping. We tasked the *Gallaway* to respond because you understand the threat the Aegix pose better than most. Besides, there aren't many Universe-class ships closer anyway."

"Why do you need a Universe—" April began, but then immediately understood. "Oh. We've got a planet-slagger."

"That's correct, Captain Idowu," Tullet said. "You are authorised to annihilate the moon of Acacia."

"Admiral," April said, "there's another colony on this moon."

"That colony has been locked down to ensure no one leaves and inadvertently takes the Aegix with them. The decision has been made. The benefits outweigh the loss of life."

"Admiral Tullet," April said, "you—"

"Deploy your planet-slagger, Captain, and do it before the Aegix self-replicate and manage to get off that moon. Admiral Tullet out."

"No!" April shouted. "We won't do it!"

"The Admiral has disconnected, Captain," Ensign Herd said.

"Son of a bitch!"

The bridge of the *Gallaway* was quiet but for the hum of ship systems and the gentle movement of air from life support.

"What are your orders, Captain?" Commander Mul asked.

April was quiet a moment longer, still regathering her composure.

"It's a geological exploration colony on the other side of the moon, isn't it?" she said eventually.

"Yes, Captain," Mul said.

"Couldn't be more than a few hundred people then?"

Mul worked his console for a moment. "One hundred and thirty-eight on the manifest, Captain."

"Ensign Herd," April said, "Get me the *Clarence* again."

"Connected, Captain."

"Captain Quaid," April said.

"Yes, Captain Idowu, go ahead."

"Can you fit a hundred and thirty-eight people aboard your vessel?"

"It'll be a tight squeeze in the cargo bay, but I think we could."

"Good. There's a colony on the opposite side of the moon, a geological exploration colony, I need you to get those people off the moon. The colony is in an enforced lockdown so you'll have to cut your way in. The Aegix aren't there yet – they can't be, otherwise they'd all be dead too."

"Captain Idowu," Quaid said, "we've been specifically ordered not to do that."

"How many people died at Agri-1 since you arrived, Captain Quaid?"

There was silence.

"You want to make up for that," April said, "at least a little? Go and save those people."

Another moment of silence.

"Acknowledged," Captain Quaid said. "We'll break them free. Quaid out."

April turned to Mul. "Prepare to launch the slagger, but hold off until the *Clarence* gets those people away. I want to check in with someone else, too."

"Okay," Mul said. "Who?"

"Ensign Herd," April said, "get me in contact with Lieutenant Commander Kira Quinn on the *FSC Deus Ex*."

———

"I currently do not have enough data points to make an analytical determination as to whether the captain and the away team have succeeded. However, simple probabilistic extrapolation would suggest that the more time that passes, the less likely the outcome will be success. Based on analysis of previous infiltrations into Alliance holdings undertaken by Federation teams, we are not yet at the point of the majority of missions resulting in failure.

We are within one standard deviation of the mean point for those missions determined to be successful. However, we are also drawing to within one standard deviation of the mean point for missions in which one or more away team members are reported as having been incapacitated or killed. Primary reported incident is being severely or mortally wounded as a result of projectile weapon. Other highly probable events include grievous bodily injury as a result of physical combat or bladed weapon, incarceration on charges of espionage up to and including execution, as well as disappearance resulting in long-term missing in action presumed dead status. I will continue to re-evaluate based on incoming variables."

Lieutenant Commander Quinn stared at Junior Ensign Hal for a moment. "Well, thank you for that in-depth analysis, Ensign. All I said was that I hoped they were okay."

"Yes, Lieutenant Commander," the android said. "I understand the sentiment. I do not have the capacity for hope, but I do find the current insufficiency in my predictive ability to be disturbing and would prefer to be able to make a satisfactory determination."

"Well," Quinn said, "that sounds like something close to hope, Ensign."

"Lieutenant Commander," Ensign Herd said. "I'm receiving a request for quantum entanglement communication from Captain April Idowu on the *FSC Gallaway*."

"Perhaps inform her that Captain Franklin is currently unavailable," Quinn said.

"It's actually you she's asking to speak with, Lieutenant Commander."

"Oh," Quinn said. "Okay then. Make the connection."

"Quantum entanglement connection established," Herd said.

"Lieutenant Commander Quinn," Captain Idowu's voice

came over the bridge speakers, "nice to speak with you again. How have you been?"

"Likewise, Captain Idowu," Quinn said. "I've been well, and yourself?"

"Good, good," Captain Idowu said, and Quinn could tell she was rushing through the pleasantries. "Are you currently on a private call?"

"Uh, no, Captain," Quinn said, "you're speaking bridge-wide at the moment."

"Go private, please."

Quinn looked at Herd and Hal, the only others on the bridge, but they made no comment. She was the commanding officer. Quinn took the earbuds from the arm of the captain's chair and slipped them into her ears, then switched the connection to the private channel.

"You're on a private channel now, Captain Idowu," Quinn said. "I'm still on the bridge though."

"Good," Idowu said. "Switch off automatic recording of this communication, please."

"Captain, Space Command regulation 67—"

"I know the regulations, Lieutenant Commander," Captain Idowu said. "Switch off recording, please."

Quinn hesitantly flicked through the touchscreen on the arm of the captain's chair and turned off the automated recording. A prompt flashed up, reminding her that Space Command regulations required all quantum entanglement communication, including personal conversations, to be recorded as part of the ship's log. She hesitated again. This was Captain Idowu, though. Quinn had spent time with her on the *Gallaway* and she was the Space Command captain she trusted the most, second only to Captain Franklin. Well, actually, she probably trusted Captain Idowu more, though she wouldn't tell Captain Franklin that. She clicked yes to disable recording.

"Alright," Quinn said, "it's off."

"Thank you," Captain Idowu said. "Now, Quinn, I understand you'll be leaving active ship service and going to run a lab researching the Synth-Hastur?"

"That's right," Quinn said. "How did you know about that? Did Captain Franklin tell you?"

"No, Admiral Merrett told me." There was a pause. "I haven't heard from Iridius. Is he there?"

"No, he's currently indisposed."

"Right," Captain Idowu said. "Well, tell him he doesn't have to pretend to be unavailable and ignore me. We can discuss things like adults." She paused again. "Then again, given it's Iridius Franklin, maybe we can't."

"No, Captain Idowu, he really is unavailable. He's off-ship."

"Right, sure," Captain Idowu said, though Quinn could tell she didn't believe it. Quinn knew Iridius wouldn't want her to tell anyone, especially not April Idowu, that he'd pretended to be a famous DJ to infiltrate an Alliance space station and steal a secret weapon.

"Doesn't matter anyway," Captain Idowu continued, "it's not important right now." Quinn breathed a sigh of relief. The last thing she wanted was to get in the middle of whatever was going on between Captain Franklin and Captain Idowu. It was bad enough being dragged into Captain Franklin's professional craziness, let alone his personal craziness too.

Captain Idowu continued. "You know I agree with you about the Aegix, that they were created to combat the Synth-Hastur but for whatever reason, likely corrupt programming, they cause damage to life rather than implementing some mechanism to protect it."

"That's my theory, and that of others, yes," Quinn said.

"Well," Captain Idowu said, "we've just responded to a colony on Acacia, a moon of Geffet. Remember that last Aegix probe that escaped? It crashed here, and has begun its usual trick of killing every sentient being."

"Oh my god," Quinn said.

"The situation is contained, there's been no evidence that the Aegix have spread. However, the Admiralty has ordered us to destroy the moon with a planet slagger. Before we do that, I wanted to ask you if you think this is the right thing to do."

"No," Quinn said without hesitation. "It's absolutely not the right thing to do. We didn't know if there were any samples of the Aegix left. I've been trying to examine Captain Franklin as much as I can, but he hasn't been completely cooperative."

"What a surprise," Captain Idowu muttered.

"He's been attempting to suppress his nanobots, and seems to have had success. Besides, his sample of Aegix is obviously different somehow. The fact that he isn't dead is proof of that. I need samples of both unaltered Aegix and the Aegix in Captain Franklin's body to try and determine what they are trying to do and why it keeps going wrong. Getting a sample of the Aegix on Acacia could be key to combating the Synth-Hastur threat."

"And if the Synth-Hastur isn't coming, or isn't a threat?" Captain Idowu asked. "Is it worth the risk to try and get samples of a synthetic intelligence that has already tried to wipe us out once?"

"Captain," Quinn said, "in the twenty-first century, when Earth was facing the grave consequences of climate change, there were many who did nothing because they refused to believe in the threat. The planet never recovered. We're in that situation again. We must act under the assumption that the Synth-Hastur is real, because if we don't, and we're wrong, then, as Captain Franklin would say, we're gronking fucked."

Captain Idowu sighed. "I had a feeling you'd say that. Which is why I reached out, I suppose. Alright, we'll try and get you a sample, but we'll need your help to figure out how to do it safely.

You need to know though – and this is why I asked you to switch off recording – doing this will be going completely against the orders of the Admiralty."

Quinn almost laughed. "Oh, that's fine. Everyone seems to be going against the orders of the Admiralty lately."

"What's he done now?" Captain Idowu asked.

"Nothing," Quinn said, though she knew she'd answered far too quickly. "I mean, who?"

"Lieutenant Commander," Captain Idowu said. "What has Iridius got himself into?"

CHAPTER ELEVEN_

GENTRIX HAD LED IRIDIUS, Mudd and the others through progressively grimier back alleys and then showed them how to access the hidden hatches into the maintenance shafts that were spaced throughout the station. This way they could move off the main streets of the station, through shafts lined with pipes and wiring looms and steaming vents – a behind-the-scenes reminder that despite appearances, this was not a city, it was a space station with all the systems required for floating in the cold, dark of space: radiation shielding, artificial gravity, life-support, waste management and more.

They had emerged in another part of the station that seemed closer to the central spire, and walked a short, nervous distance down a side street before Gentrix took them into the safehouse. It turned out to be an empty level of a building above a collection of shops, including a sex shop, a cheap hotel of single-bay sleeping pods and a distributor of gene-therapy medication. The large open space contained a few couches and chairs and a large advanced holo-display table that seemed out of place with the surrounds.

Iridius stood near the window, away from the others, staring out at the view of the artificial streets. The window was mostly blocked by a large pink neon sign, its light seeping into the room and giving everything a subtle pink hue. He had removed the DJ Chromium helmet – there didn't seem much point in keeping up the disguise anymore – and was mulling over everything that had just happened. Things had got hairy for a moment there. Latroz had been shot. Minor injury or not, Iridius had put a member of his crew in danger, and he never enjoyed that. If it had been one of the others, one who didn't happen to be naturally coated in organic armour, it might not have been quite so minor. There was always risk involved in being in space, in going on missions of just about any sort, but in all his time in command Iridius had never lost a crew member. Of course, for a large number of those years he'd been in command of a rust-bucket hauler flying cargo around, but he'd had more than his fair share of chaotic adventures in the last year, and this still felt like the closest he'd come to getting someone killed.

"Captain?"

Iridius turned from the window. Gentrix was watching him. She smirked. "You're really not good at operating undercover if you simply turn at someone calling out your rank. You're new to this, aren't you?"

"Fine," Iridius said, trying to think of some justification and failing. He blamed his sudden overwhelming guilt. Stupid guilt. "No, I've never operated undercover before."

"Oh," Gentrix said as she sidled up close to him. "A handsome man like you? I find it hard to believe you don't operate under the covers."

Iridius Franklin, galaxy-saving space captain, blushed. "I, um...you know what I mean."

Gentrix smiled again. Iridius knew she was toying with him, but he seemed unable to generate even a flicker of a witty retort. This woman broke him. Her black-hole eyes bored into him but he held strong, maintaining his composure, at least outwardly. Internally he felt like an eight-year-old with jelly legs, about to piss himself. She must surely be another species – there was no way a human could simultaneously be so effortlessly attractive and as intimidating as a deadly snake ready to strike. Iridius was drawn to her like she was some kind of siren, a sexy raven-haired witch who'd hexed him and left him defenceless before her. This wasn't just about her sensual beauty, this was actual attraction. She was magnetic. She was fiercely intelligent, powerful, and hotter than a supernova. It made her, Iridius knew, bloody dangerous.

"I wanted to thank you," Gentrix said. "I had all but taken you and your crew hostage and yet they fought to protect me – and you personally saved me."

"That's what we do in the Federation," Iridius said. "We save people."

"So I've heard," Gentrix said. "Still, you have my thanks. You acted without hesitation. Those moments are the ones that show us the truth of people."

"You're welcome," Iridius said, leaving his next thought unsaid. *Would you have done the same for me?*

Gentrix picked up the DJ Chromium helmet from where it sat on the edge of the holo-table. "I'm glad to see we've moved past the pretence that you're DJ Chromium," she said. "Why don't we continue this by you telling me your name, Captain…?"

"He is Captain Iridius Franklin."

Both Iridius and Gentrix turned at this unexpected input from Mark Mudd.

"Uh, what?" Iridius said. "How do you know that? You're a DJ."

"I think we've established that he's not a DJ, Cap," Junker said. "Gronking liar."

"Look, firstly, despite what Gentrix may currently believe, I am not an assassin," Mudd said. "I am an agent of the Federation Intelligence Bureau and have been in deep cover in the Alliance for years. The DJ Chromium identity was constructed to allow me to travel freely, and gave me an identity to build trust with the Alliance Spy Service."

"What?!" Gentrix and Iridius spoke in unison.

"What the fuck?!" Junker added, even more emphatically.

"Junker," Iridius said in warning.

"But Captain," Junker said, "I just thought DJ Chromium was a hitman, but it's much worse than that. He's a sell-out, a Federation shill." Junker rounded her attention on Mudd. "You're not even real. I'm going to kill you. I'm going to shove your head in a quantum chromodynamic discharge capacitor and invert it – turn your brain into cheese sticks."

Mudd's eyes went wide.

Iridius smiled. "Welcome back, Junker."

Junker didn't break her fierce stare at Mudd. "Thanks, Cap."

"You're Federation," Gentrix said. "This whole time. Even—"

"Yes," Mudd said. "Acting under the covers, you might say."

"Shit," Gentrix said, "and here I was thinking I was the one playing you." She sniffed. "So, all this Federation activity on my space station. To what do I owe the pleasure?"

"Wait, Alliance Spy Service?" Rangi said. "That's ASS too. Does the Alliance just not know what that means?"

"Quiet, Rangi," Iridius said. He looked at Gentrix. "We must have got lost."

"You know, a Federation space captain trying to secretly infiltrate an Alliance facility, that's in breach of the treaty," Gentrix said. "I could have you all arrested, charged and executed and there wouldn't be a damn thing your Federation could do. You break the Federation–Alliance treaty, we get to deal with you how we like. Plus, who knows what this means for broader relations. We'd be within our rights to retaliate."

"Yeah well, you know what else is in breach of the treaty?" Iridius responded. "A fucking time reversal bomb."

"Ah," Gentrix said, "I suspected as much."

Mudd shook his head. "Fucking amateurs."

"So, you're here because of the time reversal technology we've developed. I have to say, I'm surprised. How did you find out about it?"

"You launched it right in front of us," Iridius said. "It's hard to miss being sent three minutes back in time."

Gentrix tilted her head. "What? You were out there during the test? Why didn't we detect you?" She paused, realisation dawning. "I heard vague rumours about the Federation developing advanced cloaking. It's true then. You were spying on us and got hit by the temporal displacement wave?"

Mudd sighed. "Honestly. Why don't you just give her the password to whatever computer has all the Federation's secrets?"

"Shut up, Mudd," Iridius snapped. "That's right, we were out there. Everything went real wibbly-wobbly, but we've got evidence to take back to the Federation so don't try and threaten me with breach of the treaty."

"A full three minutes of time displacement," Gentrix said. "That is interesting. The effects definitely have an exponential decay then. The station only experienced about a nanosecond of temporal displacement – still enough for us to remain cognisant of the experiment though."

"Huh," Junker said.

Iridius looked at her. "What?"

"You must have to be inside the temporal displacement field to remember the initial timeline then," Junker said. "I was wondering about that after they blew up the freighter. If you're doing a weapons test to destroy a ship ten hours before you launched the weapon and it's successful, then you would have the results before the test. Lieutenant Commander Quinn could explain it better, but basically, that's having an effect before its cause, which totally screws everything up. If the freighter was gone ten hours before the test then either you wouldn't launch the weapon, in which case how could the test have happened, or you'd have to retroactively launch the weapon at the place the freighter was but currently isn't because the bomb would still detonate ten hours earlier in which case you're kind of ensuring the past event."

Iridius held up his hand. "Stop. Let's not start with this paradox talk again. It makes my eyelids twitch."

Gentrix pointed at Junker and smiled. "I like this one. She's smart. You're correct, the temporal displacement field emanating out from the detonation site smooths out the paradoxes, at least a little. Anything inside the temporal displacement field has a single timeline that folds back on itself and then keeps moving forward. So, as far as the universe outside the temporal displacement field is concerned, there is no discernible cause for the freighter exploding – ten hours ago it just blew up. But within the temporal displacement field, we on Locke Station, and you on your ship, see the launch of the time reversal bomb, and after that you fold back one nanosecond or three minutes or whatever the case may be, and then you continue moving forward in time normally. For us, the cause still preceded the effect."

Iridius looked at Rangi, who shrugged. "Yeah," he said, "let's just move on pretending we all understand. You want to talk treaty? You're building weapons of mass destruction."

"Weapons of mass destruction?" Gentrix said. "You mean like the Federation's planet-slaggers."

"How do— I didn't even know we had those until last year."

"There seems to be a lot you are unaware of, Captain Franklin."

"This is different," Iridius said. "You have a weapon capable of changing the past. You could destroy important Federation targets before the war. Jupiter's nuts, you could destroy the Federation before it even started."

"I have one goal Captain Franklin," Gentrix said, "and that is to make sure the Federation isn't allowed to commit atrocities of war again."

"What?" Iridius said. "Atrocities of war? The Alliance attacked us. The Federation defended itself. There were no atrocities."

Gentrix shook her head. "Federation sheep. So brainwashed by ideological propaganda. If the Federation fought the Federation–Alliance war in self-defence, why was the territory of the Federation so much bigger after the war?"

"I don't know," Iridius said. "I guess people came to their senses."

Gentrix turned to the table in the centre of the room. "Holo-screen on." A holographic screen projected up from the surface. "Move image to centre of room." The hologram shifted until it was in the middle of the space, right in front of them.

"Moving holographic screens," Junker said in awe, peering around the room. "Are there multiple projection points?"

Gentrix shook her head. "No, just another piece of relatively new Alliance technology that hasn't made its way to the Federation yet. Just like truth, apparently. Alepsa, play footage of Junvie VI."

The holographic projection resolved into an image of a woman looking at the viewer, as if staring into a camera. Her face and hair were matted with sweat and dirt, and she looked terrified as she began rapidly speaking. "This is Finance Officer Mehera Fentrill of Olivia Corp. I was on board the Alliance vessel *Princely Sum*. We were attacked by Federation ships and forced to ditch onto Junvie VI. This is just a civilian farming planet and we are a ship full of accountants. This is madness. The Federation came into this sector out of the blue. We've got nothing to do with any war. Someone told me the ships in orbit have launched something. They're attacking the planet now. I want to get the word out. We are civilians. The Federation are attacking civilians. There's nothing here—"

The sound of the woman's voice was drowned out by a deafening roar. She turned. The walls behind her, walls of what looked to be structural concrete, evaporated in fiery orange, revealing for the briefest second the world outside alight with fire. Fractions of a second later she disintegrated in firestorm and the projection went black.

There was silence in the room. Eventually, Iridius spoke. "Maybe that was a mistake, a one-off incident."

"Alepsa, play footage from Alliance worlds during the war with the Federation."

The holographic image split into a hundred or more individual images of planets from space, burning just as Earth had after it was hit with a planet-slagger, images of Federation soldiers marching the streets of cities, firing all around them, seemingly indiscriminately. Men, women, children, all species, it didn't seem to matter. Ships exploding. Worlds destroyed.

"History is written by the victors, Captain Franklin. But it's time you all learned the truth."

Iridius stared in horror at the holographic display as it continued cycling through images of Federation uniforms doing things that went against everything he knew the Federation to stand for – or thought he knew. He took a long moment to gather himself.

"What makes you think we're going to believe this?" Iridius said. Unfortunately though, he did believe it. Maybe a year ago he wouldn't have, but now he knew about planet-slaggers and Federation spies and his own secret stealth ship. "How do we know it's not doctored footage? Maybe you're the one who's been fed lies. What did the Alliance do during the war, huh?"

"The Alliance of Planetary Corporations did things that would make your skin crawl, Captain Franklin. The difference is, we do not try and pretend it didn't happen. We did what we needed to do to survive, but the hypocrisy of the Federation is its ability to declare itself a utopia for all sentient beings – so long as they are willing to bend to ideology."

"Look at this place," Iridius said. "There is no Federation world or space station as gronking dangerous as The Burrows. You want to talk about ideology? The Burrows is what adherence to centuries-old capitalist nonsense gets you."

"Safety," Gentrix said, "that's always the Federation answer, but you have given up your liberty in order to be safe. You can never be free if those above you keep you shielded from the truth. What I am trying to achieve here will benefit both our people. I want to ensure both sides never have to experience a war like that again."

"You can't change the past, Frost," Iridius said. "So what, you're going to attack the Federation before the war started, thinking you're saving the lives of everyone who died? The way I see it, if you change the past than you undo every sentient life. How many people's lives will be worse? How many children will go unconceived? How can you make any accurate claim that the universe will be a better place? You'll be committing time genocide."

"I know that," Gentrix said. "That's—"

Engrossed in the lively impromptu political debate unfolding between Iridius and Gentrix – actually, Rangi wasn't engrossed so much as he was confused – no one saw Mudd slide a long stick-like weapon from a holster on his leg. He lunged so quickly that not even Latroz with her lightning reflexes could intervene. Mudd drove the end of the stick into Frost's lower back. It lit up with an electric blue light and buzzed like a cattle prod. Gentrix shook in a muscular seizure, then her eyes rolled back and she dropped to the floor, unconscious.

Mudd had used a stun baton, a taser-like weapon designed to incapacitate a target without grievously injuring them. Stun batons were used primarily for crowd control. They may have been designed to incapacitate without causing permanent injury, but that didn't mean they weren't painful. In fact, they were purposely designed to inflict pain. Just before the target passed out, every muscle in their body spasmed painfully. The stun rod came from the operant conditioning school of crowd control. Sure, you wanted a rioting crowd subdued, but they also needed a good dose of negative consequences before they passed out in order to dissuade them from doing it again. Typical Alliance, Iridius thought. Federation crowd control usually involved painless neural incapacitation fields.

Latroz might not have been fast enough to stop Mudd, but she was still fast. She grabbed Mudd's stun rod-wielding arm, bending it back, and used her other hand to grab the stun rod. Mudd struggled momentarily, but Latroz was too strong. She managed to yank the stun rod free of his grasp.

"What are you doing?" Iridius said, looking from Mudd to Gentrix on the floor and then back to Mudd. He held his hand out to Latroz and she passed him the stun rod. Iridius pressed a button near his thumb and the rod sparked to life with crackling energy. "This is a bit brutal, isn't it?"

Mudd shrugged. "Sometimes you have to use non-lethal means. I didn't want to kill her. That would make this even more complicated than you've already made it. You've really stepped in the middle of it, Captain Franklin. Do you know how difficult it was to get the Alliance to believe I'm on their side? It took years of work to build enough trust to do what I'm doing and you swan in, get yourself captured in basically no time and fuck the whole thing up. I—"

Iridius extended the stun rod, jabbing it into Mudd's stomach. The DJ/secret agent looked down in disbelief and then up at Iridius. He opened his mouth to speak but Iridius jammed his finger down on the button before he could say anything. Mark Mudd tensed as his muscles locked, and then dropped to the ground. Iridius looked down at the stun rod in his hand. "Bit medieval, isn't it," he said. "Big pointy zappy stick. I wonder if he was compensating for something."

"Cap," Rangi said, "just, um, fill me in on what just happened right now? I'm sure you've got everything well under control. I'm just kind of wondering why everyone is getting electrocuted."

"Mudd was right about one thing. We've stepped in the middle of something here and the only people I know I can trust are you four. I can only see one way out of this now. We have to go see Devin Frost again, admit who we are and tell him his sister hired an assassin to kill him so she could take control of his company and use a time bomb to cripple the Federation back before the war even started. We just have to hope he's open to diplomatic talks. I mean, the guy is incredibly boring and nerdy, but at least he's not a super villain like his sister."

CHAPTER TWELVE_

"You sure you're alright to walk?" Iridius asked Latroz for the fourth or fifth time as Iridius, Junker, Rangi, Latroz and Greg made their way along the streets towards the centre of the station. Iridius had removed the DJ Chromium space suit and left the helmet behind, finally realising the benefit of being incognito in public.

"It is fine, Captain," Latroz said. "As I said before, my carapace is less sensitive to pain and heals much faster than human skin."

"I just want to make sure," Iridius said.

"Captain, may I speak freely?" Latroz asked.

"Of course you can."

"You do not need to treat me like a small human with a scraped knee."

"I...right," Iridius said.

"I will continue to speak freely. You do not appear to be acting like yourself. I would suggest you return to your normal personality trait of charging recklessly forward."

"Well, I hardly think I just charge recklessly forward."

"You usually do, Cap," Rangi said.

"No one said you could speak freely, Rangi."

Iridius and the team made their way unimpeded through the wealthier parts of the outer ring of the ASS (cue Rangi chuckling). Iridius was certain they were being watched the whole way, though. Frost Norton Security were surely monitoring their progress, and the fact that they hadn't immediately surrounded them at gunpoint like a flock of hungry and well-armed seagulls ready to kill someone for a hot chip was proof they didn't know what had happened with Frost and Mudd. Either that, or they knew exactly what had happened and were happy to let them get to CEO Frost. Maybe Gentrix didn't have Frost Norton Security Force in her pocket after all. Iridius looked up at the windows around them and caught sight of blinds opening and closing more than once – it seemed the residents here were just as nosy as in any middle-class neighbourhood anywhere in the galaxy.

Eventually, they reached the large secure door sealing the entrance to the central spire. Here, they were finally approached by Frost Norton Security. Six guards dressed in the black Frost Norton uniform moved in front of the door, weapons clutched low in front of them, clearly ready to raise them quickly and start shooting. They all wore the now-familiar visored half-helmet. Apparently no one had sent around the memo yet about how ineffective those helmets were.

Iridius stopped and held out his hand, indicating for the others to stop too. He had the sudden fear that perhaps they'd known precisely where they were going all along and hadn't bothered to intercept them because they knew Iridius and his team were walking towards half a dozen heavily armed doormen.

"Stop," one of the guards said. This one had rank chevrons that appeared to be one below the insignia on Meteon's arm.

"We are stopped," Iridius said. He also noted that the guard seemed mostly bored, rather than troubled, as though this was nothing more than a regular occurrence.

"State your business in the central spire."

"We're off to see the wizard," Iridius said.

"What?"

"CEO Devin Frost," Iridius said. "We're going to see CEO Frost."

The guard stared at him and then grinned. "Right, good one. What's your real business?"

"We're going to see CEO Devin Frost," Iridius repeated. "You're going to go into that guard station and call through to your superior. You're going to tell him DJ Chromium is here to see him and that it's incredibly important. You're going to do this now, because I can guarantee if Devin Frost finds out you didn't take us straight to him you'll be out of a job, and probably out of this space station too – and I don't mean a transfer, I mean out an airlock."

"How are we supposed to know you're DJ Chromium?" said one of the other guards. "He wears a mask all the time."

"You're a clever one," Iridius said. "Check my bio-scan. I know you will have taken one when I approached. Check it, and compare it to the one that was taken when I met with CEO Frost this morning."

The guard in charge turned to look at his subordinate. He shrugged, as if to say that he supposed that made sense. Of course it made sense, Iridius thought. He was back in action with his amazing powers of spinning bullshit.

"Seriously," Iridius said, "this is far more important than you realise. Every second you stand here like a foot bunion, the CEO of this corporation is going to be more pissed at you."

The guard stared again, but this time he didn't grin. He turned and went into his guard house. When he emerged a minute or two later, the lower half of his face was several shades paler. "Sorry, this way please Master Chromium. CEO Frost is having a car sent for you."

As promised, a car was waiting for them on the other side of the intimidatingly large door that allowed access into the central spire of Locke Station. Or, in the case of most people who lived in the outer ring, the door that would *not* allow access to the central spire. The irony was not lost on Iridius that as much as Gentrix Frost had tried to convince him that the Federation were hiding the truth from their citizens, at least they didn't have anything so obvious as a massive, multi-storey doorway locked tight like some medieval drawbridge separating those in the castle from the rest of the peasants.

The vehicle that pulled up was not a black Frost Norton Security car like they had travelled in before. This was a pearly white stretch limousine, floating on several anti-gravity plates along the length of its undercarriage. Perhaps here, where they faced less danger than out in the Burrows, Devin Frost was happy for them to travel without the protection of Frost Norton, and in a style he was more accustomed to.

As they approached, the gullwing doors at the rear of the vehicle opened. The others looked to Iridius to take the lead. He stepped forward and poked his head into the vehicle. Inside the frankly disgustingly large space were long, couch-like seats facing each other. An opaque privacy window behind the driver slid down. Iridius could see that while this may not have been an obvious Frost Norton Security vehicle, the driver was still wearing one of their stupid half-helmets. Frost wasn't letting them go completely unprotected – or perhaps completely unescorted.

"Please hop in, Mister Chromium," the driver said. "I've been instructed to take you and your team to CEO Frost."

Iridius climbed in and the rest of the away team joined him. They rode in silence through the streets of the central spire, probably because all of them wanted to say the same thing, which was something along the lines of, 'I can't believe we're riding in a limo, how many Federation away teams ride in limos on their missions? This is awesome.' Obviously that would give them away though, so they had to play it cool instead. The quiet in the back of the limo was broken only on the three occasions Iridius had to tell Rangi to stop touching things, because the helmsman was absolutely like a child who just could not stop fiddling with every knob or button he found.

When the vehicle pulled up outside Frost Norton Tower the doors opened automatically. The privacy screen did not lower again, and so Iridius took this as their cue to exit. They climbed from the car and headed to the entrance, where yet more Frost Norton Security guards opened the door for them. The android secretary who probably definitely had secret razor blade limbs greeted them with a nod.

"Please take the elevator up to CEO Frost's office. He is expecting you."

When the elevator door opened, the room in front of them was once again the ridiculous caricature office of wannabe twentieth-century business mogul Devin Frost. There was the same enormous desk, drinks trolley and couch, but this time the view out the window had changed. Gone was the high-rise view of the Manhattan skyline, replaced with a lower view of a bustling London street, complete with pedestrians passing by in suits and business attire, black cabs and the old iconic double-decker buses. Most of the view was obscured by the large shape of CEO Devin Frost, still wearing his Hawaiian shirt, standing right in front of the opening elevator doors. He opened his arms wide.

"O...M...G...," he said, spacing the letters out for painful emphasis. He looked at the away team in the elevator. "You've actually come here unmasked. I feel so honoured, you have no idea. That you would trust me, a humble fan, with your most precious secret." Devin Frost focused his attention on Rangi. "DJ Chromium, please come this way."

"Uh," Rangi said.

Frost moved into the elevator and all but physically carried Rangi along with him. "I hope this trust means you consider me more than a fan. Maybe you even consider me a friend."

Rangi looked back towards Iridius, completely confused and obviously with no idea what he should do. Iridius and the others followed Frost and Rangi into the office. For a moment Iridius considered letting it go, for tactical reasons of course, and not just because of Rangi's obvious discomfort, which Iridius found somewhat amusing.

"Excuse me, Mister Frost," Iridius said. "I'm afraid you've confused Rangi here for me. I'm DJ Chromium. That is one of my roadies."

Shocked, Frost looked from Rangi to Iridius. "OMG again," he said, slapping his forehead, "how stupid of me to make that assumption. Terribly sorry." Frost hurried to Iridius. "Please, accept my apologies. I really am quite a simpleton sometimes. My sister says I'm moronic, but I think I'm mostly just excitable. I get ahead of myself sometimes. You met my sister though, she's rarely got anything nice to say – quite a nasty woman sometimes. Remember my collection of voidball cards? She actually tried to have them shot out an airlock once because she claimed I was misbehaving. Can you imagine?"

"That's actually why I'm here, Mister Frost," Iridius said.

"My voidball cards?" Frost said. "Would you like to see them again?"

"No!" Iridius said, much too quickly and much too loudly. He cleared his throat. "I mean, as wonderful as your collection is, I'm actually here about your sister."

"Oh," Frost said. "Wait, has she been mean to you too?"

"You could say that."

"I told her you were a very important guest and that you were to be treated with respect. I should call her in here right now."

"No," Iridius said, "it's fine. I'm actually here because I have reason to believe your sister is trying to kill you."

"Trying to kill me?"

"Yes."

"Well," Frost said, moving to the other side of his desk and looking out at the fake view of the London street. "Of course she's trying to kill me."

"She plans—" Iridius stopped himself. "Sorry, did you say of course she's trying to kill you?"

"Yes, Mister Chromium," Frost said, and Iridius noticed the subtle but entirely menacing change in his voice, "of course Gentrix is trying to kill me. She's been trying to kill me for ages. Never did like the fact that I was made CEO, but I was always the higher achiever."

"You were?"

"Oh yes, Mister Chromium. Far better at everything. Don't get me wrong, my sister is very intelligent, but I was the most successful. Higher grades in my schooling. Higher aptitude results in tertiary education placement. Better results in engineering studies. Then, of course, far, far higher levels on the psychological testing – high-functioning manipulative sociopath, they called me." He turned back to face Iridius. "I don't know about all that, but I do seem to be able to fool people into underestimating me."

"Right," Iridius said, suddenly feeling like this was an entirely different situation than the one he'd been prepared for. It was like that time he'd turned up to April's birthday party at the Academy, thinking 'cocktail attire' meant it was a dress-up party, so he'd come wearing an enormous inflatable martini glass. "So, you know about your sister's schemes?"

"Yes, I know Gentrix was trying to kill me," Frost said. "That's why I sent assassins after her first. Expensive ones they were, too. Grantakian assassins who were supposedly stopped by

DJ Chromium and his entourage. Seems like this group was attempting to escape with my sister, the one you've apparently come to warn me about. I don't know about you, but that doesn't make a lot of sense, and it doesn't seem like the behaviour of a musician."

"I was abducted by your sister and was with her when your assassins attacked."

"There's also this bizarre rumour floating around that there are two DJ Chromiums onboard this station."

"That is a bizarre rumour."

"Ordinarily I wouldn't put much stock in the sort of rumours that float around the Burrows, but it does seem strange that someone carrying a DJ Chromium costume and helmet was spotted in the space port around the same time I was giving you a tour. Looked very much like a legitimate costume too, but even that isn't anywhere near enough proof to make me believe a rumour like that. But you see, there's something odd going on. You flew in aboard the *Interstella*, and you match the biometric scan of the DJ Chromium who came directly from that vessel. But I am probably the biggest DJ Chromium fan in the galaxy," Iridius was sure he heard a small scoff from Junker at that, "and although I've never met him, it's fair to say I feel like I know him. And you don't seem like him."

"Well, it's, um, like putting on a character. I'm different when I wear the outfit."

"See, you weren't much different though, were you? I showed you an incredible collection of voidball cards, and I happen to know DJ Chromium collects voidball cards, and you didn't so much as bat an eyelid at some of the rarest cards in existence."

"Well, I didn't want to seem unprofessional."

"What was your second single to go double galactic platinum?"

Iridius stared at Frost. "So, what, you're testing me now? Because of wild rumours that I'm not the real DJ Chromium?"

"Yes," Frost said, "precisely. What was your second single to go double galactic platinum?"

"I don't have to put up with this," Iridius said. "I'm trying to save your life and the lives of trillions of others. Your sister is a maniac who wants to kill you so she can take over your company and use a quantum time reversal bomb against the Federation before the Federation–Alliance war even started."

Frost chuckled in a way that Iridius was sure was completely humourless. "I see," he said. "It makes more sense now. I'd assumed you were an operative of hers, but you're an operative of the Federation. Not only that, you're an operative of the Federation with absolutely no idea what's going on – just like the whole Federation really.

"Gentrix doesn't want to kill me so that she can launch the time reversal bomb. She wants to kill me and take over Frost Norton so that I *can't* launch the time reversal bomb. That was my idea. I'm the one who wants to delete the Federation before the war. Gentrix is all against that. Oh, she was happy enough for development to go ahead, but she wants to use it as a deterrent. She wants to make development of the bomb public knowledge and forever hold it over the Federation and anyone else who wants to start a war with us, in the belief that no one will risk attacking us if there's a possibility they'll be erased from the timeline of the universe. She thinks just the existence of this weapon will mean there'll never be a war again. That sounds like utopian nonsense to me. Sounds like the sort of thing the Federation might claim. And now you've just wandered right into my hands."

Frost reached out and pressed a small red button on his desk. It was frankly astounding how quickly the room filled with Grantakian assassins. Iridius couldn't even be sure where they'd come from, but they were scuttling in along the roof, walls and floor until ten of them had surrounded Iridius and his team, with pistols in hand and daggers in tongue. "So, I'll ask again. If you're DJ Chromium, what was your second single to go double galactic platinum?"

"Uh, Stars and, um, dancing stars?"

"Stars and Dancing Stars?" Frost said. "And you're the best the Federation thought to send, are you?" He shook his head. "I thought I was just capturing one of Gentrix's people, but this is even better. A Federation spy sneaking aboard my space station gives me even more justification in launching this weapon, don't you think? I'll keep you hostage as proof. That should be enough to ensure the rest of the Alliance supports me in blowing up Earth."

"Earth?" Iridius asked.

"Yes, Earth. I mean, it's already a ball of molten rock, but that didn't happen nearly early enough for my liking. I think I'll blow it up about a hundred and fifty years ago. That should do the trick. Gets a bit confusing, doesn't it?"

"You won't—" Iridius started, but Frost interrupted him, which Iridius was partially thankful for because he realised too late that he was going to say, 'you won't get away with this,' and he didn't think he'd ever live that down.

"I mean, I'm still horribly disappointed. I really thought the Federation was a capable enemy. Anyway," Frost gestured to the Grantakians, "lock them in the brig."

As the Grantakians grabbed them and led them from Frost's office, Junker looked at Iridius.

"What?" Iridius said.

"Stars and Dancing Stars?" Junker said, completely aghast. "Honestly. DJ Chromium's second galactic platinum single was 'Galactic Boogaloo'."

"Yeah, well," Iridius said, "where were you on the voidball

thing? Besides, I didn't think who I was would matter when I was telling him his sister was trying to kill him. Where were any of you on that one, the whole Devin-Frost-is-the-real-bad-guy thing?"

The rest of the crew were silent.

"That's what I thought," Iridius said. "Fucking curveball, wasn't it? Is that a voidball term?"

CHAPTER THIRTEEN

APRIL IDOWU WATCHED as Lieutenant Commander Ish Kaku, chief engineer on the FSC *Gallaway,* leaned forward and used a small hand-held ultrasonic welder to seal up the final edge of a black composite case. It was the kind of clip-closed protective case that was often used to transport delicate scientific instrumentation, but Kaku had removed the handle, stripped the protective lining and cushioning from the inside and retrofitted it with a thick layer of the carbon nano-weaved titanium alloy used in both the manufacture of armoured EVA suits and the hull of the *Gallaway* itself. He was now ensuring it was airtight.

Inside the case was a custom-built Nanobot Attractant and Detector System dreamed up by Lieutenant Commander Quinn on the *Deus Ex.* She had called it the NADS for short, which, without Iridius Franklin or Benjamin Rangi around, she was continuing to use completely unironically. The final design was completed by Kaku and the device manufactured and assembled on the *Gallaway.* April Idowu had a far better grasp of advanced scientific concepts than Iridius Franklin, and so where the captain of the *Deus Ex* would let his eyes glaze over and wave off any explanation of how the NADS functioned, at least April had an understanding of the science involved.

Quinn had determined that Iridius's nanobots gave off several different frequencies of ultrasound when active – frequencies that didn't seem to be involved in their interaction with the technology around them – and theorised that these signals were probably the way a free air swarm of nanobots communicated with each other, and what enabled the Aegix's rapid switching between apparently distributed and centralised cognition. Quinn hadn't been able to determine what information these signals contained, if any, but she believed playing them back might attract other nanobots into the device. The detector part of the device, a miniature quantum chromodynamic energy field turned down to low enough energy levels to allow matter and energy to pass through, would then detect any objects the same size and mass as the Aegix nanobots.

So, the NADS would hopefully allow them to attract Aegix nanobots and then detect their arrival, but what they really needed was a way to collect them. That was where the outer shell Kaku was finishing came in. The side of the case had a hole 10 millimetres in diameter drilled into it. When the nanobot detector sensed Aegix nanobots entering through that hole, a small magnetically accelerated door would slide across, closing it. This would simultaneously trigger an internal laser welding array that would weld the tiny door closed, ensuring the nanobots couldn't escape. In just hours Kaku, Quinn and the hard-working technicians aboard the *Gallaway* had managed to jury-rig together an Aegix nanobot collection device. They were calling it The Rat Trap.

The rest of the plan was simple, at least in theory. They would take the *Gallaway*'s shuttle and fly down to Acacia. They wouldn't risk landing on the planet – instead, they would perform a fly-by of the Agri-1 colony, hanging the Rat Trap out the back of the shuttle on a 100-metre carbon nanotube tether that was being printed by the *Gallaway*'s advanced 3D printing lab. Once they received confirmation that the Rat Trap had been sprung, they would pull back into orbit, reel in the trap, seal it in yet another container that would be welded closed, and return to the *Gallaway*. Back on board the ship, the double-sealed Aegix container would be stored in an airlock ready to be ejected into space at the first sign that a nanobot had breached containment. April wasn't taking any chances with the Aegix, not after what the galaxy went through last time, but still she wasn't sure they were doing enough to be absolutely certain. Time was not on their side, though. They had to slag the planet before the Aegix escaped of its own accord. At least this way they had a chance of figuring out what the Aegix were trying to achieve, and how that might save them if the Synth-Hastur really was coming. She had to trust they were doing the right thing.

Maybe it was always like this, and she was only privy to it now that she was a Space Command captain, but new threats seemed to be popping up constantly, and the Federation, or even the galaxy at large, seemed ill-prepared to meet them. Everyone seemed to be rushing from one disaster to another, strapping together whatever defence they could. Had the Federation and every other civilisation in the universe always just stumbled from one narrowly avoided extinction to another? It was starting to feel that way. That also suggested that eventually one of those close encounters of the extinction kind would fall on the wrong side of the line for humanity, and for everyone else too. First there was the Aegix, which they'd only just managed to avoid catastrophe with. Then there was the looming threat of the Synth-Hastur which, according to the Aegix at least, seemed to be an even greater threat, some kind of ancient race bent on exterminating all life in the galaxy. Now, April had managed to drag out of Quinn that the Alliance of Planetary Corporations was developing a quantum time reversal and Iridius had charged off to try and save the day. She would do the same here. At least she would get Quinn her sample of the Aegix, so she could prepare for the Synth-Hastur.

"It's done, Captain," Lieutenant Commander Kaku said. "Shall I have the techs load it into the shuttle?"

April nodded. "Get it ready, attach the nanotube. I want to leave as soon as possible."

"You want to leave, Captain?" Kaku said. "You're going on the shuttle?"

April looked at Kaku. "I am. This isn't exactly a Space Command-sanctioned operation, Ish. I'm going alone."

"Captain, you can't," Kaku said.

"I'm very capable of flying a shuttle, Lieutenant Commander," April said. "I was in flight school before I transferred to the command stream. I asked you to ensure the Rat Trap could be deployed and retrieved by a single pilot flying the shuttle. Did you do that?"

"Yes, Captain."

"Then I can do it alone, can't it?"

"Captain, it's just...it's going to be dangerous. We need you here. You're the captain."

"Ish," April said, placing her hand on Ish's shoulder. "Thank you for your concern. If this was a mission given to us by Space Command then I'd likely send another pilot, but it's not. I'm doing this of my own accord and I'm adhering to the 'ask forgiveness not permission' school of starship command that seems so very popular of late. There's a reason I've kept this plan to just a few key people. The fewer who know, the better. Most of the crew will have plausible deniability if things go wrong. It's because of all this, and precisely because it's dangerous, that I'm going alone. Now, get the Rat Trap installed and attached to the nanotube."

"Yes, Captain."

"Thank you. I'll prepare the shuttle, fly down to the planet, capture some Aegix and then return. It should be easy."

CHAPTER FOURTEEN_

IRIDIUS CLOSED HIS EYES, blocking out the view of the holding cell the Grantakians had tossed them rather unceremoniously into. It had only been a short walk from Devin Frost's office. When someone had the twenty-third century equivalent of a dungeon a few doors down from their office, that was usually a sign that they weren't a good guy. Iridius was no history expert, but he was fairly sure the twentieth-century office buildings that Frost seemed so fond of modelling his office after didn't have small private prisons where the CEO could lock away anyone they pleased. At least, he didn't think they did, though some of those multi-level marketing companies did seem pretty ruthless. As the Grantakians had dragged them away Iridius had looked back at Frost, and suddenly the large man in the Hawaiian shirt had looked a lot less like a mid-thirties nerd with no fashion sense and much more like a mafia mob boss having just returned from a beach vacation.

He had to concentrate. Iridius took a deep breath, feeling for his nanobots the way he had before. It was something close to proprioception, the way someone might close their eyes and be able to sense the location of their fingers and toes. That's how it had worked with the nanobots before, as if they were an extension of himself. Now though, there was nothing.

Come on, you gronking pieces of shit. All those years of not wanting you around and you caused all kinds of issues and now, when I actually need you, you've decided to abandon me. Is this because I wanted you gone? Now you're having a tantrum and refusing to come out like a bratty kid in a time-out?

"Captain," Rangi said, "I just want you to know that performance issues are nothing to be ashamed of. Just relax. I'm sure—"

"Rangi."

"I'm just saying, it's nothing to be ashamed of."

It had only been a few minutes into their sudden incarceration before Rangi asked why Iridius didn't just Techno-Wizard his way out – use the nanobots to lower the holding cell shield and aid their escape. At first Iridius had dismissed the idea with the same excuses he'd used before – using psychotic alien bugs was too risky – but after twenty minutes of trying, and failing, to think of another way out he'd eventually relented.

"I don't know what it's like, of course, but I feel like this should be an easy one, shouldn't it?"

Iridius opened his eyes and stared at Rangi, letting his raised eyebrows do the talking.

"I just mean, compared to stuff you've done before, deflecting missiles and controlling whole ships and whatever, this should be easy."

"Yes Rangi," Iridius said, realising he should know better than to expect a glare to be enough to shut up Benjamin Rangi. "I know it should be easy, but it doesn't gronking seem to be easy, does it?"

"Right, sorry Cap," Rangi said. "I'll leave you to it. Just do your thing."

Iridius closed his eyes again. *Come on, you stupid bugs! Where are you?*

Iridius tried to push the nanobots to react to his thoughts, even just to feel them, but there was nothing. It was like the other morning when he'd woken up lying on top of his arm, having cut off the circulation for gods knows how long. It had been completely dead, a useless, floppy appendage. He could see it, he knew it was there, but no matter how hard he tried, he could not feel it or make it move. Of course, his arm had eventually come back to life with an uncomfortable barrage of pins and needles, but he suspected that wasn't going to happen with the nanobots.

Eventually, Iridius gave up with a growl of annoyance.

"Maybe they have some sort of protection against the nanobots here?" Junker asked. "Dunno how they'd do it, but they do seem more advanced than we've given them credit for."

Iridius shook his head. "No, it's not that." He sighed. "I haven't been a hundred per cent honest with you. I'm not avoiding using the nanobots because of the risk, or because I think they're creepy. I mean, both those things are true, but it's more than that. I've avoided using them because, truth is, they don't work anymore. Ever since I decided to stop using them, they haven't worked. It's like I can't get them to come back online. That's why I didn't want to use my nanobot powers to disable the *Interstella* and it's why I can't get us out of here. I don't have powers anymore."

"The classic 'superhero brought down to normal' trope," Rangi said. "How will the hero manage without his one big advantage?"

Iridius didn't have the energy to berate Rangi, so he simply ignored him.

"It's alright, Captain," Greg said after a while. "No other starship captains can do that either, and people like Captain Mayhem and Captain Jan-wei always got out of situations like this."

Iridius sighed. "Thanks Greg," he said. "Unfortunately, that's less reassuring than I know you mean it to be. I'm not one of those legendary captains."

"You saved the galaxy, sir."

"The only thing special about me was the nanobots. I wouldn't have been able to save the galaxy without them and now they don't work. They're broken, just like I break everything."

"Captain," Junker said, "are you wallowing?"

Iridius looked at Junker. Ordinarily he would have immediately denied having given up, because he was the captain and a large part of that job was at least looking like you knew what you were doing. Right now though, for probably the first time in his career, he didn't even feel like he had the fortitude to fake it. He'd almost gotten his away team killed, and now they'd been captured. They'd likely caused a diplomatic incident between the Federation and the Alliance, and the Earth was going to be destroyed, again. Well, it would get destroyed *before* he accidentally got Earth destroyed last time, so the net outcome would still be that he only got Earth destroyed once, but it certainly felt like it was going to be twice.

Ever since the Grantakians had attacked them in the street, Iridius had been questioning himself, but the moment he'd noticed the shift in Devin Frost he realised he didn't need to. Quinn had been right. He had been reckless. He'd been overconfident. He'd been convinced he could infiltrate an Alliance base and steal plans for a secret weapon of mass destruction with little more than a hastily acquired cover identity and his wiles. It had gone terribly from the start, but he'd still been ignorantly confident they could figure out their plan on the fly and succeed. It had been Devin Frost's sudden change that had really hammered home how badly Iridius had underestimated him. He had completely fooled Iridius with what now seemed an obvious ruse, one he probably used on everyone. Devin Frost was not a dorky loser, he was like the Lorenzin Flowerjaw, a creature who evolved to appear like one of the harmless ten-foot-wide wildflowers native to Lorenza. When any animal wandered across what they thought was a flower, the Flowerjaw would snap its enormous horizontal jaws shut. It could swallow animals as large as a horse in a single bite. That's what Devin Frost was in his Hawaiian shirt, an apex predator posing as a flower. Iridius was in over his head, and now his crew members would pay for his hubris too.

"What you said on the way here was right, Lieutenant Latroz," Iridius said. "I am reckless, and charging in too recklessly on this mission got you shot and got us all captured."

"Captain," Latroz said, "respectfully, my saying that you charge recklessly forward was in fact a good thing. As a Siruan I appreciate the fearless charge into battle. Why do you think I asked to serve on the *Deus Ex*?"

"I figured it was because Rangi was on the crew," Iridius said.

Latroz looked at Rangi and then back to Iridius. "Yes, this is true, I wanted to mate with Benjamin regularly, but I joined because of you, Captain. I wanted to stay under the command of a true adventuring starship captain."

"Latroz is right, Cap," Rangi said. "No one blames you for the fact we got chased by assassins with crazy tongues or that we've been captured by a sociopathic CEO in a Hawaiian shirt. We're in this together and we all know how you work. Remember what Admiral Merrett said when we got our medals? Your leadership is always dynamic. I think she means what Latroz is saying – you just kind of make it up as you go along, right?"

"I don't just make it up," Iridius said, "I—" He opened his mouth to continue, then stopped. "Listen, before we left the *Deus Ex*, Quinn accused me of wanting to undertake this mission because I wanted to be a hero again, because saving the galaxy once wasn't enough. She was right, of course, because it's Quinn and she's super-annoyingly always right. I shouldn't have brought you on this mission. It's even more reckless than usual. We could have been killed, and I have no idea how we're getting out of this one."

"But we were not killed, Captain," Greg said. "This is my first away team mission and I am glad to be doing it. I'm sure you will think of a plan. We cannot let the Alliance launch that time bomb. Also, I am finding this quite exciting."

"Cap," Junker said, apparently deciding to join the pile-on as well, "we were going to follow you into the mouth of a giant space-dog. We all could have died then. We all could die at any time in space. We know the risks. We're with you."

"Yeah," Rangi said. "We're with you, and besides, you were right, what we were doing was boring. We definitely want a galaxy-saving adventure again."

Latroz stared at Iridius. "I once led a boarding party onto a derelict ship crawling with eight-foot-long carnivorous Trill-aborgs. They have a mouth at each end filled with seven hundred razor-sharp teeth and a venomous proboscis. This is like a child's playground, Captain. I am hoping for another attack from Grantakians, to be honest."

Iridius felt the stranglehold of guilt lessening slightly. He knew they were right in a lot of ways. He could not be hesitant and soft now that they were on this mission. He could second guess his decision to undertake the mission later, and deal with the consequences of that once they got through this, and he would take on board what Quinn had said, but for now he had to focus. He had to be a fearlessly reckless Space Command captain and save the Federation and his crew.

"Right," he said, "how the gronk do we get out of this one then?"

The door to the holding cell opened and Iridius turned, expecting to see one of the Frost Norton Security guards, or maybe even Devin Frost himself, come to do some classic villain gloating and maybe outline some more of his evil plan. Instead,

Iridius was greeted with an unexpected sight. In the doorway looking in on them was the real DJ Chromium, AKA Mark Mudd. He closed the door behind him and then moved to stand in front of the shield, barring entry to the cell.

"I'm going to get you the gronk out of there," Mudd said, "but first I would like you to know that sticking someone with their own stun-baton is considered bad manners, Captain Franklin."

"Not gonna lie," Iridius said, "it was a little spur of the moment, but you'll have to forgive me for not trusting you or anyone else here. I'm trying to do the right thing for the Federation. "

Mudd shook his head in dismay. "We're on the same team, Captain Franklin. My identity had to be kept secret for obvious reasons. Years of deep cover could be blown. Your ship, the *Deus Ex*, was stationed here to monitor for any developments before my team and I arrived. We've been aware of Frost Norton's efforts to develop a quantum time reversal bomb for six months. The Federation Intelligence Bureau has spent that time carefully planning an elaborate mission to infiltrate this station, disable the weapon and steal the plans. We were confident of success until you decided to kidnap my crew, steal my ship and, well, I'm still not entirely sure what you were attempting to do – maybe ask nicely and hope they gave you the bomb?"

"Maybe if you spooks weren't so secretive and had told us that you were planning a top-secret mission we wouldn't have felt the need to intervene," Iridius said. "I'm more than aware that I've cocked this up, but your lack of communication is at least partly to blame for that."

"Well, you've cocked it up, but how would you like a chance to un-cock, Captain Franklin?" Mudd asked.

Iridius waited a moment. "Honestly," he said, looking at the others, "we're just going to let that phrasing go are we?"

"Are you going to help or not?" Mudd said.

"Yes, of course we'll help," Iridius said, "but I'm not sure how much help we'll be from in here."

"Luckily I've allied with someone who can get you out of there," Mudd said. "The same person who got me in here to see you. Despite some disagreements with a stun baton, we've all found ourselves on the same side."

"I'm not going to like this, am I?" Iridius asked.

Gentrix Frost walked, no, sauntered through the door. "Actually, Mark, Captain Franklin is the only one here who hasn't been whacked with a stun baton."

"I've apologised multiple times, Gentrix," Mudd said.

"Last baton I let you stick me with, that's for sure," Gentrix said.

Rangi laughed. "That's a stinger."

Gentrix turned to look at Rangi. "And who are you?"

"No one," Rangi said, probably faster than he'd ever responded to any question in his life.

"Well, seems like you're going to like this less than me after all Mudd," Iridius said. "What's the plan then?"

"The plan is firstly to get you out of here before we all get caught and suffer something far worse than a stun baton."

"So, we're just going to walk out?" Iridius asked. "How long before they notice we're gone?"

"Hopefully long enough, thanks to this," Gentrix said, holding up a small box. She placed it on the floor outside the cell, tucked up against the wall, and when she touched the top Iridius was suddenly face-to-face with himself.

"Gronking hell," Iridius said as he stepped back, startled by the sudden appearance of a copy of himself. He looked around and realised it wasn't just him; there was a copy of each member of the away team. All of them were staring at themselves.

"Our remote hologram technology," Gentrix said. "I always carry a few around. They come in useful more often than you'd think. I've made simple looping projections. It won't fool a biometric scan of the cell, but if they're just checking visually, it'll buy us some time."

Rangi had moved around behind his projection.

"Rangi," Iridius said, "are you checking out your own arse?"

Rangi shrugged. "Never really get a chance to see yourself like this, do you?"

Iridius shook his head. He looked at Gentrix. "I'm not sure I trust you," he said.

"I know," Gentrix said, "but sometimes that's the birth of the most valuable relationships. Our needs align, Captain Franklin. Welcome to the free market."

Gentrix pressed a panel on the wall and the shield at the front of the cell opened. She turned and walked away, and Iridius followed, but not before turning back to have a quick peek at how good he looked in his jumpsuit.

———

Gentrix Frost's office was basically the same as her – cold and stylish. The walls were a dark purple with stainless steel fittings and a curving, frankly sensual dark wooden desk. On that desk, Mudd had projected a blueprint of the secure vault facility housing the plans and prototype of the quantum time reversal bomb.

"This is the Frost Norton Secure Temporal Depository," Mudd said. "The STD."

"You are kidding," Iridius said.

"What?" Mudd asked.

Iridius looked around at the others. "He's taking the piss, surely." When there was no comment, even from Rangi, Iridius turned to Gentrix. "Really? The STD?"

"That's the name of the facility, yes."

"Did the quantum time bomb send us to a gronking dimension where nobody checks their acronyms?" Iridius said.

Mudd stared at Iridius for a moment before continuing. "As I was saying, this is the STD, a highly secure storage facility with technology able to slow the effect of entropy. It is used for storage of highly sensitive information and equipment, and is where the quantum time reversal bomb and its plans are stored."

"Yes, I know," Iridius said. "I've been in there."

Iridius felt a ping of joy at the shock on Mudd's face. *Ha, see, I know more than you think, super spy,* Iridius thought in a completely mature way.

"You've been in there?" Mudd asked. "You were in the STD?"

"Gross," Iridius said, "but yes, I was in there. So was Greg."

Mudd looked at the malignant, who nodded.

Gentrix laughed. "Voidball cards?"

"What?" Mudd interjected, clearly confused.

"That's right," Iridius said.

"God." Gentrix shook her head. "I can't believe he actually took you in there. What an idiot."

"You were inside the STD and you didn't take advantage of that?" Mudd asked.

"We were with Devin Frost," Iridius said. "The opportunity never arose."

"Plus, we did not know it was there at the time," Greg added helpfully.

"Yes, thank you, Greg."

"Well," Mudd said, "at least you'll know how secure that facility is then. Guarded elevator, coded entry, and then the vault itself is biometrically secure. If a person enters the vault and their biometric data is not stored on an authorised list on the main security server, explosive bolts blow the floor of the entire vault off and expose it to space. My team had spent months preparing to access the vault and steal the time reversal bomb. Now I'm left with," Mudd gestured at Iridius and his team, "the crew of idiots who destroyed planet Earth."

"Wait just a second!" Rangi blurted before Iridius could do the same. He wasn't going to stand for his crew being called idiots, and it seemed like Rangi felt the same.

"We're going to do a heist, aren't we?" Rangi continued. "This is the getting the team together part of a heist!"

Iridius sat back in disgust. Maybe they were idiots after all.

"This operation is not a heist, Lieutenant," Mudd said. "it is a highly planned special operation of the Federation Intelligence Bureau."

"Shit yeah," Rangi said. "I've always wanted to be part of a caper."

"As I said, Lieutenant," Mudd continued, "this is a sanctioned operation. It is not a criminal caper."

"This is it," Rangi went on. "I love it when a plan comes together."

Mudd looked at Iridius. Iridius shrugged. "It's best to just ignore him at this point."

"Right," Mudd said. "So, my team had planned to undertake the hei—" He stopped himself, looking sideways at Rangi. "Er, the mission, during tonight's concert. There was to be a meet and greet with Devin Frost, which I assume is the one you hijacked for no beneficial purpose, Captain Franklin." Iridius rolled his eyes but did not interject, despite the obvious verbal knife in the ribs. "I was going to use that opportunity to scan basic biometric data from Frost. That wouldn't have been enough to fool the vault security system, but it would have got me into the main security room. I would play the concert as planned. Frost would be there and the whole thing would act as a distraction so my team could neutralise the guards and then use Frost's biometric information to enter the main security room, where they could overwrite the security profile for the vault by adding the biometric data of one of our team members onto the server. That team member was an infiltration expert who would be able to bypass the lesser security systems and then safely enter the vault. The system inside the vault would assess them as authorised according to the newly loaded security profile. That team member would then retrieve the bomb and the plans for the bomb, extract back to the *Interstella* and we would all leave the station as planned following the end of the concert."

"Cool," Rangi said. "That was the outline the plan bit."

"Unfortunately, we don't exactly have the skill set now, do we?" Mudd said, taking Iridius's advice and ignoring Rangi. "Or the time." He looked at the clock on the holo-display. "The concert is due to start in just over two hours."

"We'd better get a move on then," Gentrix said. "Lucky you still have a Frost with the right biometrics to get into the security room."

"Plus a Space Ace to fly us out of here in a hurry," Rangi said.

"I can handle the neutralising of the guards," Latroz added.

"I can get through the basic security," Greg said.

"See," Iridius said, "we—" he looked at Greg. "You can?"

"Yes, Captain. I once hacked into the security of Rutan Station."

"Really?"

Greg nodded. "Yes, and Gagarin Station, and the Federation Senate one time."

"Right," Iridius said. "Why exactly?"

The malignant shrugged. "Something to do."

Iridius turned back to Mudd. "See? My crew might not be your highly-trained team of spies, but don't underestimate us. You think we're just the crew that may have been responsible for the destruction of Earth—"

"You *are* the crew responsible for the destruction of Earth," Mudd said. "That's a fact."

"Maybe," Iridius said, "but we're also the crew that saved the galaxy from the Aegix. We might be in over our heads right now, but here's the thing – we're always in over our heads."

"That's...great," Mudd said.

"What the hell is the Aegix?" Gentrix asked.

"See!" Rangi said. "I told you the Alliance wouldn't even know about that."

"Half a million year-old synthetic intelligence that would have wiped out you and all sentient life if it wasn't for us, this crew of idiots," Iridius said to Gentrix before turning to Mudd. "So, can you get into the facility or not?"

"I need to be playing the concert," Mudd said. "It's still imperative that goes ahead and keeps Frost occupied."

"We can handle that," Iridius said. "Someone else can play the concert dressed as you."

Mudd stared at Iridius. "You might have worn my costume and managed to pass yourself off as me for a couple of hours, Captain, but I can't teach you how to spin vinyl like the galaxy's most famous DJ in two hours."

"You don't need to," Iridius said, looking at Junker. "We've got someone who can do it already."

"Cap," Junker said, "I can't do the DJ Chromium show!"

"Of course you can," Iridius said. "You're a DJ and you're damn good at it too. You'll do great."

"You know nothing about music and you've never seen me perform," Junker said.

"Just trying to be encouraging," Iridius said. "You're DJ Rata-touille or whatever. If you're as good at DJing as you are at randomly upgrading my ship then I'm sure you'll nail it."

"Wait a second," Mudd said, turning to Junker. "You're not DJ Ratatat are you?"

Until that point Iridius had thought it physically impossible for the hard-nosed wrench-monkey to blush, but that's exactly what Junker did. "Yeah," she said. "At least I used to be."

"I remember hearing your stuff years ago," Mudd said. "Someone told me you were an up-and-coming DJ on the underground Federation scene. Your stuff was really good. I always wondered what happened to you."

"Huh?" Junker said. "I can't believe DJ Chromium heard my music. I never knew that."

"I thought you'd be screaming or something," Iridius said.

"I would have before I found out, you know," she pointed to Mudd, "that he's a complete and total fraud."

"I'm still DJ Chromium," Mudd said. Iridius could hear the faint tinge of hurt in his voice.

"Okay," Junker said, shaking her head.

"Look," Mudd continued, "do you think you could play a set of mine or not?"

Junker stared at Mudd for longer than was comfortable before she finally spoke. "I'd open with 'Under the Stars' but mix it with 'Resident Alien', stretch that real thin on the end where it goes to the piano and loop for at least four bars on the last note, get the audience begging for a resolution, and then drop really hard on the bass at the beginning of 'Electric Boogaloo'." Junker grew more animated, gesturing with her hands like she was working turntables. "Then, you know that vocal part on 'Black Sky, Black Heart', I'd bring that in under a reverb at the end of 'Boogaloo' and fade it up, letting it hang for a while under a filter and then," Junker punched her fist down, "boom! Bass drop. Then I'd love to do a remix of 'Forever Young' and 'Live a Little'." Junker was nodding her head as if the music was really playing. "Bop bop bop, pow. They've both got that pop and sizzle over a similar bass line. Then—"

Mudd held up his hand for her to stop. "You'll do great."

"I don't think I should do it though." Junker looked at Iridius. "I can't be DJ Chromium."

"Well, you've suddenly decided I can't be DJ Chromium either," Mudd said, "so someone has to."

"Yeah, fair enough," Junker said. "Okay, I'll do it."

Mudd looked shocked. "What? That easy?"

"I just realised you don't deserve it," Junker said.

"I *made* DJ Chromium," Mudd said, getting animated now.

"That's hot toasted bullshit," Junker said. "The Federation Intelligence Bureau made DJ Chromium. You never worked your way up from the underground like a real DJ. You just strapped that silver helmet under your arse and got launched into orbit by your nutsack."

Mudd looked at Iridius. "Are you going to let your crew member talk to me like that, Captain?"

Iridius smiled. "It's nice to have you back, Junker."

"Thanks, Cap."

Mudd looked from Iridius to the others and then back to Iridius before sighing. "Fine. Junker here will pose as me and perform the concert as expected. Gentrix, can you take Lieutenant Latroz and Greg and get access to the security room?"

Gentrix nodded.

"You can load my biometric data and Captain Franklin's into the security system. Greg can hack us through the first security systems. We get into the vault, secure the weapon and the plans for quantum time reversal and then get to the *Interstella*, where Lieutenant Rangi will get us out of here."

"See?" Iridius said. "It'll be fine."

"Alright," Rangi said, in a voice deeper than usual. "I'll do it. I'll do...one last job."

Mudd shook his head. "We're fucked."

CHAPTER FIFTEEN_

APRIL SAT at the helm of the *Gallaway*'s shuttle. She wasn't quite white-knuckled on the controls, but she wasn't exactly using a light touch either. She'd exuded as much confidence as she could to the crew about doing this, but in truth it had been years since she'd piloted anything at all. She hadn't even bothered keeping up her simulator hours. She just had to keep telling herself it was like riding a bike – a twenty tonne, interplanetary, nuclear fusion-powered bike that was about to do a fly-by of the most dangerous enemy she'd ever faced.

The shuttle autopilot was more than capable of following an automated flight path, which she had let it do right up until orbital insertion around Acacia. Now, as she fired thrusters to lower orbit, she'd taken manual control. This wasn't strictly necessary, the shuttle's control system could make the minor corrections necessary as they were buffeted by the atmospheric drag of Acacia, but she wanted to be hands-on. She knew it was probably a false sense of control, but even a false sense of control was better than feeling completely powerless.

It was because she knew what was down there, the Aegix. That bastard of a synthetic intelligence had taken control of her last posting, the *FSC El Nino*, and caused the deaths of her friend, Captain Roc Mayhem, and the crew she has served with for four years. If the Aegix could take control of a Universe-class starship like the *El Nino* then she had no doubt it could crush a shuttle like this as if it were little more than an annoying insect. She just had to hope it wasn't powerful enough yet. It seemed to have taken the Aegix time to build up its power last time; hopefully that was the case again. Still, she would hold the controls, and at the first indication that something was amiss she would hit the thrusters and, as Iridius would say, get the gronk out of dodge.

Of course, Ish had told her that the shuttle's control system could sense any effect of the Aegix faster than she could, and react quicker, but she was going to do it manually anyway. *You are uncomfortable when you don't feel in control* – that's what her Space Command psychological assessment had said. *This is common with high achievers who feel like they should be able to influence every outcome simply by working harder. You need to learn to accept that some situations are beyond your direct influence.* She had tried to work on that, tried to accept that she couldn't control every situation she faced as a captain but right now, fuck that. She needed as much control as she could get.

"*Gallaway*, this is Idowu. I'm preparing for descent burn."

Commander Mul came over the comms. "Roger, Captain. Proceed with burn."

April hit the controls and the forward thrusters burned for twenty-two seconds, slowing the shuttle into a descent orbit with a periapsis slightly less than a kilometre above the surface of the moon. Fifty-six minutes after the end of the burn, April hit the comms again.

"Periapsis achieved. Taking control for powered atmospheric flight."

"Roger," Mul said over the comms. "Looks good from here, Captain."

April flipped the switch for the cargo door, overriding the warning that she was opening the door during flight. She heard the mechanical sound as it began to open. The rear of the shuttle had been hermetically sealed with the bulkhead blast door, but April could check on the camera to see that the Rat Trap had dropped when the door opened as planned. It had, hanging out the back of the shuttle and fluttering in the thin Acacia atmosphere. April leaned over and flipped the switch that had been retrofitted to the control panel. The spool of carbon nanotube began unwinding. Gravity and atmospheric drag took hold and the Rat Trap began falling away from the shuttle. April took manual control for real now. She decreased the shuttle's altitude and flew by instrumented control to ensure she passed directly over the top of the Agri-1 settlement at an altitude of just 150 metres. The Rat Trap would pass less than 100 metres above the ground, hopefully capturing some Aegix nanobots in the process.

"Okay *Gallaway*," April said. "I'm approaching the settlement, altitude is 140 metres. Rat Trap looks good behind me."

There was no response.

"*Gallaway* do you copy?"

Nothing.

April's heartbeat increased and her palms grew sweaty on the control yoke. She took a breath, forcing herself to concentrate. She was about to pass over Agri-1. *Stay calm.* It could be atmospheric interference with the communication system. Everything else looked good. She had control. She exhaled, looked ahead and focused on flying. Acacia was a partially terraformed moon. Terraforming on a mass scale had never taken off in the Federation. It required too many resources and was a lengthy process, and the cost benefit had never justified undertaking a project of that scale. The galaxy was a big place and there were plenty of planets and moons of just about every composition. It was easier to just search for the type you needed, rather than going to the effort of changing one. Besides, there were ethical and environmental considerations too. The Tranmar Incident, when the Federation had begun a terraforming project that resulted in planetary instability and the extinction of geological life-forms not previously understood to be life, had triggered a brief war with similar geological life-forms from a neighbouring world. After that, it was decided that terraforming was just too much of a hassle.

Acacia was one of the terraforming projects that had been abandoned. The result was a sporadic groundcover of only the hardiest plant life, because that was all that could survive in the mish-mash atmosphere. It was enough that the Agri-1 colony could farm genetically-engineered grain crops, and it was these crops that covered the ground April saw fly past as she piloted the shuttle down towards the colony.

The shape of Agri-1 soon appeared on the horizon among the apparently endless field of bio-crop. Like most small colonies on moons and worlds of thin, toxic or non-existent atmospheres, the colony was constructed from dozens of domes of various sizes. Inside would be sealed, pressurised environments for the residents of the colony to live and work in. Often many of the domes would contain slightly different atmospheric conditions, depending on the species who lived within, but across the Federation most sentient life was similar enough, and adaptable enough, that Federation standard GAC (Generic Atmospheric Conditions) could be used. On rare occasions, a dome would be completely deadly to most life forms. These were generally for those rare sentient beings who evolved on planets with ammonia-based life, and required temperatures and pressures outside the range of most water-based life-forms. Because of their inability to live in most common environments, ammonia-based sentient beings were quite isolationist, so didn't often mix anyway. This

192 / JUSTIN WOOLLEY

was probably for the best, because something about being ammonia-based made them completely grumpy bastards. Unfortunately, April knew there would be no sentient life inside any of those domes – not water-based, not ammonia-based, nothing. The only thing that would be in there now were the piles of pink goop the Aegix left behind as it went around trying to 'help'.

April was concentrating on flying as the colony approached, keeping the shuttle from dropping into the all but endless fields of grain or slamming into the domes of the Agri-1 colony, while still keeping one eye on the small indicator light Lieutenant Commander Kaku had wired onto the cockpit display. As she crossed directly over the buildings of Agri-1, the indicator light began blinking red and April felt a sudden thrill. They'd done it. They'd managed to snag some of the Aegix nanobots in the Rat Trap. She reflexively jumped on the comm before remembering she'd lost contact with her ship.

"*Gallaway,* this is Idowu. You probably can't hear me but I've got some Aegix. Reeling them in and returning to orbit."

April leaned over and flipped the switch to begin winching the Rat Trap back into the shuttle. She pulled on the yoke and pushed thrusters to full to increase altitude. Once the Rat Trap was inside and the door closed, she could hit a main engine burn to put her back into orbit. Unfortunately, that's when everything went to shit.

Despite shuttles being designed specifically for travel from starships to space stations, planets, moons and other natural and manufactured celestial objects, they were never really designed for atmospheric flight. They had cursory wings and control surfaces for stabilisation, but not enough for full flight. Atmospheres varied so much across the galaxy that it was all but impossible to design wings and control surfaces that would be effective everywhere. On some planets they would create too much lift, on others they wouldn't create enough. As a result, the *Gallaway*'s shuttle flew like a rock that someone had glued a couple of tin-can wings to. It was the thrusters that did the grunt work of keeping it from slamming into the ground. So it was a real pain in the arse when the thrusters stopped.

It happened in rapid-fire succession. The screens over the cockpit control panel flickered, the lights in the cockpit went dark and the thrusters ceased firing. With a sudden motion that put April's stomach somewhere just under her eyeballs, the shuttle dropped. The computer immediately began howling warnings; the thruster failure alarm was immediately followed by the ground proximity alarm, and the computer began repeating that she should "pull up, pull up", as if that wasn't her immediate instinct. She yanked on the control yoke, pulled the thruster controls to zero and then pushed them back into their full burn position, hoping this might kick start them, but there was no response. She had no control at all and every screen was flicking on and off, but she could see out the front window that she was heading straight for one of the last of Agri-1's large glass domes. With no thruster control, there was no way she was going to be able to avoid the collision. But despite the wall of extraordinarily strong structural composite glass hurtling towards her, glass that would likely see her shuttle crushed like an aluminium can underfoot, April did not panic. She attempted a hard reboot of the cockpit systems and retried the thrusters, both to no avail. Ordinarily it was not advisable to fire the main engines at such low altitudes, but she tried that too, also with no response.

Seconds from impact, April made the decision to try one last thing. A starship like the *Gallaway* had massive amounts of high atomic weight materials encircling its fusion engines to contain the plasma in the event of failure of the magnetic containment system, but a vessel as small as the shuttle did not. The fusion reaction occurring inside a shuttle engine was orders of magnitude smaller than that on a starship, but it was still enough that failure of the magnetic containment would melt through everything fast. The fact that had not happened told April the fusion engine was still functioning. She vectored the main engine down as much as possible and then performed a manoeuvre that all pilots knew, despite it never being specifically taught in flight school. In fact, it was actually banned.

By pulsing the magnetic containment field quickly off and then on, there would be a brief but potent ejection of plasma from the fusion engine and out the rear main engine thruster. This technique was banned because the temperature of the ejected plasma was on the order of 100 million degrees Kelvin – about six times hotter than the sun. It would destroy the main engine nozzle, and it meant that anything behind the engine was going to have a very bad day. In this situation though, everything beneath her was already dead, and if she didn't do it, she would be the one having a bad day.

As April blew star-level temperatures out the engine of her shuttle she felt the sudden crunch of acceleration that sent her upwards but also, unfortunately, forwards. The shuttle clipped the top of the dome, high enough that it bounced off with non-critical damage, but the impact sent it into an aggressive spin. April fought to control the ship, which was all but impossible with systems bouncing online and offline like a jumping tightrope walker. The shuttle's safety features came online and April was pinned to her chair as the restraints activated. Soon after, she passed out.

CHAPTER SIXTEEN

"YOU LOOK A LITTLE SHORT, but when you're up on stage no one will be able to tell," Mudd said, eyeing Junker who was dressed head to toe in the silver spacesuit and helmet of DJ Chromium.

"I feel," Junker paused, "underqualified to be wearing this."

"Nonsense," Mudd said. "Besides, all you've really got to do is keep Devin Frost occupied while we do the job. Just think of it as a part of the mission, and not as a concert in front of thousands and thousands of my adoring fans."

"I'd say, no pressure then," Junker said, "but there isn't, because you don't deserve to wear this either."

"Can you drop the attitude?" Mudd said. "I was a musician before I was a spy. And besides, there is pressure – the future of the Federation is at stake."

"Geez, Captain," Rangi said. "His pep talks are even worse than yours."

"Maybe I could learn to spin some tunes?" Iridius said, putting one hand over his ear and scratching an invisible record with the other.

Mudd and Junker both looked at him stone-faced. "No."

"Cool," Iridius said. "Cool cool cool. I was just trying to break the tension. So, we're good with the plan then, are we?"

Mudd took a deep breath and sighed, heavy with resignation. "My team had planned this down to the minute. We'd built a replica of the vault and its security and had rehearsed every part of the mission for months to ensure we all knew the movements and could execute the operation flawlessly every time. Now, when the moment is here, we're just going to wing it."

"We're not winging it," Iridius said. "We've got a plan. It'll be fine."

"It'll be fine. You should get that on a t-shirt," Mudd said. "'It'll be fine' would have to be the most obvious famous last words I've ever heard."

"We're the crew of the *Deus Ex*," Rangi said. "We do our best work when we wing it."

"Well, I guess we don't have any better options. The concert is set to start in less than an hour. This is our window of opportunity," Mudd said. "Gentrix, can two of your guards get Rangi back to the *Interstella* so he can get prepped for a getaway launch?"

Gentrix nodded. She gestured to two of the black-uniformed guards who'd joined them. "You two take Lieutenant Rangi through the maintenance tunnels back to the space port." They nodded. "And you two," she focused on two others, "take Junker to the theatre so she can get ready for the concert."

It seemed some of the station security really were still loyal to Gentrix. They had secured several Frost Norton Security Force uniforms, two sealed maintenance suits, bags and other equipment they would need to make it into the vault. Iridius wondered how exactly Gentrix knew which of the half-helmeted security guards were the ones who were loyal to her. They all seemed more or less the same to him. But Iridius knew that was only an issue if Gentrix was telling the truth at all. It seemed very convenient that Gentrix had access to an entourage of loyal security who could go off and do her bidding without drawing the attention of the CEO. Maybe she didn't need to worry about who was loyal to her because it was all for show anyway, and they were just all part of team Devin – including Gentrix. They hadn't had much choice about allowing Gentrix to help them. Mudd wouldn't have been able to get them out of the clutches of Devin Frost without her. But even after what she'd shared about the Federation–Alliance war and how she'd thanked Iridius for saving her, that didn't mean he was ready to trust her.

It wasn't just Gentrix, her ready supply of goons and the apparent ease of her movement around the station that bothered Iridius. It was the whole thing with this concert, too. After everything that had happened – successful testing of a weapon that could change history, someone getting onto the station disguised as DJ Chromium and his sister hiring assassins – why in all the gronking black was Devin Frost still heading off to a concert? No matter how much of a massive DJ Chromium fan he was, it didn't feel right. A high-tech space heist involving a time bomb wasn't exactly something Iridius had a lot of experience with, but his instincts were yelling at him. Something about this wasn't what it seemed. The Frosts, both of them, were playing a game, he was sure of it. Iridius knew nothing about chess – he'd tried to learn once, but could never remember how all the pieces moved. But he knew what it felt like to be a pawn.

"Here," Mudd said to Junker, handing her a small plastic bag.

She held it up and looked inside. It held twenty or thirty colourful pills, each one in the shape of a celebrity's face. From where he stood, Iridius could see several classic actors from early cinema – an Arnold Schwarzenegger, a Marlon Brando, a few Meryl Streeps and a Clint Eastwood. There were a couple of US presidents, including Eisenhower and Dwayne 'The Rock' Johnson. He also spied Lady Yeet, a pop star from the previous century, and an incredibly dangerous bright red Hunter S. Thompson.

"*Improv?*" Iridius said. "Why are you giving my crew member drugs?"

"There's a couple of green ones in there that are me," Mudd said, "or at least, they're DJ Chromium. If you feel like you need help getting in character you could take one."

Junker took the bag and slipped it into the pocket of her silver spacesuit. "I don't think I'll need them, but a baggy of pills in my pocket is probably a good prop for a DJ."

Junker, Rangi and the four Frost Norton guards headed for the door.

"Junker," Iridius said.

She turned back.

"Break a leg."

"Thanks, Cap."

There was a beat. "What about me?" Rangi asked.

"You," Iridius said, "don't break anything."

Rangi gave a salute and they left.

"So," Iridius said, turning back to Mudd and Gentrix, "we're sure Devin Frost is going to go to this concert? Nobody else thinks that seems like a weird thing to do?"

"He thinks it's all going ahead as normal," Mudd said.

"Plus, he's very stubborn about these things," Gentrix said. "Stupidly stubborn. If he says he's having DJ Chromium play a concert for his birthday then that's what is going to happen."

"Alright," Iridius said, even though things didn't seem alright. "Let's do it then. Lead the way, Agent Mudd."

"Everyone get changed into a Frost Norton Security uniform," Mudd said. "Then we gear up and move out."

Gentrix stood directly in front of Iridius and began unzipping the tight jumpsuit she wore. He tried not to look. Honestly. He could hold up his hand in a court of law and be confident he wasn't perjuring himself by declaring that he had no intention of looking. In fact, when he realised she was undressing in front of him Iridius looked down at his feet, absolutely intent on untying his boots, a skill he'd learned as an eight-year-old but now apparently had no idea how to do.

He felt the burning sensation of being watched and glanced up, peeked up really, flicked his eyes up for a millisecond, and that was when any willpower he had evaporated. Gentrix Frost was watching him. Her impossibly dark eyes were fixed on his as she unzipped her jumpsuit right down the front, all the way down to just above her waist. She rolled her shoulders back and let the top half of her jumpsuit slip down. She wore a close-fitting white t-shirt underneath, which was bad enough, but then she moved her hips from side to side and the jumpsuit slipped down to her feet, leaving her standing in a tight t-shirt and underwear.

Gentrix held him in her gaze the whole time, and Iridius's face burned. It was like being held in a gronking bear trap. It felt like she was daring him to look away. He absolutely wasn't going to do that. No matter what his mind and particular parts of his body were begging, he didn't look away from her eyes. They watched each other for what was probably only a second but felt like a millennium, then Gentrix smiled and winked at him before turning away. She bent over to pick up her Frost Norton uniform and really, someone should have given Iridius a tights and a cape right then, because resisting the smouldering feminine wiles of Gentrix Frost was more superhuman than anything he'd managed to do with his nanobots. He focused on his feet again, trying to stop the blood that had filled his face and his – you know. How did laces work again?

Iridius finished dressing in the black Frost Norton Security uniform, and noticed his reflection in the glass wall. Oddly, it was only then, when he was wearing it himself, that he realised something about the nondescript black uniform. It reminded him a lot of the uniform he'd seen himself wearing when he'd been visited by Space Ghost Iridius, just before he'd crashed the *Diesel Coast* into the face of the enormous Aegix dog-ship. Of course, it hadn't really been a ghost, it had been a holographic projection of himself from the future, telling him how to escape imminent death. Actually, when he thought about it, that was only marginally less weird than being visited by a ghost of yourself.

The clothes he was wearing now were the clothes past him had seen future him wearing when he'd saved himself. Now he was present him, wearing the clothes of future him. He wasn't exactly sure what that meant – probably that, as usual, shit was about to go sideways. He was sure there was something about predestination or time paradoxes or inevitability that Quinn would be able to explain if she were here, but he couldn't worry about that now. There was nothing he could do but keep going. Shit was always going sideways, so he supposed he shouldn't expect anything else. At least now he could prepare himself that something weird was going to happen, even if he didn't know how or when.

Iridius and Mudd checked the maintenance suits the real Frost Norton Security guards had brought for them. They were bright orange suits with the Frost Norton logo on the front and the word MAINTENANCE on the back. They were sealed maintenance/inspection suits, rather than full space EVA or armoured combat suits like Iridius was used to. Not designed for long periods of space walking or exposure to toxic environments, and they had no thruster packs or ballistic protection. They were worn for working in atmosphere and pressurised environments, but would seal and provide a short-term air supply in the event of exposure to vacuum. Iridius and Mudd unpacked them from the plastic crate and slipped them into two large bags.

"Alright then," Iridius said, slipping on the stupid Frost

JUNKER STOOD at the bottom of the steps that would lead up to the theatre stage. Her knees bounced, moving with an uncontrollable need to release her nervous energy. She listened to the murmuring of the crowd floating through to the backstage area. There was always an energy of anticipation backstage before a gig, and it wasn't just the performers as they readied themselves. The noise of a crowd was always an indistinct hum, the escalation of rising conversation blending into one constant cacophonous drone. It was immediately recognisable. Listening to that sound, knowing the crowd was waiting for them, had a way of producing a kind of excited anxiety that could make even the most experienced performer just a little skittish.

Junker was not the most experienced performer, not compared to someone like DJ Chromium, but she'd had more practice than most people. Still, it had been almost ten years since her last performance as DJ Ratatat, and in that moment she struggled to recall any of the times she'd been on stage. DJ Ratatat seemed a lifetime ago – so much had happened since then. She'd joined Space Command, risen through the ranks quickly, been caught dealing with the less than savoury elements of the galaxy, been busted down the ranks just as quickly and found herself on the *Diesel Coast*, which had led to helping save the galaxy. Now, through what might be called an utterly ridiculous twist of fate, she had to DJ again to help save the Federation.

Samira Nejem was not someone who second-guessed herself. She didn't do it when she was working on starship systems, nor when she'd broken Space Command regulations. She didn't do it when she'd elected to follow Captain Franklin into what seemed like certain death at the hands of an enormous spaceship-sized dog. Now though, at the bottom of the stage stairs with the crowd noise reverberating through the walls, she realised something. This was fucking stupid. What was she doing? Could she honestly pull off faking a whole DJ Chromium set so the others could steal a secret weapon? She considered turning and walking away, but knew that wasn't an option. She took a deep breath, trying to calm herself. As far as everyone around her knew, apart from the Frost Norton guards who'd brought her here, she was DJ Chromium. She had to put on the appearance.

She'd delayed long enough; the concert had been due to start fifteen minutes ago. She could sense the crowd growing restless.

Junker looked at the theatre stage manager and nodded. He said something into a headset mic and the lights on the stage plunged into darkness. The crowd noise changed from the constant hum of chatter to the roar of cheering. Junker closed her eyes and breathed. The boom of music started, a deep, classical piece heavy enough with bass that all of Locke Station probably felt the vibrations. The intro to a DJ Chromium set. Such a stupid idea, Junker thought again as she climbed the stairs. But then, as she crested the steps onto the stage and a single spotlight stuck her, reflecting off her shining silver spacesuit and helmet and the crowd roared with even more intensity, she let go of those reluctant thoughts. The swell of the crowd noise filled her with enough adrenaline to push her anxiety aside.

Junker moved into the raised, pyramid shaped DJ booth and lifted her arms into the air. The thousands in the crowd boomed again. When Junker lowered her hands onto the decks she felt out of place. She didn't feel like DJ Ratatat anymore, but that didn't matter, because now, for this moment at least, she got to be DJ Chromium, and she didn't need a synthesised personality drug to do it because it turned out everything she knew about DJ Chromium was wrong anyway. She'd invent a new DJ Chromium. She would take Captain Franklin's lead and charge recklessly forward.

———

Latroz, Greg and Gentrix moved through the maintenance areas of the station with Iridius and Mudd as much as possible, until they had no choice but to walk the streets. They parted ways and Iridius and Mudd continued down towards the vault while they moved to the main security control room. Being dressed in the Frost Norton Security uniform paid off as they'd hoped it would. It was unlikely anyone would have paid much attention to Latroz or Greg – at least, no more attention than they'd normally pay a seven-foot-tall purple warrior woman and a walking cancerous tumour – but they almost certainly would have recognised Gentrix Frost. The Chief Operating Officer of Frost Norton was a well-known face throughout that station and, for the general population, both eye-catching and terrifying in equal measure. Wearing the black of Frost Norton Security meant she was some-where between fading into the everyday background of Locke Station and being actively ignored, because every person on board ASS Locke knew that a day when you had to deal with Frost Norton Security was going to be a bad day.

Once they made their way down several levels and in towards the central section, where the security control room was located, there was no longer an opportunity to remain incognito. The three of them approached the door beneath the Security Control Room sign and Gentrix removed her helmet.

"I've been Chief Operating Officer of Frost Norton Corporation for seven years now," Gentrix said, "responsible for the daily running of a technological development company behind some of the most advanced developments in the Alliance, including applying groundbreaking science in order to manipulate entropy and allow for the reversal of time itself. I'm not sure whether to be thankful or offended that basically my entire contribution to this mission is to stand over here and open this door."

She stepped up to the full biometric scanning system beside the doorway. "Gentrix Frost, requesting entry."

The system activated and began scanning her entire body, logging and cross-checking everything from standard biometric data used for hundreds of years, such as voiceprint recognition, iris scanning and facial recognition, to much newer and harder to mimic attributes, including full-body vein pattern structure, distribution of bone density and full body posture and proportionality scanning of every part of her body – and I do mean every part. This had been a somewhat uncomfortable metric when it had first been introduced into biometric security systems, particularly among men. This vast array of extraordinarily difficult if not impossible to mimic biometric data meant there was no hacking into this type of full biometric security.

Greg watched as Gentrix stood on the blue circle indicating the position for biometric scanning. Gentrix was right, there would be no mission if she wasn't available to open this door. Greg couldn't help but wonder then, how had Agent Mudd planned to open this door without her? Unless they had someone else who had access – one of the Frost Norton Security personnel maybe? But then, why had they needed Gentrix? Why had they needed to get her involved? As a N'hlarkic strain malignant Greg was a pacifist, entirely non-violent, and he was inclined to think the best of people. Still, he could tell that trusting Gentrix, a high-ranking member of the Alliance, had made Captain Franklin uncomfortable, and the sudden realisation that Gentrix and Mudd could have been working together the whole time made Greg wonder whether Captain Franklin was right to be uncomfortable. He would keep a close eye on her, for the sake of the mission and for Captain Franklin.

After a moment the screen beside the door displayed a green icon. "Identity confirmed, Chief Operating Officer Gentrix Fairybell Frost."

She turned to look at Latroz and Greg. "Tell anybody that and I will cut your head off."

The door to the security control room slid open before either of them had a chance to respond. There were four Frost Norton Security guards inside, monitoring the station's security. Each of them turned to look as Gentrix entered, followed by Latroz and Greg.

"Miss Frost," one of them said. Greg recognised him as Guard Leader Meteon, the one who had originally taken him and Captain Franklin to see Devin Frost. "You aren't supposed to be in here."

"The door opened, didn't it?" Gentrix responded.

"We have been instructed by CEO Frost that if you enter any secure areas you are to be arrested," Meteon said.

"You're going to arrest me, are you?" Gentrix said, a heavy hint of threat in her tone.

"I'm sorry, Miss Frost," Meteon said. "The order comes straight from the CEO."

"You understand that the CEO is currently enjoying a concert?" Gentrix said.

"Yes, Miss Frost."

"And who do you think runs things when my brother is otherwise engaged?"

"You do, Miss Frost."

"That's right," Gentrix said. "Now, I need my people here to access the security terminal."

Meteon looked at Latroz and Greg then, turning his attention to them properly for the first time. "Who are you two?" he said. "I don't recognise you."

Latroz approached Meteon. To his credit, he didn't take even a slight backwards step, which most people could not avoid when being approached by a Siruan. He did move his hand to his holster, though. "Stop and identify yourself," he ordered.

Latroz did stop in front of him. She reached up and slipped off her helmet. Meteon looked at her, his eyes narrowing in vague recognition. "Wait," he said. "Aren't you with DJ Chromium?"

"I am Lieutenant Latroz, Tactical Officer, *FSC Deus Ex,* Federation Space Command."

"Federation?" Meteon said. "What?!"

Meteon turned to Gentrix in confusion, but Gentrix looked at Latroz. "I understand you Federation types love to spout your ranks and everything, and I know you're not used to the kind of espionage thing we're doing here, but I didn't think you would actually reveal your identity."

"He asked," Latroz said matter-of-factly.

"Yes," Gentrix said, "I suppose he did." Gentrix turned to Meteon. "Now listen, there's things going on outside your remit, so you can just take this as an order to leave."

Meteon didn't move. Instead, he lifted his pistol to aim it at Latroz. He barely had it out of his holster before Latroz intervened. When she had first walked towards Meteon she'd stopped several paces away. Meteon, like everyone did, underestimated her speed and reach. Siruans were known throughout the galaxy as masters of combat, warriors possibly without equal, and yet they were still underestimated. The reason for that was relatively simple. If you got into a fight with Siruans and they had to use their full combat potential, you and everyone with you would end up dead. Vis-a-vis, none of you would be left to spread the word about just how insanely the Siruans fought. So really, all that existed in the galaxy was this vague knowledge that yes, Siruans were great warriors, but no one was really sure of the details. But this room was about to bear witness.

And so while Junker was in the theatre spinning vinyl, Latroz began doing what she did best – spinning heads.

Before Meteon could bring his pistol up past forty-five degrees, Latroz had already dashed forward and grabbed the top of the barrel, stopping its progress in its tracks. Meteon's eyes grew wide with shock. He could have sworn she was far enough away that he didn't need to worry. But Latroz's fast-twitch muscle fibres were firing faster than even the synapses in Meteon's brain. During his moment of dumbfounded shock at Latroz suddenly being in front of him, Latroz ripped the pistol from his hand. As a Venutian, Meteon was not small, and he was not weak. In fact, his general strength would be on par with the strongest humans. So he felt another moment of disbelief as the pistol was torn from his hand as easily as if an adult had taken it from a toddler. Latroz did not hesitate. She swung the pistol, cracking Meteon around the side of the skull. His head spun and his body followed as he was pistol whipped into unconsciousness.

In what was, to the casual observer, almost a black and purple blur, Latroz launched herself over Meteon's fallen body to the other three guards in the room. They had recovered from the shock of seeing Meteon knocked unconscious in a blur of Siruan movement and were stumbling over themselves to prepare for a very unexpected fight. The first of them had stood from his chair, and even managed to unholster his sidearm. Latroz didn't really think about target selection and prioritisation as she fought; instead, her instincts took over. As a species evolved almost exclusively for war, a fight like this was as autonomic as a heartbeat.

After jumping over Meteon's collapsed form, she cleared the entire room before landing in front of the pistol-wielding guard. He had been the first of the others to recover, the first to go for his gun, and so was the first to have Latroz's carapace-armoured fist punch into his face, crush his nose and send him flailing against the control console.

Of the other two guards, one was rushing for Latroz while the other went for his gun. Guns, Latroz thought, they always went for their guns, even when they were already in the shit. So stupid. In a frantic, stand-up fist fight, taking the time to reach for a gun was more than enough time for a someone to dispatch a swift butt-kicking. Don't get me wrong, Latroz loved guns as much as most war-loving Siruans, but you didn't muck around trying to get a gun from its holster mid-fight, especially in a fight with an ultra-fast Siruan. That said, Latroz's instincts told her to target the gun-dependent guard before the one rushing her, just in case he managed to get off a shot or two.

Latroz moved forward. It looked for all the galaxy like the guard madly rushing her was going to block her from the one almost wielding his gun, but then she leaped, kicked off the front guard and onto the wall, taking several steps along it before launching herself off that and straight into the gun-wielding guard. In a single movement Latroz grabbed the guard's wrist with one hand and pushed upwards. With her other hand she grabbed the guard's forefinger, which had been just about to slip inside the trigger guard. She couldn't allow a shot to go off and alert others to the commotion inside, so she bent his finger back, snapping it. He looked as though he was about to howl but she swiftly struck him in the side of the head before he could make a sound.

This had given the last of the guards a chance to recover from being used as a wall-run assist trampoline. He gathered himself and turned to find Latroz coming for him. Full credit to him, at least this one seemed to have learned how fast Latroz was. He swung a punch early enough that it might have actually connected had Latroz not simply blocked the blow as if waving away a troublesome insect. She spun the guard, wrapping her arm around his head in attempt to grab him in a sleeper hold but, her Siruan warrior bloodlust getting the better of her, she pulled too hard. There was a loud popping crack from the guard's upper spinal column. Latroz let go and the guard slumped to the ground.

"Well," Gentrix said, looking at Latroz, who stood in the centre of the room barely panting, "fuck me. I knew Siruans were brutally efficient but that was something else. I'll have to see if I can't employ a few of your kind."

"I restrained myself," Latroz responded.

"You did?"

Latroz nodded. "They live." She looked at the last of the guards, noting the way his head was twisted on his shoulders. "Except maybe that one."

"Unfortunate," Gentrix said. "I'd have preferred no casualties, but I did warn them, and they pulled their weapons first." She shrugged. "Let's get on with it. Greg, you start deactivating the entry security to the vault and I'll load Mark and Iridius's biometric information into the system so the vault doesn't eject them into space."

———

Iridius crawled through an air duct, shoving the bag containing his EVA suit along in front of him. Up ahead, Mudd was using a small cutting laser to remove the vent cover. It came loose and dropped, but Mudd was quick enough to grab the edge before it clanged to the floor below. He lowered it gently before pushing his bag out of the duct and then following. Iridius did the same, letting the bag drop and then wriggling free of the tight space.

Unfortunately his toes caught on the edge of the vent, sending him crashing unceremoniously to the floor. He swore under his breath. He was making a habit of awkwardly crashing to the floor of space stations. He made a mental note to practise jumping out of breach holes and air ducts and landing much more stylishly than he'd managed so far in his career. He righted himself, and saw Mudd looking at him.

"You're the one who saved the galaxy?"

Iridius responded with the wittiest retort he could manage at the time – he flipped him the middle finger.

Mudd shook his head, picked up his bag and moved off. "Come on. This way."

They were in a corridor – and this was certainly a corridor, it wasn't even pretending to be a street. It was only wide enough for two or three people to walk side by side, and there wasn't a single faux building facade or advertising billboard in sight. This was the business end of the spire, where it put on its fancy suit and admitted it was actually a corporate space station not a post-apocalyptic slum. The pair moved hastily along the corridor in the direction of the vault – or at least, Iridius assumed that's where they were heading. He had little choice but to trust Mudd knew where he was going, because Iridius had become hopelessly confused about their direction somewhere between the fifth maintenance tunnel and their second crawl through an air duct. Mudd had warned that they wouldn't be able to travel through the ASS's back passages the whole way – yes, that's how he phrased it – and it seemed they'd reached the point where they had to travel the ordinary corridors. They moved quickly, eager to minimise the time they spent exposed like this. They didn't run, though. That was a surefire way to draw attention. They simply moved with the determined pace of two people who had some-where to be.

There were very few others this deep in the bowels of the spire, but contrary to what you might be thinking, that wasn't a good thing. The fewer people around, the easier it was to notice the pieces that didn't fit. That was especially true in a restricted area such as this, where people tended to be more alert to things that were out of place. They passed several maintenance workers and a few people dressed in light grey Frost Norton branded uniforms, who Iridius suspected were the scientists and engineers who did most of the research and development. Iridius and Mudd kept up their appearance of being on some important secu-rity duty, and the majority of people they passed carried on without giving them a second look. Until someone gave them a second look.

A pair of scientists were walking down the white-walled corridor towards them. One of them was a human man and the other looked to be several decades younger, but he was a dipteron, an insectoid/humanoid hybrid, and Iridius had never really been good at estimating the ages of other species. Iridius thought the human probably had some amount of seniority, purely because he was an older man with a short greying beard and an electric shock of white hair that didn't appear to have been combed or cut in the last decade and that, in Iridius's mind at least, was what a senior scientist was supposed to look like. The man watched them approach from beneath his equally wild white eyebrows. Iridius noticed his eyes on them. Then he noticed the subtle shift in the man's direction. He was going to intercept them. Iridius was content with keeping his eyes forward and hopefully avoiding a confrontation. Mudd, on the other hand, was apparently not. In fact, he did the complete opposite.

"Play along," he whispered to Iridius out of the side of his mouth.

"Huh?" Iridius responded, but it was too late. Mudd had already begun moving to cut off the old man and his younger companion.

The older gentleman seemed a little taken aback by Mudd's aggressive march towards him. Mudd stopped in front of him, unwavering beneath the half-helmet.

"Excuse me," the man said. "What do you think you are doing?"

"Identification spot check, sir," Mudd said.

"What?"

"Identification spot check, sir," Mudd repeated, with very little change in the tone or cadence of his voice.

"Who do you think you are?" the man said, aghast. "In fact, I was going to ask to see your identification. I don't recognise you at all. We have a regular security detail down here."

"Frost Norton Security," Mudd said. "Don't make me repeat myself, sir." He turned to the dipteron, who moved his head in small jerking movements as he stared out from his enormous black eyes, made up of thousands of individual compounded lenses. "I'll need to see your identification. Both of you."

"Do you know who this is?" the old man said, indicating his colleague. "This is Frost Norton's chief scientist, Mozentra Mal Nerz."

No, Iridius thought, *of course we don't gronking know who that is. What were you thinking, Mudd? We're not even going to make it to the vault.*

But Mudd didn't give any sign of backing down. "Sir," he said, "we are normally security for CEO Frost and COO Frost in the Burrows and surrounds, but there have been several incidents that have mandated heightened security patrols. Identification please. Now."

The man made to object again but the dipteron held up the long hairy appendage that functioned as his arm. He spoke in a droning buzz. "It is fine Harold. They are simply doing their job. Show them your ident card please." With one of his other multiple limbs, the dipteron reached down and lifted the identity card that hung on a lanyard around his neck. With much huffing, the older man did the same. Mudd leaned forward and made a show of examining the cards.

"Thank you, gentlemen," Mudd said. "Have a nice day."

He began walking away and Iridius followed. They didn't get far before the old man called out.

"Stop. What's in those bags?!"

Iridius and Mudd stopped. Mudd turned back. He unzipped the bag and pulled out enough of the maintenance suit to show what it was. "Some maintenance suits we got asked to take to some of the guys doing something in the ventilation system. I didn't ask what for."

The old man looked at him for a moment. "Right," he eventually said, and then turned to walk away with the young-looking dipteron, who Iridius realised was actually his boss and was probably four hundred years old. Told you he couldn't pick the ages of aliens.

When they had gone, Iridius turned to Mudd. "Well, that seemed like a gronking terrible idea."

"He was going to confront us anyway," Mudd said.

"So you decided to just get it over with by making a scene, did you?"

"The best way to deal with a confrontation like that is to do it on your own terms," Mudd said. "Particularly when you're undercover. Being confident and demanding something first is usually enough to put people on the back foot. That's what most agents do wrong when they first try and infiltrate. If you're playing a role, you need to play it aggressively. If it looks like you're not going to be able to hide in plain sight you need to step forward and be seen. Counter-intuitive, sure, but it works. The easiest system to get through is still the sentient being."

"Step forward and be seen playing a role, hey?" Iridius said. "Like Gentrix Frost is with us."

Mudd stopped and turned to look at him. "You don't trust her then?"

"Do you?"

"No," Mudd said matter-of-factly. "No, I don't. I don't fully understand her motivation for helping us, and that bothers me. I intend to keep a close eye on her."

"Good," Iridius said. "Glad to hear we're on the same page with that."

They continued walking down the white-walled corridor to a set of elevator doors set in the wall a short distance away.

"So, you two have some kind of history then?" Iridius asked.

Mudd looked at him. "We do, but only in the sense of the espionage game. Both trying to get something, it seemed. I needed an in to the Alliance and she was trying to snag someone who might actually manage to kill her brother. Why? Does that bother you?"

"Bother me? What? You and Gentrix? Not at all."

"Why ask then?"

"Nothing. I mean, no reason," Iridius said, stammering. "I was just making conversation."

"Sure."

"I was."

They walked in silence a little longer before Mudd spoke again. "I'm actually surprised to hear you say you don't trust her."

"What do you mean?"

"Just seemed like you two were getting close," Mudd said. "It's not hard to miss."

"Hang on a second," Iridius said. "We're not getting close."

"Okay," Mudd said, raising his hands in mock surrender. "I'm just saying what I've noticed."

"Well, you're wrong."

"Maybe," Mudd said. "Let me just give you fair warning. Don't get pulled in by her."

"I'm not," Iridius said. "What makes you think I'm getting pulled in by her?"

"I'm just saying," Mudd said. "You're the one that brought her up and asked if she could be trusted. Don't do anything stupid like falling for her. You ever heard of a honeypot?"

They stopped outside the elevator door. Iridius looked sideways at Mudd. "Yes," he said. "I've heard of a honeypot and I'm not stuck in one."

"No problem then," Mudd said. "Call your malignant. They should have control of security by now."

Iridius turned away. Stupid Mudd. He wasn't falling for Gentrix. She was attractive, sure, smart and attractive – and seductive too, but he wasn't falling for her. Besides, how did Mudd know she was trying to use her sexuality to trap him? Maybe she actually liked him and was just very forward with her advances. It wasn't impossible that a woman might actually find him attractive. Stupid Mudd. Still, he didn't trust her, and he wasn't going to let the fact that he was falling for her cloud his judgement. Not that he was falling for her. He wasn't. He pressed the button on his earpiece communicator.

"Greg, this is Franklin."

The response came in through Iridius's earpiece.

"I'm here, Captain."

Greg was keeping communication as short as possible, just as he'd been ordered to. Their communication was encrypted, but the more often and the longer they communicated, the more likely someone would be to pick up their transmissions. Even if they couldn't determine exactly what they were saying, they would be able to locate the transmitter and receiver. Best to avoid any chance of detection.

"We're at the lift."

"Aye."

A moment passed and nothing happened. Mudd looked across at Iridius. He didn't say anything, but the implication was clear enough.

"It'll be fine," Iridius said. "Greg will come through."

"You didn't even know he could hack security systems until today. How do you know he can do it?"

"I know he can do it because he said he can. Greg wouldn't say he could do it if he couldn't."

"Yes, because you and your crew don't at all seem to be over-confident about this whole endeavour. Have you ever heard of the Dunning-Kruger effect? It says people with low competence regularly overestimate their abilities. You've got a misfit crew full of walking Dunning-Kruger graphs."

Iridius turned on Mudd with something close to Siruan ultra-reflexes. Mudd even took a surprised half-step back. Iridius barely managed to keep his voice down and it came out as a vicious hissing, like he was an angry Najani Snakeperson.

"Listen Mudd," he said, "you can talk shit about me all you want, but you don't talk shit about my crew. If someone was over-confident in our ability to get the time reversal bomb out of Alliance hands then it was me. My crew is here because that's what we do. We stick by each other, even if it seems hopeless."

Mudd lifted his hands in a gesture of surrender. "Okay," he said. "I'm just saying."

"And I'm saying you can stop just saying. The crew of the *Deus Ex* are more competent than anyone gives them credit for. You're not alone in thinking we got lucky saving the galaxy, but it wasn't luck. It was every single member of my crew doing what they're great at, what they've always been great at but that others have never been able to see. Beneath everything, they have more skill than any cardboard cut-out starship crew out there."

"Alright," Mudd said. "I get it. You're protective of your crew."

"That's the other thing. I'm not protective of them. We're protective of each other. Every person on that crew has each other's back the whole time. That's why we can do what we do. Everyone likes to think they're misfits. They aren't misfits, because they fit together. That's the problem with you spooks. You don't know what it's like to be part of a real crew. To have nobody but the other members of your ship to rely on out there in the black of space. You've got no loyalty. We're a family. I can call them a bunch of idiots because they're *my* bunch of idiots, but you don't get to."

"I said I get it. Jeez."

Iridius stared hard at Mudd for a moment longer. "Good." Then he turned back to the elevator door. Nothing had happened. He waited a moment longer before pressing his comm. "Greg, I just said all this nice shit about you. Open the gronking elevator."

"Working on it," Greg replied. "I just – hold on, that should do it, Captain."

The panel beside the elevator door lit up green and the door slid open.

"Ding," Iridius said to Mudd. "Going down."

They descended in the elevator and when they emerged, Iridius recognised the heavy vault door at the end of corridor. It was sealed tight.

"We're at the vault door," Iridius said over his comm.

"Confirm," Greg replied. "Working on vault door."

Mudd dropped his duffel bag to the ground, knelt and unzipped it. "Come on," he said to Iridius, "let's get these on."

Iridius and Mudd unpacked the lightweight maintenance

suits and slipped them on over their black Frost Norton uniforms. These were a lot easier to put on than the much bulkier suits, which were designed for combat or for long-periods of external space-walking. Although Iridius did have to zip Mudd's suit up, and then spin around and let Mudd do the same to him, in a moment only slightly less awkward than when his Aunt Wallace had made him zip up her overly tight red dress before his cousin's wedding when he was twelve. Thankfully, this time he only had to tuck in Mudd's black uniform as he zipped, unlike when he had to tuck in his aunt's actual flesh. As Iridius slipped on the helmet and clicked it in place, Greg came back over the comms.

"Door will now open with a code of zero-zero-zero-zero, Captain."

"Just like my PIN number," Iridius said. "Confirm that our biometric profiles are loaded in?"

This time it was Gentrix who answered. "They are, Captain Franklin, I did it myself."

Iridius paused. "Greg, can you confirm?"

"What," Gentrix's sultry voice said, "you don't trust me, Captain? I'm hurt."

"I can confirm, Captain," Greg said. "She did it."

"Good," Iridius said. "Just checking, Miss Frost."

"Indeed, Captain," Gentrix responded.

Iridius entered the code on the keypad and the door slid open. "Okay, we're heading into the vault. Be ready to extract as soon as we confirm we've got the package."

"You are expecting a package, Captain?" Greg said over comms.

"No, Greg," Iridius said. "It's code. That's what people say when they're doing stuff like this."

"Ah," Greg said. "In that case, I can't wait to see your package, Captain."

Iridius sighed.

CHAPTER EIGHTEEN_

WITH EVERY SHIFT in the pulse of the music, every slow break and heavy drop, Junker could feel the energy of the crowd. She had long ago lost all semblance of nerves and was fully in her element, or at least fully in DJ Chromium's element. At the beginning she had stuck very close to Chromium's original mixes, songs she remembered even better than she could remember her own original beats. Now though, several songs into the set, she felt like she had the audience in the palm of her hand. They roared and cheered, and the theatre heaved with pounding bass and flashing lights and gyrating bodies.

If there was one thing Chief Petty Officer Samira Nejem was good at, it was experimenting with how to make things better. She had always been a tinkerer, and that wasn't limited to her ongoing desire to pull things apart on a space ship. Tinkering was what had drawn her to DJing in the first place. As a DJ, you could mess with songs, deconstruct them, remix them, upgrade them. Her need to pull things apart to understand their fundamental workings and then put them back together had caused Captain Franklin no end of frustration, she knew that, but she also knew he appreciated when her wild experiments worked out, like when she'd upgraded the propulsion system on the *Diesel Coast* to give them the boost they needed to escape a barrage of missiles. Moments like that more than made up for the occasional false start, setback or minor explosion. And that was what she was going to lean on now. She felt comfortable enough to inhabit the spirit of DJ Chromium but to add her own flavour. She was going to tinker with his music, and hopefully the audience would excuse any minor explosions when they heard the end result.

She faded down the original mix of DJ Chromium's classic 'In Space No One Can Hear You Dream' and brought up the bass-heavy intro to 'Programming Language', but instead of bringing in the hook, she let loose with an absolute tear on the decks. She moved the synthetic vinyl back and forward and flicked the cross-fader with blinding speed to produce rhythmic scratches that played the main riff. It was something DJ Chromium hadn't done in years and even then, Junker knew this was the one thing she could do better than the master DJ. She had spent a long time obsessing over the scratch, and learning to use the technique as a percussive instrument in its own right. She'd given performing away before she ever got to show off her true skills, but now was her chance. As she faded in the hook, she matched it in scratches. The crowd roared like never before. They cheered for DJ Chromium, but Junker knew they were really cheering for her. She hadn't realised until this moment that she wanted to perform so badly, but at the same time she knew this would be enough, just once in front of a big crowd and she would be happy.

Junker had quickly located CEO Devin Frost where he sat in a prominent box to the left of the stage. She'd kept half an eye on him over the course of the first few songs, and then continued to glance up occasionally. Every time she looked up, Devin Frost was there in his Hawaiian shirt, nodding his head along to the beat like the galaxy's worst dash-mounted souvenir bobblehead. He seemed to be there for the duration and gave no hint that he was doing anything other than watching his birthday show, so after a while Junker stopped checking as often. That was why, when she was deep in her freestyle scratch performance, she didn't notice Devin Frost stand up and leave the box.

Several minutes later Junker noticed some sort of commotion to the left of the stage. When she looked over, she saw the stage manager was arguing with three Frost Norton Security guards who were attempting to make their way onto the stage. At first it looked like they weren't going to get past the stage manager, which for performing arts nerds the galaxy wide wouldn't come as a surprise – perhaps the only creature as warlike as a Siruan was a stage manager mid-performance. But the appearance of Devin Frost behind them soon changed this. Junker saw him and cursed herself. She'd got too lost in her musical experimentation. This was probably the equivalent of a small explosion, or at least like that time she'd tried to lift the gloom on the *Diesel Coast* by increasing the brightness of the lights, but had instead caused minor retinal burns to the entire crew. Frost was gesturing at Junker and barking something at the stage manager, who had no choice but to step aside.

Junker may have been a maintenance technician, not a tactical officer, but it didn't take an expert to realise that this might be a good time for a tactical withdrawal. She glanced to the other side of the stage and noticed four more guards there. They had cut off her exits. Devin Frost and the guards he was with were walking out onto the stage. Frost was gesturing to the sound-booth, indicating that they should cut the music. It stopped abruptly, and the crowd responded in the same way every hyped-up crowd has responded to a performance cut short throughout history, since the first tribal dances were interrupted by a tribe member with something important to say: they booed and threw things. Frost ignored them as he moved towards the elevated DJ booth in the centre of the stage.

"You!" he shouted. "You are not DJ Chromium!"

"What?" Junker said. "I am too DJ Chromium." She knew the helmet was masking her voice, but worried that if Frost got too close he might realise she was too short. "I thought you caught the impostor. You can see I'm in the middle of a performance, and as a fan you should be able to tell I'm really DJing here."

"Oh yes," Devin Frost said, "I can see you're putting on quite the performance. But as you say, I'm a very big DJ Chromium fan. You just put on a hell of a scratching showcase. The problem is, you did all your scratching with your left hand."

Ah shit.

Junker had been too into the performance to even think about that. DJ Chromium was right-handed.

"I've been practising being ambidextrous," Junker said.

"Grab him," Frost said.

The Frost Norton Security guards hurried towards the raised booth. They had blocked both sides of the stage and were closing in. There was only one chance to escape. Junker waited for them to begin climbing the steps, then unclipped her silver helmet and lifted it off. She looked to Frost, who seemed shocked.

"Not a him, dickhead!" she yelled before throwing DJ Chromium's helmet at the closest guard. It hit him square in the visor with a satisfying thunk and caused him to stumble. Then Junker jumped out the front of the DJ booth, sliding down the pyramid-shaped base and landing at the front of the stage. She leapt off into the crowd. The crowd was roaring with a combination of disappointment, confusion and excitement. She shoved her hand into her pocket and pulled out the bag of *Improv* Mudd had given her. There were a lot of old-timey action heroes in that bag and she'd seen how crazy a party could get when a lot of people decided to take *Improv* and go full Expendables. She reached inside, grabbed a handful and tossed them to the crowd around her.

"Freebies!" she shouted. "As long as you remember the guys in black are the baddies!"

Junker continued squeezing her way through the crowd, people parting for her despite the calls from the security guards for them to "stop that DJ". Those who caught the pills took a moment to look at what they had in their hands and then several of them, perhaps caught up in the moment of a DJ Chromium concert gone awry, popped the pills into their mouths. The *Improv* worked almost immediately, and those who swallowed the drugs quickly found their brain overtaken by whichever synthesised personality they'd ingested. *Improv* didn't erase the user completely – it wouldn't be among the galaxy's most popular recreational drugs if you didn't get to experience the ride while you were on it – it was more that the line between the user's personality and the synthetic caricature was blurred.

Several fans stepped forward as Junker passed, blocking the Frost Norton Security guards. There were two Arnold Schwarzeneggers, a Clint Eastwood and, surprisingly a Meryl Streep. The Schwarzeneggers stepped forward.

"I cannot let you harm the DJ," one of them said.

The Clint Eastwood stepped up next to them. "He's right, you see I can't abide you going after that lady there."

"Get out of the way," the first of the guards said. "Don't make us hurt you."

"You're going to hurt us," Clint Eastwood said, "That right, is it? Do you feel lucky?"

The second Arnold Schwarzenegger stepped forward as one of the security guards tried to push past. "Get to the chopper!" he shouted back over his shoulder at Junker.

"What?" said the confused guard, who was obviously not a fan of classic Earth movies. "What are you talking about?"

"Get her!" Devin Frost shouted from where he was standing at the edge of the stage.

The guard pulled out a stun baton and jammed it into Arnold Schwarzenegger's stomach. The man, who mostly believed he was Arnold Schwarzenegger but was actually only five feet and one inch tall, spasmed under the electrical zap. "I'll be back," he said as his eyes rolled into his head.

Next to him, the man under the Clint Eastwood delusion swung a wild right hook, catching one of the guards on his exposed jaw. The guard, perhaps not expecting a skinny man wearing a tight white t-shirt and a fluorescent headband to hit like a man straight out of the old west, stumbled back into another guard, who stepped forward and, rather than using the end of his stun baton to subdue the wannabe action star, simply hit him around the head with it.

"Hey!" The shout came from someone who had accidentally swallowed a Meryl Streep. "That is brutality."

The guard pointed the stun baton at the man. "Stay out of this."

"We will stand on principle," Meryl Streep man said. "We will stand against this brutality."

"Who do you people think you are?!" Devin Frost shouted from the stage, his frustration evident. "Get out of the way!"

"I think I'm Meryl Streep," Meryl Streep man said, then shouted, "And I am a righteous bitch!" He sprang forward and slammed a punch into the guard's stomach before he could react. As the guard buckled over Meryl jumped, spinning in the air and landing a roundhouse kick to the side of his head, sending his helmet flying. The other guards reacted by lashing out with their batons. In response, more people in the crowd threw themselves forward, even those not possessed by the belief that they were action stars.

With her improvised distraction proving more effective than

she'd even hoped, Junker ran up the steps between the rows of theatre seats towards the exit. She shoved her communication earbud in as she ran.

"Captain," she said, breathless and hurried. "Captain, this is Junker. I've been compromised. You'd better hurry!"

———

"Junker," Latroz said from where she was monitoring the situation inside the security room, "what is your situation?"

Latroz had tuned one of the monitors to the surveillance cameras in the theatre. She could see Devin Frost on the stage. In the crowd, a brawl had broken out in the front rows between several Frost Norton Security guards and concert-going patrons.

Junker's voice came over the comm. "You could say it's pretty gronking bad." She was sucking in air, huffing as if running. "I'm heading to the *Interstella* ready to extract, but I'll try to take them on a bit of a runaround."

"A chasing of the goose!" Greg said.

"Yes, Greg," Junker puffed. "A chasing of the goose."

"Captain Franklin and Agent Mudd," Gentrix said, "you need to grab the prototype and the plans and get out of there now. The time line for extraction has moved up."

"Copy," Iridius said over the comm. "I heard Junker. We're in the vault. Searching for the prototype now."

Just as Iridius finished his transmission, another voice came over a speaker in the security room. "Security room, this is CEO Frost. There's a situation in the concert hall. Have you sent backup? I need you to find a woman dressed as DJ Chromium and check the Federation crew members in the holding cell. I think it's one of them. Security reset on all levels."

Without hesitation Gentrix held down the button to respond. "I don't think I'll be doing that, Devin."

"Gentrix?" Devin's voice was surprised, and then immediately angry. "What do you think you're doing? Trying to have me killed again so you can run things?"

"Oh please, Devin, you giant baby. You've been trying to kill me since you were like thirteen. Anyway, killing you isn't the point, and I don't care about running the company. The point is to stop you from erasing billions of lives in the galaxy's biggest moment of revisionist history."

"Wait," Devin said, "you're working with the Federation? You hate them as much as anyone."

"I hate war, Devin," Gentrix said. "I thought having the temporal reversal bomb would act as a deterrent, but if you use it on Earth you're no better than any warmonger throughout history, Federation or otherwise. I thought you'd see reason, but obviously I was wrong. So perhaps it's best if you don't have the bomb."

"And what are you—" Devin said before stopping. "What do you mean they're gone?!" He was talking to someone else. Gentrix glanced at the monitor in front of Latroz and saw a Frost Norton guard on stage with him. He was reporting something to Devin, and Gentrix had no doubt what it was – they'd finally discovered that the holding cell contained nothing but a holographic projection of the prisoners. "Where are they, Gentrix?" Devin said. "Are they in my vault?"

"Should I insult your intelligence by telling you I don't know what you're talking about?" Gentrix replied.

"You know, sister," Devin said, "it's quite amazing how easy it is to make people underestimate you. Sentient intelligence throughout the galaxy always want to think the best of themselves, and that usually means being quick to believe they're smarter, more cunning and generally better than anyone else they meet. You just have to give them a few examples of ineptitude, make it clear you might not understand some simple concepts, and they never think you're a threat. They think they'll always have your number."

"I don't need you to wax philosophical about the way you ensure everyone underestimates you. I already know you do that. I already know you aren't the idiotic geek you go around pretending to be."

"Oh, I know that," Devin said. "You're far too cunning yourself to fall for such a simple gambit. Besides, of everyone in the whole galaxy, how can I conceal my true self from my own sister? You know me too well. But that's the rub for you, isn't it? I have the better of most people as soon as they believe I'm an inattentive fanboy who just happened to inherit our father's corporation. They believe me undeserving and incompetent. As a result, it's easy to control them because they believe themselves too intelligent to be controlled by me. But with you, Gentrix, I needed to take a different tack. I needed you to know what I was doing with everyone else. I needed you to believe you were too intelligent to be controlled by me. And in doing so, you underestimated me the same as everyone else."

"What are you saying Devin?" Gentrix said. "Are you trying to tell me you've been playing me all along? On me, you're trying to play that?"

"I don't need to play that. It's the truth."

"Is that right, Devin? I don't think it is. I know all your little schemes. I control enough of Frost Norton to be told everything, including all the times you tried to go behind my back."

On the monitor, Devin Frost looked straight up at Gentrix in a way that was incredibly disconcerting, like he knew exactly which security feed she was watching and exactly where that camera was. He reached into his pocket and pulled out a small micro-tab, a miniaturised tablet computer. "If that was the case, you'd know about the secondary security system I have in the central tower, including the vault, and you'd have known to shut it down. Otherwise, when I press this button a full security breach will be generated inside the vault and your new Federation friend will get sent into space. My agent has already secured the package."

Gentrix felt her stomach drop as a flood of realisation hit her. Devin had said Federation friend, singular. She slammed her comm on. "Iridius, get out of there!"

Devin Frost pressed the button.

———

Iridius and Mudd had secured themselves to the wall with a magnetic tether line connected to a spool of thin but high tensile strength wire on the back of their maintenance suits. Again, these tethers were not meant for serious space walking, but were a common safety line for maintenance workers. The line would not provide any additional life support, but if something went wrong and you found yourself drifting off into space you were still connected to home and your corpse would float away into deep space as a perfectly preserved desiccated prune for all eternity.

Iridius and Mudd searched through the locker drawers that slid out from the large cylinder in the centre of the vault. There were lockers containing other prototype equipment, including a vial of something glowing blue labelled 'entropy-reversal anti-ageing cream', some kind of improved cleaning agent for food manufacture 3D printers, and several drawers containing Devin Frost's collection of voidball cards. Eventually, Iridius pulled open one of the lockers and found himself looking down at a metal canister about 800 millimetres long and 200 millimetres in diameter. It was labelled with the Frost Norton logo, and had a symbol similar to that used on hazardous materials, but this one had a small diagrammatic representation of an atom, a nucleus surrounded by three whizzing electrons leaving a trail. This was not at all scientifically accurate, but had long ago become the accepted symbol for quantum physics. Iridius looked down at it. There were some coiled wires at one end and a small display panel that was currently off. It certainly looked bomb-ish.

"I think I've found it," Iridius said.

Mudd hurried over. "Yep," he said. "That matches the description I've been given." He pulled open the next locker. "Here's a datavault with an access port. Just as the intel said. This'll be the plans." He passed Iridius a small drive. "Plug this in, it's set to automatically extract the data and then corrupt the vault. It should only take a couple of seconds."

Iridius took the drive and plugged it in while Mudd unclipped the prototype time bomb from the other locker, placing it inside one of the bags they'd carried the maintenance suits in. The drive blinked with a green light and Iridius pulled it out and dropped it into the bag Mudd held. Mudd zipped up the bag and slipped it onto his back.

"Alright," Iridius said, "that's the prototype bomb and the plans. Enough to put the Alliance back a bit and give the Federation a chance to catch up and build a deterrent of our own. Let's get out of here."

But Mudd didn't reply. Iridius saw his mouth moving, but no sound came across their comm line. They were supposed to be on a suit-to-suit open channel. They must have had a malfunction.

"Hang on," Iridius said out of habit, even though he knew Mudd probably couldn't hear him. "I'm going to reboot my comm." He looked at Mudd and tapped the side of his helmet where his ear would be, a common signal to indicate you were experiencing communication issues. Mudd should take that as an indication to reboot his comm system too. But Mudd didn't do anything. He didn't move. He just watched Iridius, and the way he was looking at him gave Iridius a rush of concern, that sudden flooding gush of panic like when you realise you've left your wallet behind.

"The comm is fine, Captain Franklin," Mudd said. "I was just talking to someone else."

"Right," Iridius said, hesitating. "And who were you talking to exactly?"

Mudd said nothing.

"What's going on, Mudd?" Iridius said, a question he didn't really expect an answer to, and one he didn't really need to ask, because he already knew the answer, even if he didn't know the specifics. Mudd was betraying him. One way or another, for one reason or another, Iridius was being blindsided.

Mudd shrugged. "Just playing my role."

Iridius already knew he was knee-deep in the shit, and could sense that things were about to get even thicker, so it only came as a partial surprise when Gentrix Frost's voice burst onto his comm line. "Iridius, get out of there!" The surprise was not that Iridius was about to be neck deep in stinking betrayal, it was that apparently Gentrix had absolutely nothing to do with it.

When Iridius looked at him again, Mudd, who'd also heard Gentrix's warning, had a disgustingly self-satisfied smile on his face. Mudd grabbed hold of the handle of one of the storage lockers with both hands, bracing himself hard against it. In that moment Iridius knew exactly what was going to happen. He was too far away to grab hold of anything. He opened his mouth to give Mudd a spray, but before he even got the first syllable into telling him he was a no-good two-faced piece of the sentient excrement left behind by Azlonian mega-wombats, the floor fell into space.

Through his helmet, Iridius heard the eruption of explosive bolts all the way around the diameter of the vault. The room reverberated with a cascade of small detonations along the base of the walls. Iridius tried to run, but before he could take more than a step, the floor beneath him was ripped away into space. He heard the roar of explosive decompression as the atmosphere inside the vault was sucked out into space in a rapid and ultimately pointless attempt to equalise pressure across the entire universe. The sound lasted only a fraction of a second before the oppressive silence of vacuum took over.

Iridius was falling. Well, actually, he was tumbling out into space with no real downward vector anymore, but the floor had been the last thing he'd considered 'down', so being shot out into space in that direction was as good as falling. He heard his breath, fast and frantic inside his helmet as he spun, catching sight of Mudd holding tight to the locker handles back inside the vault. The tether holding Iridius to the inside of the vault was unwinding rapidly from the spool on the back of his suit. After a few seconds of wild freefall, the 30 metres of tether line ran out and sprung taught. Iridius grunted as he came to a jolting stop and the recoil sent him floating back the other way, if a lot slower than before.

Iridius instinctively kicked his legs and waved his arms, but with no medium to swim through all this did was make him look even more like a flopping fish hanging from a line. Eventually the tether line grew slack enough that as he floated around, he could grab it. He pulled himself, hand over hand, along the tether line so that he faced the vault, then began manoeuvring his way back.

Mudd was still inside the vault, looking at him.

"So, I don't suppose you're going to pull me in then, are you Mudd?" Iridius said.

"No," Mudd's voice came over the comm line. "I don't suppose I am."

"Who are you working for? Devin Frost?" Iridius asked as he continue to pull himself back towards the gaping hole in the bottom of the ASS.

"You're really not very good at this if you need to ask that,"

Mudd said. "Of course it's Devin Frost. I've been a Federation Agent for twenty years, and a double-agent for the Alliance for about eighteen of those. The plan was always for my team to be captured, giving the Alliance justification to retaliate. We certainly had to adjust things when you and your meddling crew got involved and Gentrix decided to grow a conscience, but things have worked out in the end. Devin Frost is still going to get to have his cake, and the Federation will have to eat it."

"Weren't you born on Earth, Mudd?" Iridius said. "If Frost has his way you'll be erased from existence."

"You don't understand much about the science, do you?"

"No," Iridius said. "I understand fuck you, that's what I understand."

"Frost has assured me I'll remain within the temporal displacement field when he eventually gets to Earth. My timeline will continue just fine."

Iridius continued pulling himself in. He was only a quarter of the way there. He watched Mudd move towards the spot where his tether was magnetically secured to the wall. "Don't you do it, Mudd," he said.

"Just look on the bright side, Captain Franklin," Mudd said as he reached down and grabbed the tether. He switched off the mag-lock on the end and then held it up to show Iridius. The only thing connecting him to the space station was now in the hands of his betrayer. "Once Devin Frost has rewritten history, you being left to float away into space and die probably won't happen anymore."

Mudd threw the end of the tether out into space, casting Iridius hopelessly adrift.

CHAPTER NINETEEN

SECONDS after the vault floor was blasted off into space, and even before Iridius had been sent adrift, Gentrix was already in motion.

"Let's move," she said, bending over and taking a pistol from one of the fallen guards. "Both of you grab a weapon and stay together. We need to get to the space port." She turned back. Greg and Latroz hesitated.

"What about Captain Franklin?" Latroz said. "Why should we be taking orders from you?"

Gentrix flicked the monitor in front of them from the chaotic scene Junker had left behind in the theatre to an outside view of the space station, looking down the length of the central spire. The floor of the vault could be seen tumbling end over end off into space, or at least falling down towards Lentrani II, where it would eventually be gravitationally captured and burn up in what little atmosphere the planet had. More importantly, there, harder to see because it was a lot smaller but obvious nonetheless, was the shape of a person in a bright orange maintenance suit dangling from a tether line. A tether that they could see had been disconnected.

"Maybe that is Agent Mudd and not Captain Franklin," Greg said with trademark optimism.

A crackling communication came over their headsets, the sound of short-range radio battling through interference, cutting in and out as it drifted out of range. "God damn gronking Jupiter's nuts," could be made out through static and drop-outs. "Gronking shitting fucker cut me loose. Can you—" But that was all that could be made out.

"Alright," Greg said. "So it is Captain Franklin."

"That puts me in command of the away team," Latroz said. "You are not in command of us, Gentrix Frost."

Gentrix jumped on her comm. "This is COO Frost, all forces execute Operation Exodus. I want the *Interstella* clear to leave immediately when I arrive with two others. Consider all other Frost Norton Security Force members as hostile. I'm getting off the station. Clear a path."

Behind her, the door to the room opened. Gentrix spun. Two uniformed Frost Norton guards were standing in the doorway.

"Miss Frost, you are under—"

Gentrix lifted the pistol and fired. Two shots. One into the chest of each guard. At first it looked like she had simply and far too nonchalantly shot and killed two of her own employees. Even if they had been loyal to her brother, that still seemed a little much. As they shook and then dropped to the ground it became clear she had switched the pistol to fire electro-stun rounds. Each pistol could only fire six of these rounds before requiring a reload.

Gentrix turned to look at Latroz. "I said, let's go."

She glared at Latroz with an intensity that was matched only by the fury of a Siruan Battle Warden. Every young Siruan girl spends seven years being educated in the ways of war and battle, and it was the Siruan Battle Wardens who were responsible for that training, ancient warriors who had proved themselves in countless conflicts and spent the remainder of their lives heartlessly and brutally shaping the warriors of the future. Latroz had seen only one other creature with a glare as ruthlessly cutting as that of a Battle Warden, and that was Greg's mother-in-law – and now, perhaps, Gentrix Frost.

Latroz turned to Greg. "I believe we should go with Miss Frost."

Greg nodded. He looked at Gentrix. "I will not carry a weapon though, Miss Frost. It is against everything my strain be—"

"Fine," Gentrix said, cutting him off. "I don't care why. Let's go."

As the three of them headed out into the corridor and began running down it, an alarm began blaring. Three long whooping blasts followed by an electronic voice. "This facility is entering lockdown. Return to your homes or shelter in place."

Up ahead, they could hear the sound of distant gunfire.

"Inform me of the tactical situation please, Miss Frost," Latroz said as they moved.

"I've long had an exfiltration plan in place," Gentrix said. "For if things ever went, well, like they just have. My people will start an all-out battle to allow me time to get off station, then they will attempt to either take control of the facility or, should that prove untenable, abandon station. I have an account ready to distribute money to all of them. They will be rewarded for their assistance."

As they continued, the sound of gunfire increased in volume until they emerged onto one of the wider faux-streets of the central spire. Two groups of Frost Norton Security guards were engaged in a firefight across the street. Full assault rifle fire was criss-crossing the open space, ending in shattering sprays of glass and cracking thuds into walls. Latroz's eyes lit up at the sight of war. Greg's lit up as well, but for the opposite reason.

"That does not appear to be a wise activity inside a space station," Greg said.

"It is glorious," Latroz muttered.

"We aren't getting involved," Gentrix said, realising that Latroz badly wanted to get involved. "It's all a distraction for us to get out of here. Come on."

"How do you tell which side is which?" Greg asked as Gentrix led them off down a side street. "They are all wearing the same uniforms."

"My people know who's who," Gentrix said. "Besides, that makes it a more effective distraction. Just consider anyone who shoots at you to be on the other team."

A whistling sound cut through the air, followed by another and another, then bullets pinged into a nearby wall. Latroz, sensing the dangers of battle faster than any of them, shoved Gentrix with one arm and Greg with the other, all but launching them down another side alley. She spun, pulled the pistol she'd taken from one of the guards in the security control room and fired back a few suppressing shots, giving her time to back into the alley as well. Her shots reverberated with loud cracks. Latroz clearly had no intention of switching her pistol to stun.

"You see?" Gentrix said. "Just like that. This way, into the maintenance tunnels."

Gentrix hurried ahead, Greg following closely behind, but Latroz didn't follow.

"I will cover your escape," she said. "You get back to the *Interstella*."

"No," Gentrix said. "I might not know your Captain Franklin all that well, but I can already tell he'd kill me if I let you do that."

Latroz didn't move.

"Lieutenant," Greg said, "we need you with us. I know you want to fight, but sometimes you need to challenge your nature. Besides, Lieutenant Rangi is waiting for you."

Latroz didn't move.

"Lieutenant, please," Greg said. "It's your instincts as a Siruan telling you to stay behind and fight but your crew need you. You're more than a Siruan fighting machine to us."

Latroz looked at Greg. She took a moment of consideration and then nodded, moving after them. Gentrix led them to another of the maintenance entrances that were scattered throughout the station. They wound their way through the tight spaces behind the scenes of the central spire, twisting tunnels of pipes and wiring looms lit by dim orange lights.

"Getting from the central spire to the outer ring will be the issue," Gentrix said, ducking under a crossbeam of pipework. "There are only four access tunnels, and I'm sure they'll already be guarded. My people can get us from the other end to the space port, but the central spire is mostly Devin's turf. Getting into a tunnel will be a challenge."

The maintenance tunnels led them most of the way. It wasn't a direct route, they were forced to weave their way along the access tunnels between major power hub locations and life support systems, but eventually they emerged near the entrance to tunnel two. This was not the major access tunnel between the outer ring and central spire, but a less commonly used one, which Gentrix hoped meant it wouldn't be as well-guarded. As she stopped and peered around the corner towards the entrance to the tunnel, Gentrix saw that it *was* less well-guarded – less well-guarded than, say, the Kondoplarian Galactic Museum of Priceless Artifacts.

Gentrix turned back to the others. "There's eight guards at the entrance."

"Armed?" Latroz asked.

Gentrix nodded. "Rifles."

"I will have a look," Latroz said, moving to the corner and taking a moment to recon the guards at the tunnel entrance. She turned back to the others. "Down there." She pointed to a small side alleyway. "We hide."

The three of them moved to the alleyway.

"Alright," Gentrix said when they were tucked away with their backs to the wall. "I suppose you have a plan?"

"Growing up, all Siruans must participate in hours and hours of simulated virtual reality combat," Latroz said. "There were always situations where one must sneak past multiple guards, and it was often the correct approach to use a distraction. Large groups of guards always send one or two to investigate, a number easily overcome. We can then use their weapons against our remaining foes."

"Video games?" Gentrix said. "You're talking about video games?"

Latroz looked at Gentrix with a blank expression. "I have never played a game in my life. I am speaking of virtual reality combat in which one must overcome enemies to reach an end objective."

"Sounds like video games," Gentrix said.

Latroz didn't respond. Instead, she fired her pistol into the air. The round cracked against the roof.

"Huh? What was that?" they heard one of the guards say. "I heard something."

Latroz closed her eyes, tuning in her heightened Siruan senses.

"Probably just the wind."

"I better check it out."

"You two, go and have a look."

Two of the guards did exactly as Latroz had anticipated and made their way around the corner towards the alleyway where Latroz, Gentrix and Greg were hiding.

"Probably just the wind?" Gentrix whispered. "What fucking wind? We're on a space station."

"I told you," Latroz whispered back. "Just like a simulation."

As the two guards approached the entrance to the alleyway, Latroz launched out at them like some massive purple crocodile exploding out of the water. She grabbed one guard, wrapping herself around him, her hand planted firmly over his mouth to stop him calling out. She fired her pistol at the other one but, in a very unSiruan move, she had switched the pistol to fire stun rounds, which were much quieter than normal rounds. So actually, it was completely in keeping with the Siruan way, because it was the tactically superior move. The stunned guard dropped in a floppy mess while Latroz held the other one in a choke hold until he too collapsed to the ground.

"Huh," Gentrix said. "You didn't kill them."

Latroz let out a little growl. "Sometimes you need to challenge your nature, I suppose. Killing your enemy is more efficient, but I understand it is sometimes frowned upon." She picked up one of the guards' rifles and passed it to Gentrix, then grabbed the other herself. "These do not have a stun setting," she said to Gentrix. "So, I may not have a choice in the next phase."

Gentrix nodded. "I understand that."

"We attack then. There is no cover. I will fire for suppression. Follow after, and attempt to fire for effect."

Latroz rounded the corner and moved with speed towards the tunnel entrance. She opened fire with the assault rifle and rounds peppered the wall, pinging off the tunnel entrance. She fired wildly, but deliberately. Her shots sprayed in a wide pattern, covering the area, driving the guards back. With no time to react, three of the guards dropped immediately. The remaining three stumbled back, but raised their rifles and began firing. Their shots were wild too, but not with Latroz's calculated precision. Their rounds ricocheted off the roof and walls with desperate abandon.

Gentrix moved up behind Latroz and fired more purposefully, dropping one of the remaining guards. Latroz brought her aim to one of the others, felling him. This left only one guard, but as Latroz drew closer he managed, even under the intense pressure of two approaching assault rifles, to score a hit. The bullet struck Latroz in the shoulder, ripping through her natural carapace armour which, though extraordinarily strong for an organic body part, could not withstand an assault rifle round. Latroz roared in pain and fell, and her rifle and pistol spun away on the hard floor.

Gentrix immediately dropped to the ground, landing hard, and heard the crack-whistle of bullets passing just over her head. She hadn't been hit, but with Latroz down she knew she had become the target. She raised her rifle, knowing the guard would already be bringing his sights down to where she lay. As she looked, she saw it was too late. The guard's assault rifle was already pointed directly at her.

But before the guard could fire again, he started shaking violently. It took Gentrix a moment to realise that he'd been hit with a stun round. She looked to the side and saw Greg, with Latroz's dropped pistol in his hand and a look somewhere between determination and horror on his face. After a moment he dropped the pistol and wiped his hands on his clothing, as if he'd been handling some creepy-crawly that freaked him out.

"Greg," Latroz said as she rolled over and sat up, grimacing against the pain. Her shoulder had been torn open, a mess of shattered purple carapace and dark red blood, and her right arm hung limply at her side. "You used a weapon."

Greg looked from Latroz to Gentrix and then back again. "You were going to get shot," he said. "I could not allow my crewmates to get shot." He looked shook. "I needed to challenge my nature, too."

"Thank you," Gentrix said. "You've both saved my life now. Let's get out of here before you need to do it again."

Gentrix and Greg helped Latroz to her feet and the three of

CHAPTER TWENTY_

WELL, this was shit.

That was about the only way Iridius could sum it up as he tumbled through space. He was turning slowly, end over end, head over feet. The enormous shape of ASS Locke would appear in his vision, lights shining against the dark shape of Lentrani II, and then he'd continue spinning, revealing the empty forever of space. Locke Station. Space. Locke Station. Space. Each time he tumbled back over to face Locke Station, it was a little further away.

Iridius followed his training, trying to avoid watching everything in the far distance spinning around him. That was a surefire way to fill a space suit with vomit which, he knew from personal experience, was very unpleasant. He orientated himself by watching the HUD on his helmet. A maintenance suit like this had only the most basic of heads-up displays, showing suit pressure and remaining oxygen levels. Still, this was enough to inform him that things were going to go from shit to gronking shit very soon – in eighteen minutes, in fact, if his air supply read-out was accurate.

Despite trying not to look at the station whenever it came

into view, both to avoid motion sickness and also because that station had proven itself a pain in his ASS, Iridius still noticed the flash of movement as a ship roared out of one of the landing bays. Even from the brief glimpse he got, it was obvious which ship it was. The flashing lights, pulsating through every colour of the rainbow and possibly a few that weren't part of the rainbow at all, revealed it as the *Interstella*.

Iridius had no idea whether that was his away team managing to make a drastic escape or if it was DJ Chromium getting away. The *Interstella* flew out of Locke Station at high speed, which didn't really tell him much, but it looked to be heading away into space, which wasn't a good sign. He'd hoped that if it was his crew, they might have come and collected him – if they even knew where he was. Surely these suits have some sort of automatically activated distress beacon? Then again, maybe that was Federation thinking. The Alliance was all about money. Maybe a single maintenance worker wasn't worth the cost of an emergency beacon to them. Iridius soon lost sight of the *Interstella* as he rotated over again.

Sixteen minutes of air left. What did one do while waiting to die? Iridius felt surprisingly calm. Maybe it was because most of the other times he'd nearly died had been a lot more hectic. Over the years he'd survived floods of excrement, numerous spaceship malfunctions, killer toy dogs, a battle for the galaxy and long-tongued alien assassins. He'd honestly thought it would be some chaotic fight or chase scene that would see him die in a single moment, one that would take him by surprise, but instead he was going to float away into space and slowly asphyxiate. That was such a boringly normal way to die in space. Nonetheless, it was kind of peaceful.

Turning back towards the station again he saw the colourful lights of the *Interstella* again. They were distant now, perhaps far enough away that at any minute the ship would be enveloped by the bubble universe of a BAMF drive and vanish, leaving the annoyed universe to rapidly fill in the hole left behind in reality. It didn't vanish though. Instead, it appeared to be stationary. It was difficult to tell at this distance though, and Iridius soon lost sight of it.

For five more minutes nothing remarkable happened. He continued floating in the same rotation he would likely experience for all eternity, or at least until Devin Frost changed the past. But then Iridius felt a twinge in his leg. One point of his quad muscle vibrated, rapidly twitching of its own accord. This was followed by a similar fasciculation in his bicep, then his calf and even his tongue decided to buzz. It hadn't happened for months, but the feeling was immediately familiar. His nanobots were activating.

"Oh," he said, his voice echoing in the stuffy confines of his helmet, "now you decide to wake up, do you? Bit gronking late. What am I supposed to use you for now?"

Iridius's annoyance was quickly overshadowed by concern as the buzzing and twitching of his muscles was joined by an electric jolt in his head – that was new. When it passed, what was left was a feeling Iridius could only describe as a heaviness, something like having your skull jammed full of steel wool. That, and the none-too-subtle existential dread that had settled on him. Surprisingly, given his current situation, it wasn't a sense of dread for himself, it was for everything, the entire galaxy. There was something coming. It was something massive – no, that didn't even do it justice. It was something so cosmically enormous that solar systems felt like scattered marbles. Something that overwhelmed him with enough horror that he thought he might piss his bright orange maintenance suit if he continued to dwell on it, despite not even knowing what it was. But that wasn't true, was it? He knew, deep within himself – or at least his nanobots knew – that it was the Synth-Hastur. The threat that all but a few had tried to ignore was making its approach into the Milky Way, and Iridius understood immediately that he'd been wrong to ever dismiss it. This was a threat beyond anything imaginable, beyond nanobots and time bombs, beyond human comprehension, and now he was going to die having been unceremoniously dropped out of an ASS and he wouldn't have a chance to warn anyone.

Some five head over feet flips later, when Iridius's 'oxygen remaining' display ticked down to four minutes left, he still could not shake the feeling of unease that had settled on him. His nanobots had not only awoken, they'd gone altogether batshit. He tried to ignore the hyperactivity of his muscles, and also tried – although this was far more difficult – to ignore the feeling of the Synth-Hastur encroaching on the edge of the galaxy like a thick black fog. Iridius saw the *Interstella* in the distance flashing irreverently against the black before being suddenly replaced by a flash of light and a disconcerting but rapidly filled-in hole in space. Iridius burped against his rising nausea. Whoever had been on that ship had gone now, but what had taken them so long? The answer became clear as the space directly in front of him shimmered. It resolved into a long, triangular starship, painted grey with white lines darting back along its length. Its name was stencilled on the side, its beautiful, beautiful name: *FSC Deus Ex.*

And Iridius slammed straight into it.

He bounced off at an oblique angle, but didn't float far because a side hatch opened and a figure in a Federation EVA suit emerged, using small thruster bursts to fly to Iridius and grab him. The darkened faceplate slid up to reveal Junker smiling behind the helmet. She winked at him and then fired a thruster burst to take them home.

Inside, as the airlock equalised, Iridius pulled off his helmet.

"You been slackin' off out there, Cap?" Junker said. "Takin' a little pleasure float?"

He looked down at the display on his wrist and then up at Junker. "I still had two minutes of air left. You could've made it much more dramatic."

"Glad to have you back," Junker said. "Everyone is on the bridge."

When Iridius walked onto the bridge of the *Deus Ex* the crew were, just as Junker had said, thankfully all there. He noticed Latroz had her arm in a sling, her shoulder covered in a hard healing-promoting cast.

"More than a scratch this time? Iridius asked.

"A graze," Latroz said.

"Welcome back, Captain." Quinn stood up from where she sat in the captain's chair. "You have the conn."

"Thank you, Quinn," Iridius said. "Also, you were right. Let's get that out of the way."

"I know."

"About more than just my recklessness with this mission, too," Iridius continued. "The Synth-Hastur are real."

Quinn's eyes went wide. "You've confirmed it. How?"

"My nanobots seem to know."

"They're working again?" Rangi asked from where he sat at the helm.

"Apparently."

"Bit late," Rangi said.

"That's what I said."

"The crew of the *Interstella* have already taken their ship and will be returning to the Federation Intelligence Bureau with a full report on Agent Mudd's betrayal," Quinn said. "What are your orders?"

Iridius sat in the captain's chair and looked around. The only thing out of place on the bridge was the surprising sight of one Gentrix Frost standing and watching at him.

"First, what are you doing here?" Iridius asked.

"I pulled out," Gentrix said.

"That's what he said," Iridius immediately responded.

Gentrix cocked an eyebrow and smiled. "I have extracted myself from the Frost Norton Corporation and cannot help but think my time with the Alliance is at an end. My brother will see to that. I haven't got anywhere else to go. I was hoping I could tag along."

"As an Alliance spy?" Iridius asked. "Not a job position we need filled."

"I was hoping I'd proved myself trustworthy to you by now," Gentrix said.

Iridius nodded. "You have. Welcome aboard, Miss Frost."

"There's a ship leaving Locke Station," Latroz called out from the tactical station. "Small frigate, standard Alliance type. It's headed away bearing one nine three."

"It's Devin," Gentrix said. "That's his ship, the *Neverlander*. He'll have the temporal reversal bomb."

"They're initiating BAMF," Latroz said.

Iridius instinctively reached for his nanobots to try and stop them but he was a fraction of a second too late.

"They're gone," Latroz said.

Iridius was quiet for a moment. "So, let me spell this out. We've got a sociopathic Alliance CEO on the way to Earth with a time-reversing bomb, and meanwhile the most terrifying thing in existence has just entered the galaxy ready to destroy literally everything, and I've got to decide what to do?"

"A good summary, yes, Captain," Quinn said.

Iridius took a moment. This was it again. The burden of command.

"Rangi," Iridius said, "BAMF us to Earth. We stop Frost first. Then we worry about the Synth-Hastur – whatever that actually is."

CHAPTER TWENTY-ONE

IRIDIUS STARED out the dark-tinted window of his cabin, not that he could see anything other than his own reflection in the glass. The *Deus Ex* was in BAMF transit, tucked within its temporary bubble universe and cheating its way around relativity as it moved towards Earth. The windows of every spaceship automatically tinted when travelling FTL to avoid the potential corneal flash burn that could occur if anyone was unfortunate enough to catch a glimpse of the extreme white light as cosmic background radiation was brought into the visible spectrum. This was a phenomenon that only happened faster than light, and was more pronounced with higher speeds. And the *Deus Ex* was certainly travelling at high speed. Taken relative to the prime universe, actual reality, the ship was moving at six thousand times the speed of light, some six and a half trillion kilometres per hour, which is pretty fast by just about anyone's standards. At that moment, however, it was not fast enough for Iridius.

Devin Frost was aboard his ship, the *Neverlander,* in its own bubble universe somewhere slightly ahead of them, en route to destroy Earth a hundred and fifty years ago. Gentrix had assured them that the *Neverlander* was a standard Alliance fast frigate with a top speed almost identical to that of the *Deus Ex*, so at least Devin wouldn't be pulling any further ahead. Still, it was going to take almost twenty hours for them to reach Earth, and despite knowing it would take Frost the same amount of time, Iridius felt impatient. It felt like he was losing time to the enemy. The vast distances involved in space travel always meant there was a lot of time spent in transit, feeling helpless even though you were moving desperately fast. Iridius felt like Dorothy trying to run home but watching it move further away. The *Deus Ex* would arrive just after the *Neverlander*, and Iridius just had to hope he could drop a metaphorical house on the bad guy before he managed to do worse than any wicked witch ever had. Until then, there was nothing he could do but pace around his cabin and stare out the window at the hidden nothingness of a BAMF bubble.

Most of Iridius's restlessness was due to a desire to put an end to this, to do whatever he could to stop Devin Frost's maniacal plan, because he was ninety per cent confident he was the good guy here, and stopping the villain's evil scheme was what the good guy was supposed to do. But there was also a ten per cent chance that this was his fault. He felt a duty to intervene because maybe his shotgun attempt to sneak aboard Locke Station and steal the time reversal bomb had led directly to this new threat to billions of lives. He had thought he was doing the right thing, but then, as they say, the road to hell is paved with reckless attempts to save the day.

Still, Mark Mudd had betrayed them, not just Iridius and this crew but the entire Federation, and he would likely have done so whether Iridius had been there or not. According to Gentrix it had always been her brother's plan to arrange some complicated incident with a Federation spy in order to provide the political justification to strike at Earth with the time reversal bomb. Iridius getting involved hadn't escalated anything. In fact, even Quinn had admitted that just as the Aegix would have found a way off Iota Persei E with or without Iridius's help, it was likely Devin Frost would have attempted this anyway. All they could say for certain was that Iridius had managed, with trademark reckless abandon, to once again put himself in a position where he might be able to help. That was some consolation to Iridius, but he had set out to prevent the Alliance from deploying that weapon against the Federation and he had failed, crazy CEO with a rogue secret-agent DJ or not. Perhaps, as much as he wanted to be an adventuring space captain, it was time to admit he was doing more harm than good.

All this reflection on his latest misadventure was being compounded by his continuing feeling of utter doom. The sense of foreboding that had settled over him while drifting in space had not let up. There was no doubt about it, this feeling of dread was coming from his nanobots. They had emerged from their apparent stubborn stasis to tell him in no uncertain terms that the Synth-Hastur were here and that it was time to be afraid, because maybe if you were afraid, you idiots might actually do something. He should have believed Quinn. Of course he should have believed Quinn, she was a genius and he – apparently like most people in the Federation chain of command – was a knucklehead. They should have acted earlier, he knew that now, and he would see that action was taken even if he had to smash down the doors of the Federation Senate to get them off their arses. The Aegix had caused widespread devastation, but it turned out it *had* been trying to do the right thing. Huh, Iridius realised, he and the Aegix were the same. Both blundering forward with a view on the right thing but leaving disaster in their wake. For the record though, Iridius was just a loose cannon. The Aegix was proper batshit crazy.

A knock on his door pulled Iridius away from the window. That was strange. If anyone wanted him they'd usually just call him over the comm. The only person who might knock on his door was Quinn, but she was supposed to be on the bridge as Officer of the Watch. Despite having been in command of the ship the entire time he'd been gone, she insisted he was the one who needed some rest. She never seemed to need much downtime – maybe he should check whether she was actually an android like Hal.

Iridius walked to the door. Hopefully she didn't want to talk about leaving the ship, because he hadn't quite worked out how he was going to convince her to stay yet, and whenever he knew a conversation was going to get emotional, which he was sure that one would, Iridius liked to be well prepared with a point he needed to make, so he could push through the emotion without it making him all gooey and gross. That said, there weren't many topics of conversation Quinn would want to engage in that he felt like dealing with at the moment. The Aegix, the Synth-Hastur or the fact that his nanobots had woken up and were going crazy were all things he knew Quinn was dying to poke and prod him about. He'd hoped to avoid any of that until at least after they'd dealt with Frost.

He'd already started speaking before he opened the door. "You know you were the one who told me to rest." But he stopped. It was not Lieutenant Commander Quinn at the door. It was Gentrix Frost. "Sorry," Iridius said. "I thought you were Quinn."

"No, not Quinn," Gentrix said as she entered Iridius's cabin without being asked, sliding past him. "I like her though. There's a lot more going on in that brain than she lets on. You might need to help boost her confidence though."

"I tried that," Iridius said. "It wasn't the right approach. She's fine the way she is."

Gentrix turned back. "Meek?"

"Thoughtful. Measured. Not reckless."

Gentrix considered him for a moment. "Fair enough." She looked around the space. The *Deus Ex* was a small ship and there wasn't much space for large quarters, even for the captain. Iridius's room was only about the size of a dorm room, although admittedly it was the dorm room that someone down the hall lucked out and got, that was always bigger than yours and maybe had room for a couch along with the desk and bed.

"You Federation types really take the socialism to heart in the bedroom, don't you?"

"I'm not sure how I'm supposed to interpret that?" Iridius said.

"I mean, it's sparse in here."

Iridius shrugged. "It's everything I need."

"Is it though?"

"What is it you want exactly, Miss Frost?" Iridius asked, feeling like he'd had enough of the games played by the Frost family.

"Please, Iridius, it's Gentrix – no need for the formalities. I came by because I wanted to thank you. In all the chaos on the station I never had a chance to thank you for saving my life."

"You did thank me," Iridius said. "And I don't need thanks, anyway. I already told you. The Federation Space Command helps people. I don't know what happened in the Federation–Alliance war and I may not know all the motivations of those above me, but I know what I believe the Federation stands for, and that is helping people, no matter who they are." Iridius paused, then added, "Except for your brother, and maybe not the Grantakians now. They can sod off."

Gentrix smiled. She moved close to Iridius, placed her hand on his chest. "I'd still like to thank you," she said. "I told you that's why I came by, and in case you haven't noticed yet, I'm not meek."

Gentrix leaned forward; she was almost the same height as

Iridius. She didn't hesitate, and Iridius was all but caught off-guard. By the time his brain caught up with the reality of what was going on, Gentrix's lips were against his and it felt good, really good. She slid her hand around the back of his head, entwined her fingers in his hair. This was when his brain caught up with reality, and he quickly pulled away.

"Stop," Iridius said. "Wait. You don't have to thank me like that."

"I know," Gentrix said. "That was just an excuse to get into your bedroom." She moved forward again but Iridius leaned back. She looked at him, her smoky eyes full of desire, but also now a touch of confusion. Why did he constantly find the need to stop beautiful women from kissing him? In that moment it seemed dumber than usual. "You don't want to?" Gentrix asked.

"No, I mean yes, I mean, it's not that," Iridius said. "It's just, I'm not sure it's the best idea."

"I'm not part of your crew," Gentrix said. "And I know you're attracted to me." She pushed her body into his suggestively. "I can feel it. So, what? Is there someone else?"

Iridius's mind turned to April, and to whoever the fuck Teth was. Was that it? Was he denying himself this because of April? She'd moved on. Why shouldn't he?

"No," Iridius said. "There's no one else. It's just, I'm the captain of this ship. I have responsibilities."

"Doesn't that get lonely," Gentrix said, "being in a relationship with just your ship? Being alone out here in the black?"

Iridius nodded. "Yeah," he said, surprising himself with his honesty. "It does. I said that to someone once. That it was difficult being alone as the leader."

"Yes, it is." Gentrix looked at him with sincerity. "I know that feeling, you know." She paused. "I find it difficult being vulnerable, Iridius Franklin. I might come across as a femme fatale but the truth is, I'm lonely too. I have been for a long time."

"Well, if we're being honest..." Iridius took a breath. "I might try and be the swashbuckling space captain, but I don't feel the need to sleep with every woman I come across. I'm not interested in being lured in one time by your feminine wiles. I want something meaningful."

Gentrix stared at him, and Iridius was certain he could just about see the layer of ice that encased her melting away. "Okay then, Iridius B. Franklin, let's start again. I'd like to spend some time with you, get to know you better."

Iridius smiled. "I'd like that."

Gentrix moved in close to him again. "Can we still have sex?"

"I'd like that too."

Iridius leaned in this time and they kissed long and passionately. Gentrix pushed him towards the bed until they fell back onto it, Gentrix heavy on top of him, but then she stopped, and pushed herself up to hover over him. "By the way, what does the B stand for?"

Iridius just smiled and pulled her back down.

CHAPTER TWENTY-TWO_

As the FSC *Deus Ex* was BAMFing its way to Earth, Captain Iridius B. Franklin was, at least for a short while (but hopefully not too short, even though he was out of practice) managing to forget the overwhelming feeling that something very bad was coming.

Unfortunately, some seven hundred and sixteen thousand light years away, a species that had yet to make contact with any other space-faring race was coming face to face with that something very bad. The Woontranki were mostly humanoid, very similar in appearance to Earth's orangutans but with an extra pair of limbs. They had reached the point in their technological development where they understood orbital mechanics well enough and had access to powerful enough rocket engines to take those first steps off their homeworld and into the expanse of the galaxy.

Like a child learning to crawl and then to walk and then to run, every culture that reaches the technological level required to become space-faring experiences several historical moments that are long remembered. There was the first of their species in space, the first to set foot on another moon or planet, first contact with another species, first interstellar war, and the first hamburger store on their homeworld (side note: several historians strongly believe the hamburger is what cemented humanity's place as a dominant force in the Federation). For the Woontranki, this was just such a historical moment. Only hours ago, a small, single seat capsule had been blasted into space on the back of several solid-fuel rocket boosters. Inside was the first Woontranki astronaut, the first of their people ever to reach the threshold of space.

This astronaut's name was mostly unpronounceable in Galactic Standard Language – which you may have gathered by now was basically the same as Earth English. This, of course, was for reasons to do with the most common sounds able to be made by anatomy throughout the galaxy, and not at all to do with the arrogance of humanity or a convenient shortcut for a science-fiction author. Anyway, for our purposes the best phonetic approximation for the name of this unfortunate traveller was Kah Ren.

Kah Ren orbited her homeworld in wonder. Her flight was the accomplishment of hundreds of years of technological development, and she would be remembered in the historical record of the Woontranki for as long as their species existed. This was, as it turned out, only about another two minutes. Because Kah Ren was not only the first of the Woontranki in space, she was also going to be the first of her people to make contact with another race. It was just a shame that race would be the Devourers of the Stars, the Great Living Storm of Steel, the Lords of Interstellar Space, the Harbingers of Forever War, the Synth-Hastur. For the Woontranki this also meant their first contact with another species could technically be considered their first interstellar war, not that they had much of a chance to retaliate. It also meant, in a tragedy they'd never understand, the Woontranki would never get a hamburger store.

As Kah Ren rounded her planet on the beginning of the third

of her history-making orbits, she saw through the small window at the front of her capsule movement on an enormous scale. In fact, what Kah Ren saw was so enormous that it was entirely difficult to comprehend. A body as large as her planet was moving towards her and her homeworld. It was black, but a kind of opalescent black that stood out against the darkness of space. She communicated back to her equivalent of ground control.

To translate:

Kah Ren: "Uh, there's something out here."

Ground control: "We're picking it up on radar now. We thought it was a glitch. It just appeared from nowhere."

Kah Ren: "It's no glitch. It's...I don't know what it is. It's some sort of sphere. A planet or something."

Ground control: "It can't be a planet."

Kah Ren watched as the enormous cosmic black pearl that couldn't have been a planet continued moving soundlessly towards her. It shimmered with fractals of light that at first she thought were natural reflections, but then she saw that they were actually emanating from the sphere.

Kah Ren: "It's...it's beautiful."

And that's what she thought in the beginning. She thought it was beautiful, at least until it opened its mouth.

The sphere cracked and hinged open around the centre like a planet-sized Pac-man. There were no creatures on the Woon-tranki homeworld that had tentacles, so Kah Ren had no reference for what she was looking at. Inside the gaping maw of the planet-sized creature were tens of thousands of wriggling, lashing tentacles, each one large enough to envelop whole mountain ranges with suction cups made to secure the flicking appendages to the surface of an entire world.

A strange low-frequency sound filled Kah Ren's headset, like the resonating of the universe itself.

Kah Ren: "Ground control, do you read? It's opening."

But there was no reply, only the continuing sonic rumble that was barely audible through her headset.

"Are you trying to communicate with me?" Kah Ren asked, hoping that perhaps the thing could hear her. "Listen to me!"

The Synth-Hastur could hear her if it chose to, but it did not bother. That would be like a human trying to listen for the bacteria when they washed their hands. Kah Ren, the entire Woontranki species, every species of living creature on their homeworld, were given no thought or consideration.

"I demand to be addressed!" Kah Ren screamed into her headset. "I want to speak to whoever is in charge around here!"

The Synth-Hastur had opened so wide that its mouth could envelop the entirety of the Woontranki homeworld. Everything was on a scale so immensely huge that Kah Ren had difficulty comprehending what was going on. It was as if the universe was crushing in on them. For those on the ground, it must have seemed as if the sky itself had decided to bite down on them. Kah Ren screamed for ground control to respond. She screamed for the Synth-Hastur to respond. Soon, as it became clear this thing intended to eat her planet, she just screamed, and then sobbed, until her mind simply broke. It was not like being a boat on a vast ocean, it was like being a grain of sand dropped into the ocean, surrounded by it, dissolved in it until there was nothing else.

Kah Ren's small capsule was soon enveloped inside the mouth of the Synth-Hastur. The light she had seen and once thought beautiful was now a barrage of sensory overload as various colours flashed around her – blues and purples and greens. She had no idea what was going on anymore. She had no idea who or what she was anymore.

The Synth-Hastur's tentacles whipped out and slammed onto the planet, crushing forests and mountains and submerging through oceans until they struck the sea bed. It gripped the planet to pull it inside its mouth, where it would strip everything from its biosphere.

Kah Ren's tiny capsule would be crushed any moment, but before it did, she had one last thought about the outcome of space flight.

Well, this was shit.

CHAPTER TWENTY-THREE

PING.

Something at the edge of Iridius's perception pinged. It took a moment to orientate himself before he realised he must have dozed off, and that Gentrix Frost was lying curled up and naked under the tangled sheets beside him. Well, that had been an unexpected turn of events. Certainly not unwelcome, but in that moment Iridius was thankful that Gentrix was forward in her approach, because as much as he wanted to consider himself a brave space captain, he wouldn't have had the directness to make that advance. He might not have got the rest he probably needed, but it was worth it.

Gentrix's eyes opened. She smiled. She suddenly seemed light years away from the intimidating vixen he had first met on Locke Station.

Ping.

Ah. That's what had woken him. Iridius rolled over and hit the comm button beside his bed.

"Yes?"

"Sorry to wake you, Captain." Quinn's voice came over the comm. "You're needed on the bridge. We're five minutes out."

Iridius rubbed his face. "Five minutes out?" He felt a sudden rush that jolted him completely awake. Five minutes until they arrived at Earth to confront Devin Frost and his time bomb. "I thought I told you to call me up when we were twenty minutes out!"

"I know, Captain," Quinn said. "We have been trying to reach you."

Iridius grumbled, feeling annoyed but knowing it was entirely his fault. "Acknowledged. I'm on my way."

He climbed out of bed and began throwing on the nearest clothes he had to hand – the Frost Norton Security Force uniform, which was bundled in a pile on the floor. He probably should have put his FSC uniform on, but this was the closest thing, and he didn't have much time. He hopped on one foot as he pulled the black pants on and then grabbed the shirt, turning back to Gentrix as he zipped it up.

"You should get dressed too," he said. "We might—" Iridius stopped as he saw Gentrix standing before him, fully clothed in her black uniform already. "How did you do that so fast?"

"Probably still slower than you pulled them off, Iridius."

Iridius sat on the bed and pulled on his socks and boots. "We might need you to talk to your brother."

"I'll try," Gentrix said, "but I don't think it will help."

The two of them hurried to the bridge. As Iridius stepped through the door he felt every pair of eyes on him. It wasn't unusual for people to check who was coming onto the bridge, but none of them, except Ensign Herd, who was almost as much technology as he was human, and Ensign Hal, who was one hundred per cent technology, managed to hide their raised eyebrows or cheeky grins as Iridius walked onto the bridge with Gentrix. Rangi, obviously, had a goofy grin from ear to ear, but he didn't, thank the stars, say anything.

Quinn stood from the captain's chair and let Iridius sit down.

Gentrix stood next to him, and Iridius couldn't help but notice the side-eye Quinn was giving her as she moved to her XO station. Iridius had to fight the urge to say something. He had to remind himself it wasn't personal. His second-in-command was being wary of this newcomer. Quinn hadn't been with them on the away mission. She hadn't seen the way Gentrix had become a trusted part of their team – or if not part of their team, at least a trusted ally.

"Captain," Quinn said, "there's something you should know, but I thought you should rest after the away mission before I told you." She looked at Gentrix and then back to Iridius. "Captain Idowu is missing in action."

"What?" Iridius asked.

"That Aegix probe that was considered lost turned up. It crashed into Acacia, a moon of Geffet. Captain Idowu was piloting a shuttle solo, trying to recover some of the Aegix nanobots, and contact was lost. Her shuttle crashed on Acacia. The *Gallaway* has had no contact with her, but they confirm there is a life sign down there. Commander Mul has specifically requested your aid. He believes you may be able to affect the Aegix and get her out."

Iridius stared ahead, rubbing his chin. "How long ago did this happen?"

"We received word from the *Gallaway* not long before we picked you up."

"You should have told me straight away, Quinn," Iridius snapped.

"I was concerned about you, Captain."

"I'm not a child, Quinn," Iridius said. "I don't need a nap before you give me bad news."

"I wasn't concerned about that, Captain," Quinn said. "I was concerned that Captain Idowu being in danger would cloud your decision-making ability and that you'd go off and try to save her. I was concerned you'd be reckless and stupid again."

The bridge was silent. Proper, stunned silence.

"I thought you said she was measured and thoughtful," Gentrix said. "But you were right, certainly not meek."

Quinn opened her mouth to speak but Iridius held up his hand, stopping her. "No, don't." Iridius had no idea whether she was going to apologise or keep tearing strips off him. Either way, it didn't really matter. "You know I'm not very good with this stuff but, Space Command Regulation 13B, isn't it?"

"Every enlisted member of Federation Space Command shall treat with respect their superior or one having authority over them," Quinn said.

"Yeah," Iridius said. "That's the one, but me recklessly ignoring regulations is your point, isn't it? But I've told you before, Quinn, and I promise you it's true – I only recklessly ignore regulations when I think I'm right. Gronk knows I've ignored 13B plenty of times. That's why I'm going to let you ignore it too, because you're right, or at least you believe you're right. And that, when you're in a position of command, is as good as the same thing because it's basically all you've got. I've done enough dumb shit that I completely understand your expectation that I'm going to do some more dumb shit."

"Especially if April Idowu is involved," Rangi said.

"So, who is April Idowu?" Gentrix said, looking at Iridius.

"I'll fill you in later," Iridius said.

"I understand Captain Iridius Franklin and Captain April Idowu were once lovers," Latroz said.

"Yes, thank you Lieutenant," Iridius said. "That was a long time ago, so let's just leave it there, shall we?"

"Yeah, then they were both on the *Gallaway* for a while, where we're pretty sure they almost got back together," Rangi said.

"That didn't...how..." Iridius paused. "No, we were never going to get back together."

Gentrix looked at him. "Should I be worried?"

"No," Iridius said.

"In a situation of mating conflict Siruan women fight in ritual combat," Latroz said. "The first to draw blood is declared the victor and they can elect to behead their opponent if desired."

"Look, first of all, and I should think this would go without saying, there will be no beheading," Iridius said. "Second, no matter my relationship with Captain Idowu," he looked at Gentrix, "not that I have one, I'm not going to let that affect my decision." Iridius turned to Quinn. "Lieutenant Commander Quinn, I understand why you are upset with me but listen, we're going to air this out right now. You aren't leaving my crew. We're going to stop this idiot and his little time bomb and then we're going to face the Synth-Hastur and we're going to do it together. You have the best understanding in the Federation of the Aegix and how they might work, so you're staying here."

"Captain, I—"

"Furthermore," Iridius continued, "I'm sorry you think I pushed you when you didn't want to be pushed, and I'll be more open with you in the future, but I'm going to push you again now because the galaxy needs your help. As for what happened with your Aegix countermeasures not protecting the fleet, you don't get to blame me. I already blame me. You need to accept responsibility for your part in that, Quinn. Something you tried didn't work. But at least you tried something. Out here that's basically all we have most of them time."

Quinn looked at the ground.

"Quinn, you are my right-hand on this ship – gronk, you are my brains on this ship – and I need you here with me."

Quinn looked at Iridius and nodded.

"But," Iridius said, "never keep important information from me again."

"Yes, Captain. What should I tell the *Gallaway*?"

"April has crashed landed alone on a moon infested with Aegix, and because it's the Aegix I'm likely the only one who can deal with them, otherwise she's dead," Iridius said. "Do the *Gallaway* crew believe she's still alive?"

"They don't know," Quinn said.

Iridius took a deep breath. "Tell them..." he paused. "Tell them I'm sorry. Rangi, how long until we drop out of BAMF?"

"Popping the cherry in fifty seconds, cap," Rangi replied.

"None of this changes the plan," Iridius said. "First priority is stopping Frost before he pre-destroys Earth – if he does that, everything else becomes moot anyway because a bunch of us won't exist anymore and who knows what state everything will be in. We're going to drop out of BAMF close to Earth. We can't risk allowing Frost time to launch the weapon. Unfortunately, that means we won't have a chance to go stealth. They'll know we're there straight away and we'll have to deal with them straight away."

"And what is your plan for dealing with my brother exactly?" Gentrix asked.

Iridius smiled at her. "Same as always. We wing it. Welcome to the team."

———

Fifty seconds later, Iridius sat in the captain's chair drumming his fingers mindlessly on the armrest – the only external sign of the nerves he felt. As the BAMF drive shut down, the bubble universe around the *Deus Ex* became unstable and disintegrated, causing the ship to collapse back into the real universe. The orange crackle of the *Deus Ex*'s overloading shields cleared from the bridge's view-screen to reveal the equally orange glow of Earth. The planet that had birthed blue jeans, rock 'n' roll and clicky ballpoint pens was still a ball of molten rocky slag. Ten months after a planet-slagger caused a quantum fission catalytic exothermic reaction that ignited the planet's atmosphere to such extreme temperatures that oceans evaporated and much of the surface was turned to magma, the planet was still burning, the surface a bubbling, inhospitable hellscape.

"Well," Iridius said, "for once the fact that Earth is a bubbling inhospitable hellscape is actually a good thing. It means it hasn't been destroyed in the past yet. At least, not further in the past. Where is the *Neverlander?*"

"Ship coming around from the far side of Earth now, Captain," Latroz said. "It was using the fluctuating magnetic field from the molten surface of the planet to mask itself. Missile lock on us. It's firing. Ten missiles incoming."

"Evasive manoeuvres, Rangi," Iridius ordered.

"Aye."

"Railgun defences online," Iridius said.

"Aye, Captain," Latroz replied. "They're online. Shields at ten per cent post-BAMF and recharging at full power."

The *Deus Ex* was agile – far more agile than the *Diesel Coast* had ever been, and Iridius had seen Rangi do some impressive things with that ship. What he could do with this one was next level. When Benjamin Rangi was flying at his best it was almost enough to forget what an utter pain in the arse he was the rest of the time. Rangi's hand flicked across the controls. He released the manual flight yoke, rarely used by pilots on anything larger than a shuttle, and flew directly towards the missiles. The incoming missiles lit up with red reticles on the view-screen – they were coming straight for them with a closing speed of 30 000 kilometres per second.

Just before Iridius was about to take back all the nice things he'd just thought about Rangi and ask him what in all the gronking black he was doing, Rangi rolled the *Deus Ex* over ninety degrees and fired thrusters to put the nose down. In an atmospheric flight vehicle, this would have caused enough g-force to squish most species, but in a starship the artificial gravity field simply modulated itself to compensate before stabilising again, and the crew barely felt anything. This was one of the misnomers about flying a spacecraft in combat – being in a vacuum meant the ship could move in any direction in any orientation, and the ability of the onboard systems to cancel out any g-force from high-stress manoeuvres gave people the impression that it should have been easier to handle. From the perspective of pure physical strain on the body this was true, but the six degrees of freedom in movement, plus not having any of the normal feedback in gravitational or acceleration forces, made it far more difficult to keep yourself orientated. Even with all the advanced navigation and guidance systems, it wasn't uncommon for space battles to be lost because the pilots or helmsmen became momentarily disorientated.

Rangi's manoeuvre meant that the top of the *Deus Ex* was orientated to the incoming missiles and they were also moving in this direction. Iridius understood why Rangi had done this. It was risky, but it gave almost all of the ship's anti-missile railguns an opportunity to fire. Rangi was trying to cut down the number of missiles, hopefully all of them. The *thunk-a-thunk-a* of the railguns reverberated through the ship as they shot at the incoming missiles.

"One down, two down," Latroz reported. "Six, seven. Proximity alert. We do not have shields, Benjamin."

Rangi took the warning and engaged a burst of fire from the main fusion engine. This enormous acceleration vector was enough to overwhelm even the artificial gravity dampening, and Iridius felt momentarily pushed back into his seat. The ship shook violently and the bridge crew were tossed around. As Iridius gripped the arms of his chair, Gentrix tumbled on top of him. Iridius grabbed her.

"You alright?"

She nodded.

"Are we hit?" Iridius asked.

"Negative, Captain," Quinn said. "Close-range detonation. I'm seeing minor hull damage and some impacts on the main engine nozzle, but no breaches, and systems all look fine."

Rangi brought the *Deus Ex* up to high speed and then began turning aggressively. The riskiness of trying to eliminate all the incoming missiles and not managing to do so became clear. The two missiles that remained were left close to the ship and were getting closer.

"The *Neverlander* is pulling back from Earth," Quinn said.

"Devin is putting himself the right distance away," Gentrix said. "He wants to stay within the temporal displacement field but far enough away that he only experiences a few seconds of displacement."

"Proximity alert still," Latroz said. "Missiles within 5 kilometres and closing."

Rangi fired the ship's thrusters to turn again. It wasn't strictly possible to lose something in space, there wasn't exactly anywhere to hide, but the purpose of evasive manoeuvres like these was to deplete the missiles' limited fuel supplies until they ran out of delta-v – that is, they no longer had the capability to change their velocity. In this situation though, it did not look promising. The remaining two missiles were close, too close for the railguns to fire lest they detonate the nuclear warheads and cause another, more damaging, close-range detonation. The missiles were sticking right on their tail, gaining all the time. They would hit before Rangi could out-turn them.

"Shields?" Iridius asked.

"Fifty-five per cent recharged," Latroz responded.

And here was the major difficulty with chasing someone through BAMF. Arriving second meant your opponent had a major advantage: they could fire on you before you could fire on them, and the time it took for shields to come back online after a BAMF jump meant you were immediately on the backfoot. Iridius had heard once that most games had a slight advantage to the player who went first – even chess had something like a five per cent advantage to whoever played white. Space combat was just like chess, really: whoever goes first has an advantage, and everything moves in stupid ways.

"*Neverlander* slowing," Quinn said. "Looks like they're at their intended firing distance."

Iridius sighed. Devin Frost was smart. Iridius had no doubt he'd anticipated they'd follow, and he'd no doubt planned this: fire on them as they came out of BAMF, keep them busy while he detonated the time bomb. He'd probably even calculated how close the *Deus Ex* could get to ensure it stayed outside the temporal displacement field and would experience whatever sweeping changes would run through the galaxy's timeline. Devin Frost had been smart enough to fool Iridius into thinking he was stupid. Hell, Devin Frost probably played chess. He was relying on the first-turn advantage. He'd underestimated Iridius though – chess players didn't have superpowers.

"Rangi, take us in towards the *Neverlander,* full speed."

"Cap, the missiles..."

"I said, take us towards the *Neverlander,* full speed."

Rangi didn't hesitate again. "Aye, sir."

He turned the ship. The missiles turned with them and then flew right towards their back end. There was no way they could avoid them now. Iridius reached out with his nanobots, felt the missiles behind him. His leg twitched.

"Missiles are turning away," Latroz said. "Both are curling off. Out of range detonation."

Everyone looked at Iridius, who still had his eyes closed. He opened them to see Benjamin Rangi turned away from the helm, grinning at him. "Ho-ly Jupiter's nuts," Rangi said. "Are you back? Is Techno-you-know-who back?"

It was one of those rare times when Iridius found Rangi's shit-eating grin endearing. He let himself smile in return. "Yes, Lieutenant, Techno-Wizard is back."

"Woo!" Rangi fist-pumped the air. "I love this shit!"

Gentrix was staring at Iridius. "Something tells me I haven't quite got to know you after all, Iridius Franklin."

"Something else to explain later," Iridius said. "Ensign Herd, hail the *Neverlander,* see if they'll take our call."

"Aye, sir."

Iridius looked at Gentrix. "I need you to talk your brother down," he said. "Otherwise I'll have no choice."

Gentrix nodded.

"CEO Devin Frost has responded to our hail," Ensign Herd said.

"Put it bridge-wide, Ensign."

"Aye, you're on, Captain."

"CEO Frost," Iridius said. "I have to say I preferred your welcome on the ASS Locke. Not quite as many missiles."

"That's because I didn't know you were a Federation spy come to steal my property, Captain Franklin," Devin Frost replied. "I only like people stealing my property when it's all well planned out in advance and I'm pulling the strings. Still, it all worked out in the end, didn't it?"

"That depends what you're expecting to happen," Iridius said.

"I'm expecting my sister to be with you," Frost said. "You're going to get her to talk to me, try and convince me not to launch this weapon blah blah, but it's not going to work. You see, I don't really care for my sister. I don't really care for anyone. Perks of being a high-functioning sociopath, I suppose."

"Devin," Gentrix said, "when you were five years old you tried to stab me with a fork. That was the first time you tried to kill me. If you insist on acting like that same brat all your life I'm going to have no choice but to knock you on your arse like I did then."

"Ah, sister," Frost said, "I'm not entirely sure what's going to happen when I blow up Earth – I mean, neither of us were born on Earth, so I assume you'll still be around. I wonder if I'll be aware of both timelines. No one really knows. I guess that's the beauty of scientific progress – we'll find out. So long, Gentrix and Captain Franklin."

"Frost!"

"He's gone, Captain," Ensign Herd said.

"Missiles away from the *Neverlander* again," Latroz said.

Iridius looked at Gentrix. "That wasn't really what I had in mind when I said you should try and talk your brother down."

Gentrix shrugged. "I told you, appealing to his better nature doesn't work. He doesn't have one."

"Keep us moving in, Rangi," Iridius said. "Get us closer."

The view-screen lit up with red, showing the incoming missiles. Iridius swept them aside as if sweeping clear a desk. They spiralled off, smashing into each other, flipping away.

"So, why didn't you just do this kind of thing on the station?" Gentrix asked.

"It's a long story," Iridius said.

"He pissed off the alien bugs in his blood and they went on strike," Rangi said.

Iridius shrugged. "Not that long I guess."

"*Neverlander* is firing a weapon," Latroz said. "Spectral profile matches a quantum temporal reversal bomb. It's heading for Earth."

Iridius reached out with his mind and his nanobots, trying to feel for the bomb, and in that moment he felt a pang of panic, something he should have anticipated, just like last time the quantum temporal reversal bomb was unguided. His plan had been to steer it away from Earth, just as he would with a missile, but this bomb had no propulsion of its own. Once in flight, it was a simple projectile, like a railgun round. There was nothing he could do to affect its flight path. It was time to change tack. He felt for the *Neverlander*. He pressed into it with his mind, letting the nanobots seize control. He almost had it, but something like a starship was so complicated, with so many systems, it was difficult to find what he needed. It felt as if everything was blurred together. Just like the Aegix, distance was limiting him.

"Get us closer, Rangi, give me more speed," he demanded.

Second by second, he felt things become clearer.

"We're going to be too close, Captain," Quinn said. "No matter what happens, we're well within the temporal displacement field. I have no idea how far back we'll be thrown if that bomb detonates."

"It's us or the Earth, Quinn," Iridius said. "I failed to save it once, that's not happening again."

There. They were finally close enough that Iridius could sense the propulsion systems of the *Neverlander*. If he couldn't control the bomb, then fine. He'd control this whole gronking ship instead. He fired the main engine as hard as he could. The *Neverlander* took off in the direction of Earth and the temporal displacement bomb. That's the thing with a projectile weapon that doesn't have its own propulsion. In space, it's just going to keep on going at the same velocity, and luckily, this prototype bomb didn't seem to be going that fast, certainly not the speed of a railgun round. If you fire an engine, you keep accelerating. The *Neverlander* accelerated after the bomb, drawing closer and closer to it as they both headed for Earth. Iridius hadn't done any calculations, he had no idea if the *Neverlander* was going to reach the bomb before it reached Earth, but that was what winging it was all about. As if she knew what he was thinking, Quinn answered the question.

"The *Neverlander* will reach the bomb 1020 kilometres from Earth."

"See?" Iridius said. "I told you, you are my brains."

Moments later, like a missile chasing a ship, but with the sizes massively reversed, the *Neverlander* slammed into the back of the quantum time reversal bomb. It burst in that same expanding sphere of purple light, the *Neverlander* vanishing as it was destroyed. The disturbing purple light swept towards the *Deus Ex* and then enveloped it. Iridius saw the scene around him repeated ad-infinitum, overlays of time and reality in a mess of strobing imagery.

Years, seconds, forever. Time had no meaning.

Then things snapped back to normal.

"Report?" Iridius immediately asked.

"No damage," Quinn said. "All systems functional."

Earth was still there in the view-screen, but Iridius immediately noticed the difference. It was still a ball of molten rock, it was just burning even more brightly. As if it hadn't been burning all that long.

"When are we?" Iridius asked.

Quinn was staring at her console. "Um," she looked up, "we're temporally displaced ten months."

Iridius nodded. He'd already suspected the answer. "The fleet battle with the Aegix is happening at Tau Ceti soon, isn't it?"

Quinn nodded. "About fifteen hours from now."

"Rangi, set a course for Tau Ceti, far enough away that we can arrive and go full stealth. I've got someone to visit. Gentrix, have you got one of those remote holographic projectors still?"

She nodded. "What's going on?"

"Some paradoxical bullshit."

"The visit you said you got from yourself?" Quinn asked. "That's you, now."

Iridius nodded. "I figure I need to go to Tau Ceti on my fancy stealth ship and tell myself how to get out of the situation I'm about to get into on the *Diesel Coast* so that I can survive and we can go on to do all this stuff. Kind of convenient that this is when we got sent to, isn't it? Just the time when I need to go save myself."

"Well, not really," Quinn said. "It's not a coincidence because it's already happened. You've already been saved, so we were always going to get here so that you could go and save yourself. It's a paradox, but it isn't a coincidence."

"Quinn," Iridius said, "what I don't understand is why I don't or didn't or won't – I'm not sure which tense to use anymore, to be honest – do something to save everyone in that battle. Why don't we go there and tell them to fall back? Tell them the jamming signal won't work and then just go and destroy the Aegix. We could save all those people who died."

Quinn shook her head. "No, that doesn't happen because I'm going to tell you not to do it. You're right, Captain, I have to take responsibility for that and we can't change it, otherwise we're just the same as Devin Frost was going to be. We have no idea what the butterfly effect might be."

Iridius nodded.

"Makes sense," Rangi said.

"No," Iridius said. "It really doesn't. Don't anyone pretend us being blasted back in time so that I can save my past self is normal. Now let's go Rangi, get us to Tau Ceti."

CHAPTER TWENTY-FOUR_

Iridius was standing in the ready room of the *Deus Ex*. This was where Gentrix had set up the remote holographic projection equipment. Out there, in space, the battle for Tau Ceti was raging. People were dying and they weren't going to save them because that would mess up the timeline, even though Iridius was about to save himself, which he was sure sounded like messing up the timeline but apparently it wasn't because it had both already happened and was going to happen. Fuck this time travel shit.

"Okay," Gentrix said, "this will ping the location and project the inverse for you so you'll see a representation from where your hologram will be standing. Make sense?"

"Sure," Iridius said. Nothing really made sense anymore, but he'd resigned himself to just go with it.

"I'm switching it on," Gentrix said.

And Iridius was projected onto the bridge of the *Diesel Coast*. From where he stood, he saw a blue, partial representation of the bridge. He felt a moment of nostalgia looking around at the clunky old girl that he'd captained for so many years. Then he saw the image of himself floating in front of where the viewscreen would have been, although it wasn't in the image he could see. This was the moment when he'd accepted he was going to die.

"Ahem," Iridius said.

The image of past him didn't move.

"Ahem," he repeated.

Past-Iridius slowly turned. His eyes were wide. He looked like shit. But Iridius had to remind himself he'd just been through the ordeal of the Aegix. A lot had just happened to past him.

"Am I already dead or something?" Past-Iridius said.

"Jupiter's nuts," Iridius said. He'd been through a lot and was convinced he was about to die, but god he was an idiot. "I hate that we say that. If you were dead you'd *be* the ghost, you wouldn't be looking *at* the ghost, would you? Plus, I'm not a ghost."

"What are you then?" Past-Iridius said. "Why are you on my ship? Why do you look like me?"

Man, I really was concerned about this intruder rather than the fact that I was about to die, hey? Iridius thought.

"You remember this ship is about to hit that giant dog, right? We don't have time for this. Don't speak, just listen. This is where it starts getting weird."

"*This* is where it gets weird? Earth was incinerated by an artificial intelligence modelling itself on a fluffy white dog and it's just *starting* to get weird?"

You've got no idea. "God, I'm annoying. I told you to shut up and listen." This was just as weird for Iridius as it was when he'd been on the receiving end. He wanted to get it over and done with. "I'm from the future. This is a holographic projection. I'm actually hidden on a completely cloaked ship nearby. I'm here to tell you how to survive this so that you can go on to become me and then come back and tell you – us – how to survive this."

Past-Iridius opened and closed his mouth, apparently

confused. So he should be. "There aren't any ships that have managed full cloaking."

"Future, remember?" Iridius said. "We've got about thirty seconds. Go down the steps into the cargo bay. Damage to the hull has caused one of the last escape pods to come free. It'll be floating across the bay but its life-support is still operating. Get in it."

"It won't keep me safe once we hit the Aegix."

"Just do it," Iridius said. Wow, he complained almost as much as his crew did. "Trust me, I have the benefit of knowing exactly what happens. An explosion will cause the pod to be hit by debris, knocking it free. After that you'll get a little nudge from a few other objects. Go now."

Past-Iridius took a moment but then began moving, pushing himself off consoles to float towards the doors off the bridge.

"Remember to breathe out so your lungs don't burst," Iridius added, as an afterthought – a strange afterthought, considering he knew he'd told himself that, but he'd almost forgotten anyway. He looked at Gentrix and nodded. She shut down the projector.

"Alright," Iridius said. "I should be fine now."

The two of them returned to the bridge where the crew was waiting.

"All done, Captain?" Quinn asked.

Iridius nodded. "It was weird, but it went exactly as I remember."

"There goes your escape pod," Latroz said.

On the view-screen of the *Deus Ex* the crew watched the *Diesel Coast* slam into the enormous open mouth of the Aegix dog-ship. With the detonation of the *Diesel Coast*'s nuclear drive, the front of the Aegix ship ruptured. The fleet bombarded it with missiles and the Aegix exploded in a colossal conflagration of nuclear explosions.

"Cool," Iridius said. "I missed that the first time. Nice to see that stupid dog blow up."

"I guess that's that then," Quinn said. "What now, Captain?"

"Now," Iridius said, "we figure out how to get back to the future."

TO BE CONTINUED...

ABOUT THE AUTHOR_

Justin Woolley has been writing stories since he could first scrawl unreadable words with a crayon.

Now he is the author of novels for both adults and young-adults including *Shakedowners,* the *The Territory Series, We Are Omega,* and Warhammer 40K fiction for Black Library.

Justin lives in Hobart, Australia with his wife and two sons. In his other life he's been an engineer, a teacher and at one stage even a magician. His handwriting has not improved.

Keep up to date with all Justin's news and releases by subscribing to his newsletter here:

https://www.justinwoolley.com/signup

Made in the USA
Middletown, DE
10 January 2022

58376339R00172